When Sleuthing Spells Trouble

A Nick and Nora Mystery

T. C. LoTempio

BEYOND THE PAGE
PUBLISHING

Praise for the Nick and Nora Mystery Series

"This mystery is rock star exciting—Nick and Nora are a hoot. I was hooked from start to finish!"
—Laura Childs, *New York Times* Bestselling author

"Nick and Nora are a winning team"
—Rebecca Hale, *New York Times* Bestselling author

"A fast-paced cozy mystery spiced with a dash of romance and topped with a big slice of 'cat-titude.'"
—Ali Brandon, *New York Times* Bestselling author

"Nick and Nora are the purr-fect sleuth duo!"
—Victoria Laurie, *New York Times* Bestselling author

"Excellently plotted and executed—five paws and a tail up for this tale."
—*Open Book Society*

"Nick brims with street smarts and feline charisma, you'd think he was human . . . an exciting new series."
—Carole Nelson Douglas, *New York Times* notable author of the Midnight Louie mysteries

"I love this series and each new story quickly becomes my favorite. Cannot wait for the next!"
—*Escape With Dollycas Into a Good Book*

"I totally loved this lighthearted and engagingly entertaining whodunit featuring new amateur sleuth Nora Charles and Nick, her feline companion."
—*Dru's Cozy Report*

Books by T. C. LoTempio

Nick and Nora Mysteries

Meow If It's Murder
Claws for Alarm
Crime and Catnip
Hiss H for Homicide
Murder Faux Paws
A Purr Before Dying
Bell, Book and Corpses
When Sleuthing Spells Trouble

Urban Tails Pet Shop Mysteries

The Time for Murder is Meow
Killers of a Feather
Death Steals the Spotlight
Cats, Carats and Killers
A Side Dish of Death

Tiffany Austing Mysteries

A Dish Best Served Dead

Cat Rescue Mysteries

Purr M for Murder
Death by a Whisker

<u>Acknowledgments</u>

As Always, thanks to my agent, Josh Getzler, and his team, and to my editor, Bill Harris. Thanks always to the loyal readers who keep coming back for more and help keep Nick and Nora alive!

For my cousin Paul Ferrante, who loves to write as much as I do!

Prologue

Cruz, California
September, Six Years Earlier

The house was as still as death.

That was Velma Cutter's first thought as she pushed open the back door and stepped into the spacious kitchen. She paused, head cocked, listening. The only sound she heard was her own breathing, and she frowned. It wasn't unusual for Dr. Blackthorne to be at the hospital around this time, but surely Mrs. Blackthorne must be somewhere. Her black Ferrari was in the driveway, and a light was on in the upstairs bedroom.

"Mrs. Blackthorne? Dr. Blackthorne? Anyone home?"

No answer.

Velma shrugged out of her thin jacket and hung it on the hook behind the door, then got an apron out of one of the cabinets and slipped it on. As she smoothed it across her plump belly, she thought that perhaps Mrs. Blackthorne might have gone for a quick run. The woman was a fanatic about staying in shape—and she did a good job of it, judging from her petite frame—a decided contrast to the husband, who was at least twenty-five years older than his wife and about twenty pounds overweight. She'd been working for the Blackthornes for the past two years, and so far the arrangement had proven quite satisfactory. She came early in the morning, did the cleaning and any other chores that needed to be done, had her afternoons free, and then returned around five thirty to prepare their dinner. If they hosted a dinner or a cocktail party, of course, she was expected to cook and serve, and clean up afterward—but the pay more than compensated for any inconvenience.

As far as Velma was concerned, it was a job made in heaven, even in spite of all the arguing that had been going on between the couple lately. The one two nights ago had been particularly intense. It had ended with Dr. Blackthorne storming out of the house, Mrs. Blackthorne trailing behind him shouting, "If I find out you are cheating, I'll kill you! Do you hear me?" The doctor hadn't even turned around, just jumped into his BMW and sped off, nearly taking the mailbox with him. Mrs. Blackthorne had looked a bit embarrassed when she'd come back inside, and Velma had felt a rush of sympathy for the woman.

Still, their private life was none of her business, unless it should affect her employment.

Velma opened the bottom cabinet and pulled out the roasting pan. Tonight was Dr. Blackthorne's sixtieth birthday, and Mrs. Blackthorne had requested she prepare his favorite, a crown roast of pork. Velma opened the large double-door refrigerator and started pulling out the ingredients she'd need—garlic, a Spanish onion, celery, the chestnut-and-pear stuffing she'd prepared the day before; and of course, the thirteen-rib pork loin. She got her spices out of the large center cabinet: kosher salt, rosemary, sage, and extra-virgin olive oil. As she assembled everything on the spacious marble countertop, she stood back and frowned. Something was missing—oh, yes, the dry white wine she needed for the sauce. She hurried across the hall into the living room and over to the large redwood bar at the far end near the fireplace. There were about ten bottles of wine stacked behind the bar, all of them red.

She frowned. She could probably use one of the reds, but then she ran the risk of getting a lecture from Dr. Blackthorne on how white wine was the natural partner for the delicate flavor of pork. Mrs. Blackthorne probably wouldn't be too pleased either. No matter what differences they'd had lately, she'd want everything to be perfect for the old boy's special day. The prospect of heading back out to the liquor store didn't exactly thrill her, either, unless . . . Her spirits lifted as she remembered Dr. Blackthorne kept a private stash of his personal favorite, Cloudy Bay Vineyards 2009 Te Koko, a delicious yet pricey Sauvignon Blanc, in the cabinet in his study. Dr. Blackthorne prized that wine almost as much as he prized that bronze bust of Sigmund Freud that sat on the low shelf behind his desk. Dr. Blackthorne probably wouldn't be thrilled she'd used the wine for pork gravy, but what the heck?

You only turned sixty once.

Velma hurried down the hall toward the doctor's study, pausing when she was a few feet away. The door was closed, and a thin stream of light emanated from beneath it. Raising her hand, she rapped her knuckles peremptorily on the door.

"Dr. Blackthorne? Mrs. Blackthorne? Are you in there?"

No answer. Velma reached for the knob, and then gasped as her fingers touched something sticky. She pulled her hand back and her breath caught in her throat.

Her fingers were tinged with a red sticky substance that could only be . . . blood.

The feeling of trepidation she'd felt earlier returned, stronger this time. She tamped down the butterflies that stirred in her stomach and pushed open the study door. "Dr. Black—" she began, and then the words died in her throat as she struggled to take in the tableaux before her.

Dr. Blackthorne slumped over in his chair at his desk, his head caked with blood that dripped all over him and down onto the expensive Oriental carpet. And, lying not two feet away was Mrs. Blackthorne, her hand curled around the bust of Freud, its base smeared with blood.

<u>Chapter One</u>

Cruz, Present Day

"Anna, this is a very impressive résumé."

I flicked an auburn curl out of my eyes and scanned the paper I held in my hand. "You've waitressed at Le Cruset and A Touch of Venice the last three years, and in high school you held down part-time jobs at all the popular food chains." I tapped at the paper with the edge of one nail. "Plus, you're one semester away from graduating Mission College with a degree in culinary arts." I hesitated and then added, "You might be a bit overqualified for this job."

A bit was putting it mildly. Anna Weathers was *extremely* overqualified for the position I was hiring for—namely, another part-timer to help out at Hot Bread, the sandwich shop I'd inherited from my mother. My sideline catering business had picked up the past few months, due in part to some very good publicity I'd received from catering for a soap opera that had filmed some episodes here in my hometown of Cruz, California. My current part-timer, Mollie, had told me a few weeks ago that she was going to have to cut back on her hours in order to prepare for college boards. I had other help, of course: My BFF, Chantal Gillard, helped out in between her shifts at Poppies, the flower store she co-ran with her brother, and managing her own New Age and homemade jewelry businesses. Although she insisted that working part-time for me was no problem at all, I felt guilty about taking her away from her own thriving enterprises. That left me with my sister Lacey. She was currently living with me and helping out but I knew that wouldn't last either. Her former employment had been as a sketch artist on the St. Leo Police Department, but budget cuts had put the kibosh on that career. However, a few weeks ago our head of Homicide, Dale Anderson, had asked for her résumé, so I figured it was only a matter of time before she hung up her apron for a sketch pad and pencil. I'd been able to manage nicely with just the four of us, but in recent weeks it had become evident that not only my regular business but my catering sideline were expanding to the point where I needed at least one other dependable person on staff—emphasis on *dependable*.

"I don't view myself as being overqualified, Ms. Charles," the plump brunette in front of me said with an eager smile. "I look on every job I have as a positive learning experience. My plans are to eventually start my own catering business, and who better to learn from than one of the best. You." She flashed me a wide, toothy smile.

She seemed sincere enough, but still, something about her just didn't hit me right. "You do understand this position is only part-time, right?"

Her dark curls swung to and fro as she nodded. "Oh, that's fine. Part-time's all I'm really interested in right now, anyway. My last semester consists mainly of working at the school kitchen two days a week, so I'm available to be here the other five days as much as you need me." She flashed me another wide smile. "I'm really very interested in working for you, and in learning from you."

I tapped my pencil against the table. Anna was certainly a dream come true in almost every respect. Maybe that was what bothered me. She seemed a bit *too* good. Plus, she was laying on the flattery a little thick. I always wondered about people who did that.

"You wouldn't make a lot of tips here, like you did waitressing," I said. "Would that present a problem for you?"

The smile widened. "Not at all. I live at home, and my expenses are pretty minimal. I socked away a lot of the tip money I made at my other jobs against future expenses. Plus, I got a partial scholarship."

Memories of the three jobs I'd held down while attending college floated through my head. I'd worked part-time at the *Chicago Tribune* doing everything from fetching coffee to running copy. And when I hadn't been doing that, I'd stocked shelves at the nearby Barnes and Noble. I slid the résumé back into the manila folder. "Well, I guess that pretty much covers everything, except . . ." I paused, uncertain how to broach my next question. The most important one of all. I let out a deep breath and asked, "How are you with cats?"

"Cats?" Her eyes widened and the toe of her shoe started to beat out a steady *tap-tap-tap* on my black and white parquet floor. "Well . . . okay, I guess. Why?"

"Ow-orrr."

We looked down. One large black and white paw emerged from beneath the table, and then another. A few seconds later a black and white head popped out. "Ow-owrr," the cat said again.

"Anna, this is Nick. He's, well, he's sort of the store mascot." *And my partner in crime solving, in addition to being my furry guardian angel,* I added silently.

It was hard to tell just what Anna was thinking as Nick wriggled all the way out from underneath the table and squatted beside my chair. My tuxedo is a bit on the tubby side, but it's more muscle than fat, although Nick does love to chow down, especially on my leftovers. He cocked his head to one side and slitted his golden eyes, regarding the newcomer thoughtfully.

"My," Anna said finally. "He's certainly . . . big, isn't he?"

"Owwr?" Nick's eyes popped, and he sat up, his black plume of a tail bristling behind him.

"Something seems to have upset him," Anna observed. "Look at how the fur on his tail sticks out. Cats get like that when they're upset about something, right?"

That's because you've insulted him, I wanted to scream, but instead I said calmly, "Nick is very sensitive, particularly about his build. He doesn't like to be called big, or large or substantial . . . well, you get the idea."

She looked from me to Nick then back to me. "He understood what I said?" she asked.

I gave a dismissive wave. "He's in the shop a lot, so if you work here, it's important that you two get along."

From the expression on Anna's face I wondered if the appearance of Nick might be a deal breaker for her, and I was surprised at how elated that thought made me feel. She looked at me again, and this time her expression melted into another sunny smile. "I wasn't exactly expecting to be interviewed by a cat, but it's fine." She shrugged. "My aunt has a cat named Percy, and one of my besties has a Chihuahua. I get along with animals."

At the word Chihuahua, Nick's ears went up, then flattened against his skull. His lips pulled back, displaying his sharp white teeth. "Grrrr."

Anna let out a laugh that sounded more like a nervous titter. "I guess he doesn't like dogs?" She reached out a French-manicured hand. "Hey there, Ned. You're a good boy, aren't you? You're probably a great mouser." Her fingers stretched toward Nick, who was now sitting on his haunches, watching her. I caught the gleam in his eye and I rose from my chair, pushed Anna's hand out of the way just as Nick raised his claw and swiped the air.

"Geez!" She scraped her chair back and stood up. "You didn't mention he was vicious."

"You called him Ned. His name is Nick."

She tugged at her navy jacket and reached for the voluminous tote bag on the floor. "Your cat might be smart, but I'm sure he's not *that* smart."

I saw Nick's eyes narrow. As Anna's fingers closed over the tote's strap, Nick's paw shot out again. Anna whipped her hand back just in time to avoid a nasty scratch, dropping her tote in the process. Her iPad tumbled out, and before she could reach for it, Nick had plopped his portly body *smack!* right on top of it.

Anna looked at Nick dubiously. She reached out a tentative hand toward the iPad, and Nick opened his mouth, displaying a generous amount of fang. Anna jumped back. "Great," she muttered. "I need that iPad. My whole life is on that thing."

"Come on." I tugged at her elbow. "Just move away and wait a few minutes. He'll get tired of sitting on it and get up, and then I can get it for you."

Anna regarded Nick with a deep frown. "Are you sure? He looks pretty comfortable to me."

Indeed, Nick did look comfortable, spread out full length across the iPad, his paws folded neatly in front of him. Anna took another tentative step forward and he raised his head, let out a low hiss. Anna jumped back as if she'd been stung.

"You know what?" She glanced quickly at her watch, and then slung her tote over her shoulder. "I'll stop back later and pick my iPad up. I have another appointment that I don't want to be late for." She started edging toward the door, her gaze still riveted on Nick.

"Okay then. I'll give you a call on your cell once I retrieve it." I paused. "Shall I put you down for a second interview?"

Nick raised his head, peeled back his lips and let out a loud hiss.

Anna squared her shoulders and faced me. "No offense, Ms. Charles, but I don't think this is the job for me after all. Not if I'd have to work with *him*." Her hand shot out, and she pointed a finger directly at Nick. Nick stared at her for a moment, then lifted his paw and began to wash his face. Anna made an exasperated sound, turned on her heel and stormed out the door, letting it close behind her. The minute she was gone, Nick rose, stretched, and padded over to where I stood. He hunkered in front of me, raised his paw, and resumed his grooming.

I picked up my pen and mimed drawing a straight line. "Cross her off the list." I bent down and picked up Anna's iPad, then folded my arms across my chest and looked at Nick. "I'm not sure whether to scold you or thank you."

Nick paused in his ablutions to regard me with his golden gaze. Then, with a flick of his white whiskers, as if to say *No problemo, human,* he rose and padded off to his favorite spot in front of my refrigerator.

I sighed. "She wouldn't have worked out anyway. Now that I think of it, I can't see her getting along with Lacey. Two divas working here I don't need." I set the iPad on the counter, walked back over to the table and picked up the manila folder. I opened it, removed Anna's, and tossed it into the wastebasket. Then I looked at the one that remained and said, "Ricky Hawkins's mother was in here yesterday and said that he already got a part-time job at that new patisserie in Monterey." I pulled out Ricky's résumé and added it to the trash bin. "So now I've got zip. No prospects at all." I eyed the cat. "Feel guilty at all, Nick?"

Nick shifted his position slightly, opened one golden eye, and then shut it again. Apparently not.

The bell above the shop door jangled. I scraped back my chair and turned toward the counter, thinking perhaps Anna had ventured back for her iPad, but instead I saw Louis Blondell coming through the door. Louis was the editor for *Noir,* an online true crime magazine that I wrote for in my spare time, and I figured the purpose for his visit today was twofold: to eat lunch, plus a gentle reminder that my article for this month was seriously overdue. As he approached the counter, I held up my hand. "Before you say a word, it's been a very busy month here."

"So I gathered." He removed the newspaper he had tucked under his arm, set it on the counter, then leaned forward on both elbows. "It's been weeks since I've heard from you, so I thought I'd drop in, make certain you were still in business. Oh, and I'll have a Jimmy Kimmel. Light mayo today."

That was no surprise. The roast beef, provolone and hot peppers on rye was one of Louis's favorite sandwiches. As I pulled the rare roast beef out of my display case and set it on the slicer, Louis said, "So, it's just the fact your business is booming that I haven't heard from you? Writer's block has nothing to do with it?"

The last time Louis and I spoke about this, I'd told him I had a hard time thinking of a topic that might be as popular as my previous series of articles, about becoming a private eye. He'd told me to take some time to think about what I wanted to do next, but we both knew I'd far exceeded the limit. Fortunately, my back door banged open just then, and my sister Lacey flew in like a mini-tornado, her arms full of paper bundles. "I'm back." She dropped the bags on the back table with a resounding plop, then made a beeline for my side counter. "Where's the remote?"

"Right here." I pulled it out of my apron pocket. She hurried toward me and reached out, but I held it out of her grasp. "Oh, no. No watching TV until those groceries are put away."

"Then it'll be too late. Gimme." She made another lunge for the remote, and again I lifted it out of the way of her questing fingers. She stamped her foot and cried, "Oh, come on, Nors. Don't be like that. We'll miss it."

I looked at her, my eyes narrowed. "What will we miss?"

She jumped up and stretched out her hand, but I pulled the remote out of reach once again. "Oh, for pity's sakes!" She stuck her tongue out at me and angled her head toward the clock on the wall. "It's a live broadcast." Her hand shot out and she wrenched the remote out of my grasp, pointed it at the TV and turned it on. The screen flickered to life, and she smiled in satisfaction. "Good. It didn't start yet. I think you'll be interested in this, Nors." Her gaze traveled to Louis. "You too," she added.

I squinted at the large gray brick building that appeared on-screen. "Isn't that . . ."

"CCWF? It sure is," Louis answered.

CCWF, or the Central California Women's Facility, is the largest female correctional facility in the United States. Located in nearby Chowchilla, it also houses the State of California's death row for women. Out of the corner of my eye I saw my sister shudder. No doubt she was thinking how close she'd come, not too long ago, to being a resident there herself. I opened my mouth to speak, but shut it quickly as a tall blonde-haired man, holding a microphone with the Channel 6 News emblem on it, stepped forward. He looked straight at the camera and said, "This is Eliott Elkins, special correspondent with Channel Six News. I'm here waiting outside the gates of the Central California Women's Facility in Chowchilla, where Mariah Blackthorne will shortly emerge, after serving five and a half years behind bars following her manslaughter conviction in the death of her husband, Dr. Christian Blackthorne."

A dark sedan with tinted windows emerged from behind the main building of the prison. About a half dozen reporters, Eliott Elkins in the lead, made a beeline for the car. As they approached, the passenger door was flung open and a slim, dark-haired woman in a form-fitting navy blue trench coat alighted and faced them. At that same moment, the prison gates slowly swung open. Strobe lights flashed and microphones and cameras jostled as the woman stared at the gates for a moment before walking through them.

"Being in prison didn't diminish her sense of style," Lacey observed. "That's a Burberry coat, if I'm not mistaken. And those shoes! Definitely Louboutins!"

The woman tore her gaze away from the gates, focusing instead on the crowd of reporters. "I am Mariah Blackthorne," she said, her voice clear and strong, "And I am happy to finally be going home to Cruz."

"Ms. Blackthorne." Eliott Elkins pushed his way forward, wielding a microphone right under the woman's nose. "Ms. Blackthorne, are you hoping that returning to Cruz will help you to recover your memory of the day your husband died?"

Mariah regarded Elkins silently for a moment, then reached up and snatched the microphone from his hand. In a clear voice she said, "I have been advised that may or may not happen. I am hopeful, however, that being back in familiar surroundings might prompt a change in my situation. Of course, there are no guarantees, so I would ask all of you to respect my need for privacy at this time. Thank you."

With that, she handed the microphone back to Elkins, then slid gracefully back into the car and pulled the door shut. It sped through the gates, the reporters and cameramen racing after it.

"Wow," Louis said after a minute. "That was certainly the last thing I expected to see. I knew she was coming up for parole, but I never expected her to get it. She must have had some heavy hitters go to bat for her with the parole board."

Lacey frowned. "Her case never went to the jury, did it?"

"No," said Louis. "The turning point was when Mariah testified she'd overheard her husband on the phone that morning telling someone that if she were pregnant, it was her problem. Phone records confirmed a call from a burner cell placed to Blackthorne's private number at the time Mariah indicated. Her lawyer argued that it provided reasonable doubt that someone else could have committed the murder. The jury was made up of mostly women, and my personal opinion is that the DA was afraid at least one of them would turn sympathetic and think Mariah had done the world a favor, getting rid of a cheating, unfaithful husband. So a deal was offered, and Mariah's lawyer convinced her it was in her best interests to take it."

"I followed that case too," I said. "I even asked Mom to send me the local papers. Mariah's lawyer did a better job defending her than I would have thought, considering his specialty is estates and family planning, not murder trials. I always figured his lack of experience in the criminal arena was the main reason they snapped up copping to manslaughter instead of murder two."

"Mariah's convenient case of amnesia didn't exactly help her cause," Louis added. "When she was examined the doctors didn't find any evidence of a physical assault on her."

"Now you sound like the prosecutor," I chided him. "I believe her doctor testified she suffered from PTSD—posttraumatic stress disorder. You don't necessarily have to be hit on the head to acquire it. The body can just go into shock and the patient tries to forget the traumatic event. It's usually temporary, but it can be a permanent condition, depending on the circumstances."

Louis's expression was thoughtful. "If one listens carefully to that pretty speech she gave, it sounds as if her main reason for returning here is to try and remember what happened."

"I don't blame her," I said. "I know if it were me I'd want to remember. Besides, she never struck me as the killer type."

"Public opinion was divided on that front," Louis said. "Mainly because most reporters played up the 'spoiled woman who married money' angle. Some believed that she was a cold-blooded killer, while others thought it was something done in the heat of the moment. It was about fifty-fifty as to whether the amnesia angle was genuine. Mariah was an actress before she married Blackthorne, you know."

"If you can call some regional theater, a toothpaste commercial and a six-week stint on a soap opera, where her character got pushed off a building, an acting career," I remarked. "She was branded mediocre, which is why I don't think she faked her memory loss."

Louis stroked his chin thoughtfully. "This case is still interesting, even after all these years. Lots of unanswered questions." He looked at me significantly. "It's a real mystery."

I sliced his sandwich in half and looked up at him. I knew exactly where he was going with this. "Yes, it is. But right now I have no time to investigate it."

"Why not? In case you've forgotten, you owe me an article."

"I haven't forgotten. Investigating that case, though, sounds as if it will require a great deal of time, something I don't have a lot of right now. I've got three catering jobs lined up in the next two weeks, in addition to running the shop every day."

"Oh, yeah, about that." Lacey flushed guiltily. "I forgot to tell you. Mazie Heerema had to cancel her daughter's bridal shower. Seems that Yvonne's fiancé decided to run off with her best friend instead. And Cloris Calhoun's aunt had to go in the hospital, so she eighty-sixed the plans for that surprise eightieth birthday party. So you've only got Fred Paisley's retirement, and that's three weeks out."

A broad smile creased Louis's face. "Well, looks like your busy schedule just lightened up, Nora."

I ran my hand through my tousle of red curls. "Maybe so, but there's another reason not to pursue this. Or didn't you hear Mariah Blackthorne's request just now? When she asked everyone to respect her privacy?"

Louis waved one hand in the air. "Oh, that remark was meant for members of the press."

I set Louis's sandwich in front of him. "And just what might I be?"

He reached into his pocket for his wallet. "Why, the *unofficial press*, of course. Besides, you're forgetting about your reputation as an amateur sleuth, not to mention you're a newly minted official PI. Who knows, maybe Mariah Blackthorne will seek you out and request your services."

I took the ten-dollar bill he held out to me. "I hate to burst your bubble, but I'm pretty sure the chances of Mariah Blackthorne coming in here are slim to none, let alone asking me to investigate her husband's death."

A loud merow sounded from underneath the rear table, and then Nick wriggled all the way out and faced me, his tail waving like a metronome. He raised one paw in the air. "Merow."

"Sounds like Nick disagrees," Lacey said and laughed. "And his instincts are usually pretty spot on."

I laid Louis's change on the counter and then shook my head at the cat. "Sorry, buddy. I think your psychic radar's off this time."

He stared at me for a moment, then deliberately turned his back and skulked over to the corner, where he arranged himself in a ball, his back to me. I turned around and saw both Lacey and Louie looking at me with slack expressions and I said defensively, "Oh, he'll get over it. He can't be right all the time, you know."

"Maybe so," Louis said as he picked up his sandwich. "But if I were a betting man . . . I'd put all my money on that cat."

Chapter Two

It was almost one thirty before the last of my lunch regulars departed. My sister vanished upstairs, claiming she owed our Aunt Prudence a long-overdue letter. I didn't doubt that, but I also had an idea that activity would take a backseat in favor of calling either Peter Dobbs or Hal Frey, two lawyers who both had gigantic crushes on her. She was currently dividing her free time between both of them, enjoying all the attention. I glanced over at Nick, sprawled comfortably in his favorite spot in front of my refrigerator. His eyes were closed but I was fairly certain he wasn't asleep. I walked over and looked down at him, my hands on my hips. "Nick."

No response.

I tried again, a little louder. "Nick."

Still nothing.

"I know you can hear me. Listen, it's quiet right now. How would you like to help me do some research on Mariah Blackthorne?"

His head rose, cocked to one side. "Er-owl?" Which I took as kitty speak for: *Are you serious?*

"I am," I said. "I read every article I could at the time, and while the circumstantial evidence seemed overwhelming, Mariah Blackthorne just didn't strike me as likely to kill someone. Then again, I've covered enough murder trials in my time to know that unlikely people can lose control and do something entirely out of character in one split second that could change their lives. In fact, that could be the root cause of Mariah's amnesia."

He let out a soft merow as he struggled to his feet, and I grinned. "Well, all right then. Let's get to it."

My trusty laptop was on the rear table. I went over, slid into the chair in front of it and booted it up. I heard a soft *thunk* as Nick launched himself onto the table and stretched out full length next to my laptop, his paws crossed in front of him, his golden gaze riveted on the screen. I was just about to call up Google when the bell above the shop door jangled. "Rats," I muttered under my breath. "Guess our research will have to wait a bit."

Nick made a soft *grr* as I closed the laptop's lid. I started to rise, but paused as the sound of raised voices reached my ears.

"Amazing. They let her out on parole, and she comes back here. Imagine! It takes nerve to return to the scene of the crime."

"Oh, really, Carm. You talk as if she were Lizzie Borden, for goodness sakes."

"Hah! She might as well be."

I recognized the voices. One belonged to Carmela Reis, a svelte, good-looking blonde who was recently divorced. The gossip chain maintained she'd made out exceptionally well, enough so that she'd recently opened up a beauty supply slash perfume store right across the street from Cruz High. A good business move, I thought, because who buys more cosmetics than a teenaged girl?

The other woman was Gillian Spence. She was the total opposite of Carm, introverted and round-faced with stringy dirty-blonde hair. I didn't know much about Gillian, other than she'd moved here to Cruz after her husband left her. She never talked about her marriage, so I assumed it was a sore point. I knew that the Cruz gossip chain favored the scenario that her husband had left her for another man and if that was true, I understood her reluctance to share details. She'd bounced around at a few jobs but for the past year had clerked at Pages Past, the used bookstore near Poppies. She usually stopped into Hot Bread for a sandwich once or twice a week. The two women were as different as night and day but were friends, proving that old adage that opposites attract. I stepped forward with a bright smile. "Ladies. What can I get you?"

Carm jerked her thumb at Gillian. "How about a big dose of reality? Can you imagine she's actually sticking up for that murderess?"

"Whoa, whoa," Gillian cried. She held up both hands. "I'm not sticking up for anyone. All I said was we shouldn't condemn people when we don't know the whole story."

"Hah! No one does, not even Mariah Blackthorne . . . supposedly." Carm tapped her finger against her temple. "That so-called amnesia of hers is a bunch of hogwash, if you ask me."

Louis's words about public opinion on that subject came to mind, and I looked at Carm. "You think she's faking?"

Carm goggled at me. "Don't you? I mean, why else would she have taken that sweet deal? She knew darn well if she didn't, she'd probably spend most of her life in prison. The prosecution had her hands down. I was positive the jury'd bring in a guilty verdict. You could have knocked me over with a feather when the DA offered that plea. I mean, ten years with a chance for parole in five?" She let out a snort. "Ridiculous."

"There were, what do they call them? Mitigating circumstances," cut in Gillian.

Carm belted out a sharp laugh. "You mean the phone call Mariah overheard? The one from the supposedly pregnant mistress? I'll admit Mariah was pretty convincing on the stand when she testified to it, but still, it was only her word. If you want my opinion, the DA dropped the ball. He was afraid of a hung jury, so he just wanted a quick conviction of any kind. As long as Mariah did time, he was happy. Justice, my foot." She let out a sharp snort. "Guess I should look up her lawyer if I ever get in a jam. He sure was a miracle worker."

"Oh, for goodness sakes, Carm." Gillian thrust her hands into the pockets of the pink and gray sweater she wore. "Stop beating a dead horse. She got a plea, and now she's out on parole. So what?"

I leaned forward. I had to admit, I was a bit curious about why Carm seemed so passionate over a woman she'd never met.

"I'll tell you so what," Carm said vehemently. "The press is going to start sniffing around here and dredge up that case all over again. Cruz doesn't need publicity like that. It'll be bad for business." Her voice dropped to a conspiratorial whisper as she continued, "As a matter of fact, there was a woman in my shop today, and I'll bet a week's worth of receipts she was a reporter for one of those gossip rags. I overheard her on her cell phone. She was talking to someone about dogging Mariah's footsteps until she got at the truth of what happened that night. Sounds like a loser proposition to me."

"Really? A reporter?" Gillian's brows drew together in a frown. "Hmm, maybe you're right after all. Who needs reporters nosing around, bothering people and asking a lot of questions."

"My point exactly!" Carm cried triumphantly. "The woman should have moved to New York or Philadelphia or Seattle to get a fresh start. Better yet, she should have moved out of the country, where she wouldn't be known. I bet she *wants* the attention, gets off on it or something."

"I doubt that," said Gillian. "And even if she did, who are we to judge? I'll bet Blackthorne deserved what he got," she added. "Shrinks can be the pits. I saw one for a bit, so I know. They talk out of both sides of their mouths."

"Some do, some don't," responded Carm. "But Mariah could have just divorced the guy instead of killing him. Unless, of course, she signed a prenup and would have walked away with zip."

"Good thing you didn't have a prenup," Gillian shot back. "Then you wouldn't have been able to take your husband to the cleaners and open your store."

Carm's eyes blazed, and I decided to interrupt before things got really ugly. "Speaking of your store," I cut in with a smile at Carm, "word on the street is it's fantastic. You seem to have a real hit on your hands."

Carm preened, her argument with Gillian temporarily forgotten. "Thanks. I think so. I've got a good mix of products, all ranging from inexpensive brands to the more upscale ones." She gave me a critical glance. "You should stop by, Nora. I offer a ten percent discount to new customers, but for you, I'll give fifteen."

"That's very generous, Carm," I said. "I'm afraid I don't use much makeup, though. Usually just lipstick and eyeliner, sometimes a little blush."

Carm leaned over to peer at me more closely. "You've got great skin. So do I. Some others aren't so lucky." She slanted a glance Gillian's way. "I keep telling Gil that she should come in for a makeover."

Gillian's hand flew to the side of her face. "What's wrong with my makeup?" she cried defensively.

Carm shrugged. "Nothing, sweetie. You don't look bad at all, but I could make you look even better. The no-makeup look is in, you know."

Gillian lifted her chin. "No, thanks," she said. "I like the way I look. Besides, I can't afford all those fancy foundations and blushes you sell."

"Aw, c'mon," Carm said, her tone wheedling. "I'll give you the first one free."

Gillian gave her head a vehement shake. "I don't need a makeover. It's not like I'm trying to attract a man, after all. I'm through with all that nonsense after the last go-round."

I could sense the bitterness in Gillian's tone and apparently Carm did as well. She moved closer to Gillian and laid her hand on her arm. "You mean your husband, right? Sorry, I didn't mean to dig up old wounds. It's just that, well, I get so passionate about my products."

"It's okay. I get a little too self-conscious sometimes." Gillian pulled at a loose thread on her sweater and added, "I know you're entitled to your opinion of Mariah Blackthorne, but all I'm saying is we shouldn't judge what people do when we don't know all the facts. Besides, even if it should turn out she did murder her husband, she can't be tried again or resentenced for the same crime. I saw it in a movie with Ashley Judd. It's called double jeopardy."

Carm frowned and looked at me. "Is that true, Nora?"

"It's true Mariah couldn't be tried for the crime again," I said. "But if she should remember what happened that day and someone else is responsible, that person could be tried for the crime."

Now Gillian frowned. "You're kidding? After all this time? I thought there was some sort of time limit on that stuff."

"You mean a statute of limitations. There are on felonies and misdemeanors, but not for the more serious crimes like murder or sex crimes."

"Hah!" Carm leaned over to give Gillian a poke in her ribs. "Guess you didn't learn as much as you thought from watching those Perry Mason reruns."

Gillian made a face, then slid her gaze to me. "What about you, Nora? What do you think about Mariah Blackthorne's return?"

Carm looked at me, a spark of interest in her eyes. "Yeah, I'd be curious as to what you think, Nora. After all, you used to report on crimes like that, right?"

I wasn't about to get in the middle of another heated discussion, so I just shrugged. "Truthfully, I've been so busy with the shop lately I've hardly had the time to keep abreast of current events."

Carm shot me a look that plainly said she wasn't buying it. Gillian, on the other hand, clucked her tongue sympathetically. "Well, it's better to be busy than not, especially in these times," she said with a wise nod. She nudged Carm and pointed to my blackboard. "What do you want to eat? Everything sounds so good, especially that John Stamos sandwich."

Carm waved one hand impatiently. "Those specialty sandwiches are always good, but I'm in the mood for something simple, like maybe . . . grilled ham and cheese?"

"That does sound good. Make that two." Gillian glanced at her watch. "Oh, shoot, I forgot Irene has to leave early today. I've got to get back to the store." Her lips twisted into a rueful grin. "We've been pretty slow lately, and Irene's been making noises about cutting my hours down to bare bones."

"Oh, Irene's always threatening to cut her staff's hours," Carm said with a dismissive wave of her hand. "That old bat has the first dollar she ever earned framed on her wall, I'm certain of it." She gave Gillian's arm a squeeze. "Don't worry, Gil, if she cuts your hours I can always use you a couple days a week. My business is booming, although who knows what will happen now Mariah's back in town."

Gillian's lips twisted into a rueful smile. "You just want to convince me to change my makeup."

Carm grinned. "Yeah, that too."

"I'm sure your store will do just fine," I interjected smoothly. "Teenaged girls love makeup and perfume, and they won't really care who Mariah Blackthorne is."

"I guess that's true," Carm said a bit grudgingly. "And speaking of part-time help, I should be getting back too. I've got a new part-timer starting today."

I prepared their sandwiches quickly, and once they'd departed made a beeline back to the rear table. I'd barely sat down before I heard a familiar scraping sound. Scrabble tiles started flying out from underneath the table faster than I could snatch them up. There were seven in all, and I arranged them on the tabletop, chuckling as I saw what they spelled out: trouble. Nick's head popped out from underneath the table.

"Merow."

I bent down and gave him a quick scratch behind the ear. "You could be right about that, Nick, and I guess Louis was right with what he said about public opinion. Carmela certainly feels strongly against Mariah, doesn't she? I really wouldn't have thought that of her. She's always seemed so easygoing."

Nick blinked twice. "Mrrrr."

"Yes, I know, there's just no accounting sometimes for the things people get on a soapbox over. Well, one thing's for sure. Mariah Blackthorne had better steer clear of Carm's store, or Carm just might eat her alive. Now, where were we? Oh, yes. Refreshing my memory on trial details."

"Merow."

I called up my favorite search engine and typed "Mariah Blackthorne Trial" into it. A plethora of news articles came up. Nick hopped onto the chair next to mine and watched as I clicked on several, skimming over them. In one the reporter—male—had focused on Mariah's appearance, calling her a "knockout" and remarking that she was a combination of "classy and gorgeous." From the accompanying photo, taken of Mariah at the defense table, I had to agree. She sat tall and regal, her dark hair spilling across her shoulders. Her hands were clasped in front of her, and I noted that she still wore her wedding band. "The High-Society Widow" was the caption underneath the photo. News articles like that had probably gotten under Carmella's skin.

I skimmed several more articles, but the one from the *Monterey Observer* seemed to have the most information regarding the background of the case itself. I leaned forward and read the article:

Woman Accused of Murdering Husband in Cold Blood Faces Sentencing

Cruz, CA: Mariah Wilton Blackthorne, who two weeks ago pleaded guilty to a charge of manslaughter in connection with the brutal slaying of her husband, psychiatrist Christian Blackthorne, faces sentencing today.

Dr. Blackthorne was found dead in his study by the couple's maid, Ms. Velma Cutter. He lay sprawled across his desk, his skull bashed in. Mrs. Blackthorne lay unconscious not five feet away from the body, her hand curled around what authorities later determined to be the murder weapon.

Upon initial questioning Mrs. Blackthorne claimed that she could not remember events leading up to right before the murder. Earlier in the day, she'd been preparing for a special dinner party for her husband's birthday; however, during the course of the morning she overheard a conversation that confirmed her suspicions that her husband had been having an affair. According to Mrs. Blackthorne, she was so upset that she went for a drive along the coast to think things through. Upon her return to the house later that day, she went into her husband's den to have a discussion and saw him sprawled over the desk. She went over, saw that he was dead, and then blacked out. She has no recollection of how she came to be on the other side of the room, or how she came to be clutching the bronze bust that was proven to be the murder weapon.

Mrs. Cutter, summoned as a hostile witness, testified that on more than one occasion she'd heard Mrs. Blackthorne express concern that her husband might be unfaithful. Next up, Dr. Paul Lassiter, Blackthorne's partner, could not confirm or deny the rumors of Blackthorne's infidelity, but he did testify that the suspicion was a niggling thorn in the marriage. Lassiter testified to witnessing several incidents where Mrs.

Blackthorne and her husband argued, and Mrs. Blackthorne on at least one occasion threatened her husband's life. However, even Lassiter could not entirely discount the possibility that Blackthorne might have received a call from a woman that morning.

Following Lassiter's testimony, Leon Childs, Mrs. Blackthorne's attorney, and the DA met behind closed doors. It is rumored that Childs and the DA might have reached an agreement for Mrs. Blackthorne to plead guilty to manslaughter and the ten-year sentence it carries.

I frowned at the screen. "Neither the housekeeper nor Blackthorne's partner did Mariah any favors with their testimonies, although the housekeeper was viewed as hostile. Lassiter seemed particularly vicious toward Mariah, though . . . maybe to call attention away from himself? Any thoughts, Nick?"

I glanced up and saw that Nick had moved over to sit in front of my large picture window. Some robins had made a nest in one of the branches of the tall elm on the street in front of my shop, and Nick spent his afternoons watching them and tapping at the window as they flew past, making guttural sounds in his throat. Now he raised his paw and tapped his nails against the glass. After a few seconds he pressed his face against the windowpane and let out a loud hiss.

"Hey, stop that, Nick. You'll scare the birds."

"Meower," he said. He tapped again at the window, more insistently this time.

I scraped back my chair. "Okay, okay. What's got you riled up?" I walked over to the window and peered out. The street was deserted save for a large, dark blue sedan parked across from my shop. The car looked vaguely familiar, but I couldn't quite place it. I put my hands on my hips and looked at Nick. "There's nothing out there, Nick."

He swiveled his head to give me a golden stare before jumping off the counter and heading toward his food bowl, tail held high.

I returned to my laptop, where I typed "Paul Lassiter—testimony Blackthorne trial" into the search engine. There were several articles, and they all said pretty much the same thing. Lassiter testified that on several occasions Blackthorne had mentioned that his wife was on the verge of "losing it" and that her possessiveness and jealous tantrums had him on edge. He spoke of a dinner party he'd attended at the Blackthornes', only a few weeks prior, where he'd overheard a particularly violent argument between them over Blackthorne's supposed infidelity. Not many details were given. It seemed to me as if he were deliberately painting a picture of Mariah as a jealous wife, prone to fits of anger.

My cell phone started to vibrate. I ignored it and kept on reading. A few minutes later the landline in the shop rang. Still I kept on reading. The call switched over to my answering machine, and after the beep I heard a familiar voice boom out, "Nora! If you're there pick up! It's me."

Me was Hank Prince, a dear friend and my old CI from my Chicago reporting days. I scraped back my chair and made a dive for the phone. "Hank! What a nice surprise! What's up?"

"You sound a bit out of breath. Is this a bad time?"

"No, not at all. I was just researching a possible article for *Noir*." I tucked the phone under my chin and eased one hip against the counter. "Say, I thought you were planning on taking a trip out here soon."

"I was, but my plans got changed. I'm needed here in Chicago. It's an urgent case."

"Aren't they all?"

He chuckled. "True, but this one really is urgent." He paused. "I'm calling because I kind of need a favor."

"Really? That's a switch. Usually it's the other way around."

"First time for everything. So, what do you say? Or are you too busy? Have you gotten yourself involved in another mystery?"

I glanced over at my laptop with the account of Mariah's trial still up on the screen. "Sort of, but you know I'll help you, whatever you need. You're always there for me, after all."

"I was hoping you'd say that," Hank said. "A friend of mine desperately needs your help. I'll let her fill in the details. She should be at your shop very soon. I've known her a long time—years, in fact. She didn't do what they think she did. Mariah's innocent, she wouldn't hurt a fly."

"Did you say her name is Mariah?" That wasn't a common name. He couldn't possibly mean Mariah Blackthorne, could he? I was just about to ask his friend's last name when I heard a burst of loud static in my ear. "Nora?" I could make out Hank's voice, faint and very far away. "Bad connection. I'll have to call you back."

There was a last burst of static and then the line went dead just as the bell above my shop door jangled. I glanced up, and sucked in a breath as I saw two women framed in my doorway. One I had never seen before. The other I'd seen only a few short hours ago on my TV screen.

Mariah Blackthorne.

Nick's head popped out from underneath the table. "Merow." *Told ya.*

Chapter Three

I set the phone down and stepped out from behind the counter. The two women were turned slightly away from me, studying the board where I posted my daily specials. I took a tentative step forward, and Mariah suddenly swung around to face me. Her face broke into a wide smile and she held out her hand. "You have to be Nora Charles," she said. "I've heard a lot about you. It's nice to meet you at last. I'm Mariah Blackthorne."

"Yes, I know who you are." I took the proffered hand, shook it and winced. Mariah had a pretty strong grip.

The woman standing beside her cleared her throat—loudly. Mariah released my hand and gestured toward the other woman. "Pardon me. This is my friend Elle Gardner. She was good enough to pick me up at the prison earlier and bring me here."

I realized then why the dark sedan across the street had seemed so familiar. It was the one I'd seen Mariah ride off in. Elle didn't offer her hand, merely nodded. I nodded back, and then Mariah cleared her throat. "Hank did call you, right? He told me he would."

"He did call," I said, "but unfortunately he couldn't say much other than a friend of his needed some help. There was a bad connection, and he got cut off before he could tell me any details."

"Oh, dear. I imagine it was a bit of a shock, then, when you saw me here in your shop?" Her brows drew together and her lips turned downward in a worried expression.

"Maybe a little bit," I admitted. We stood there awkwardly for a few moments and then I gestured toward one of the front tables. "You should sit down. Are you hungry? Can I get you something?"

Her worried expression morphed into a smile. "How nice of you to ask. I am famished. I couldn't eat a bite this morning. Too excited about finally being free, I guess." She squinted at my board, then pointed. "The Betty White sounds good. Grilled chicken breast and provolone on a wrap. I'll have that."

Elle nodded. "That does sound good. Make that two."

"Great. I'll just be a few minutes. Sit anywhere and make yourselves comfortable."

I hurried back behind the counter, pulled out the ingredients for the sandwiches. As I prepared them, I could hear the two women talking in low tones. I poured hot coffee into two oversized mugs and set them on a tray with the sandwiches and a bowl of sugar and a small pitcher of cream, and carried it over to the table. "Coffee okay?" I asked as I placed the tray down.

"Perfect," they said in unison, and each took a mug. Elle sipped hers black, but Mariah added some cream and two spoonfuls of sugar, then took a sip. She leaned back in the chair with a contented sigh. "Like heaven. Prison coffee is nothing like this." She drained her cup, held it out. "Could I have a refill?"

I took her cup and went behind the counter. I'd just finished pouring the coffee when I felt my apron pocket vibrate. I pulled out my cell and saw I had a text from Hank: *Sorry about that. Hit a dead zone. Mariah will explain. We'll talk soon.* "You bet we will," I murmured. I slid the phone back into my pocket, poured a mug of coffee for myself and carried everything back to the table. "I hope you don't mind if I join you?" I asked.

Elle frowned, but Mariah smiled affably. "Not at all. Please sit down."

I slid into the seat opposite Mariah and took a moment to study her. The thought passed through my mind that Carm would undoubtedly have approved of Mariah's makeup, even though underneath the carefully applied foundation she was pale, and there were dark circles underneath her eyes that no amount of concealer could hide. That notwithstanding, I had to agree overall with the reporter's assessment of her. Mariah certainly radiated class. It was hard to believe that she'd spent the last five years in prison.

Elle pushed her plate with a half-eaten sandwich to one side and scraped back her chair. "I'm going to go outside to the car," she said. "I have some calls I should make, and I know you want to speak to Ms. Charles privately." She bent over and squeezed Mariah's shoulder. "Take all the time you need."

Once Elle had gone, Mariah looked me straight in the eye. "I know you must have many questions. I know I would if I were in your position."

"I do." I met her gaze. "I guess my first question is, how do you know Hank?"

Her laugh tittered out, not unlike the one of a very young bird. "That's an easy one. Hank and I go way back, to when my name was Wilton. We went to high school together in Chicago. My parents moved out here my senior year of high school. My father got a huge promotion, so . . . ." She spread her hands. "It all happened at a very inopportune time, just when

Hank was starting to come out of his shell. Believe it or not, he was painfully shy, especially around girls. It took him until the end of junior year to ask me for a date." Her eyes took on a faraway look. "We made up for lost time, though, until my father lowered the boom—we were moving to California. We swore to keep in touch, and we did for a while, but, well, you know how it is when you're teenagers. I think the phrase 'out of sight, out of mind' had to be invented by one." She tilted her head to one side and remarked, "I'll admit you surprised me, Nora. I thought for sure your first question would be, 'Did you kill your husband?'"

"That would have been a rather pointless one, considering you don't remember if you did or didn't, correct?"

Her lips twitched slightly. "Correct. But most people ask anyway." She studied me for a few moments and then said, "When Hank mentioned your name I googled you. I read some of the articles you wrote for the *Chicago Tribune*, and for that magazine, *Noir*. The Lola Grainger case, and the one about the PI they thought committed suicide. Hank said you have a definite talent for deduction and I have to say I agree."

"Thanks, but I didn't solve those alone. I had help." A loud meow sounded from the depths of the kitchen. "Come on out, Nick."

A few seconds later a black and white face peeped out from the doorway leading to the kitchen. "Meet the other half of the Charles investigative team," I said.

Nick trotted over to the table and squatted, tail wrapped around his forepaws, his head cocked, studying us with wide golden eyes. Mariah looked down at him with a smile. "Nick Charles, eh? He's well-named. Why, I believe he's even more handsome than Bill Powell." She turned her gaze to me. "It's a good thing he didn't come out when Elle was here. She's not fond of animals, and she dislikes cats in particular."

Why was I not surprised? My tubby tuxedo, no doubt, had sensed a hostile presence and chosen to remain out of sight.

Nick got up and went over, rubbed his body against Mariah's ankles. She reached down to stroke the top of his head, and he let out a loud, rumbly purr. "I had a cat myself, once. A gray tabby. Her name was Trixie." Her tone grew wistful. "We gave her to my aunt when we moved to California. I missed her for a long time. She was a good cat, and smart. Like your fellow here." Mariah slid her gaze to me. "It's funny, but I can see how your cat would be a help to you. I can't explain it. There's just something . . . almost human about him. Maybe I should get a cat." She looked at him for a few moments, then turned to me and held out her mug. "Could I trouble you for another cup?"

"No trouble at all."

I took Mariah's mug and refilled both hers and my own. When I returned, she said, "I'm sure you're wondering how Hank and I reconnected after all those years. Actually, it sounds like something out of a Nora Ephron movie. It was about seven years ago. We both happened to be staying at the same hotel in Boston. I was accompanying my husband on a lecture tour—one of the few times I did—and Hank was working on a case. We ran into each other in the elevator." Her lips twisted into a wry grin. "We just started talking, as if no time at all had passed, and then later that night we met for a drink while my husband was giving his lecture."

"And then?" I prompted as she paused.

"And then," she sighed, "we went our separate ways. I had my life with Christian, and Hank had his work, which he told me was very fulfilling. I didn't hear from him again until after I got sent to prison. Hank wrote to me there, pretty much every week. He wanted to do an investigation back then, but I told him no. What was the point? Public sentiment was high that I had committed the crime, and I couldn't remember otherwise." She paused and then added, "I always had an idea, though, that Hank might have done some digging on his own, but with no success. Anyway, when I wrote that I was being considered for parole, he wasted no time contacting the board and giving a statement. I'm certain it went a long way toward their decision to release me." She looked straight into my eyes, and I saw a lot of pain there. "I've paid the price for my husband's death whether I had something to do with it or not. I don't feel, however, that I can move on with my life unless I get some sort of closure. In my heart I don't believe I had anything to do with it, but, if I did, I need to know it, and if I didn't, I need to know that too. Hank said he'd come out and help me, but now he can't get away, and so . . ." She paused and raised an eyebrow at me.

"He suggested me," I finished.

"That's correct." Her hand shot out, covered mine. "I realize this is an imposition, that you have a business, a life for goodness sakes. This is probably the last thing you want to do."

"I wouldn't say that," I said. "At one time I made my living investigating cases just like yours. I was working in Chicago at the time of your trial, but I managed to follow most of it. Personally I thought you got a raw deal."

Her lips twisted into a half smile. "That's nice of you to say. Most people painted me as a money-grubbing, hack actress loser who'd landed a rich husband and iced him when the going got tough. Most people think I'm faking my memory loss but I assure you, it's genuine. Oh, I've tried to remember over the years. I consulted with several psychiatrists while in prison. One even set me up with a hypnotist, but apparently I'm not a good candidate. So it's all still a big blank."

"Public opinion can be hard to change," I said, thinking about what Carm had said earlier. "Tell me what you do recall, then."

She let out a long sigh and stretched her arms wide. "We'd been arguing a lot. I challenged him more than once about his philandering, and he always denied it, even hinted I might be paranoid on the subject. That morning I was walking past his study when I heard him on the phone. I couldn't make out all the words, but I could tell from his tone he was upset. No, more than upset. Angry." She let out a breath. "He was quiet for so long I thought he'd hung up, and then I heard him say, 'Here's my final word. You have more to lose than I do. If you are pregnant, and I do mean if, it's your problem, not mine,' and then he slammed the phone down."

I raised an eyebrow. "Are you certain that's what you heard?"

Mariah nodded. "Oh, yes. I was grilled up and down on it by the DA. I know he was disappointed when he couldn't trip me up. That's absolutely what my husband said."

"What did you do then?"

"I considered confronting him, but then I figured what was the use? He'd only deny it as he'd always done. Christian had always maintained so strongly that he'd never cheated on me . . . I was in shock. I couldn't face him right then, I couldn't even bear to be in the same house with him. I had to get out of there. Calm down before I asked him about it." Her fingers twined themselves in her thick hair, and she gave an errant curl a tug. "I decided to go for a drive. Driving always clears my head. I went to McCogan's Bluff."

I knew the place. It was a quiet, secluded area, set far off the main highway. High school kids went there to make out, and both Chantal and I had indulged in that activity there back in the day. It was definitely not a tourist trap. "And no one saw you?"

She shook her head. "No. I just sat there for hours, thinking about my life in general and what I was going to do next. I knew I had to confront him at some point, but I just wasn't ready. I had fifty people coming to my house later for a celebration, so I decided to just table everything and put on a happy face, and just like Scarlett O'Hara, I'd think about the whole mess tomorrow. When I got back to the house, everything was so quiet, I thought maybe he'd gone out. I hadn't seen his car. I started upstairs, and that's when I saw the light on in the den. The door was open, just a crack. I pushed it open and went in, and that's when my memory gets fuzzy. I had an impression of a body slumped over the desk and . . . there was something else."

"Something else? Like what?"

"That's the bad part," she said with a tight smile. "I don't know. Something I saw or sensed, like a slight sound, or a smell perhaps. I keep thinking it's something I should be able to remember, but I just can't recall. Then everything went black, and the next thing I remember was waking up on the floor with police surrounding me."

"They found you clutching the murder weapon. You have no memory of that? You don't recall touching it at all?"

"No." Her jaw clenched. "I gave him that bust, too. Had it specially commissioned for him as a Christmas gift the first year we were married. He loved that thing. Said once he'd die if anything ever happened to it. Ironic, huh?" She traced the outline of the checkered tablecloth with the edge of her nail. "There's a light at the end of this tunnel, though. Most of the shrinks I spoke with said pretty much the same thing. Once I was back in familiar surroundings, something could trigger my subconscious and there was a good chance my memory might return."

I raised an eyebrow. "Assuming you're innocent and the real killer is still out there, you could be setting yourself up as a target."

Her chin lifted. "It's a chance I'm willing to take, if that is the only way to get results."

"Do you have any ideas who might have wanted your husband dead?"

She pursed her lips and tilted her head to one side, considering my question. At last she said, "My husband really wasn't a very nice man, Nora. He made a lot of enemies, including his business partner, Paul Lassiter." Mariah fairly spat the name. "He professed to be my friend as well as Christian's, but when push came to shove, he could not wait to throw me under the bus."

"He said that he overheard you threaten your husband. Was that true?"

She was silent for a few moments before she responded. "It wasn't a threat in the strictest sense of the word. It was more like something said in the heat of the moment. Christian could give as good as he got. I imagine I could say there were just as many times when he threatened *me*, and I know for a fact Paul overheard some of those arguments too. He said nothing about *them*, though," she hissed, and then added with a significant glance, "or about the many arguments he himself had with Christian, that ended with each of them threatening the other as well."

"What did he and your husband argue about?"

"Their business, mostly. Christian was desperate to expand, add another location, put in more hours, hire another associate. Paul liked things the way they were. He didn't think an expansion would be beneficial. They argued about money as well. Paul thought they should have been showing bigger profits. And, speaking of money, I don't expect you to do this for nothing. I'm perfectly willing to compensate you for your time."

I held up my hand. "Oh, I couldn't take money from you, Mrs. Blackthorne. For one thing, I'm not a practicing PI. For another, I owe Hank a lot. I'm doing this for him, and also because I would love to write up the story of your innocence for *Noir*."

"Let's hope that you get that opportunity." She put her hand up to her mouth and stifled a yawn. "Goodness. I'm afraid I'm more tired than I realized. I probably should get going."

We both rose and walked to the door. "Are you staying at the Cruz Inn?"

"Actually, no. My lawyer managed to convince a judge to rule that I could return to my house." Her lips curved upward. "I'm anxious to see it. I know there were a few attempted break-ins while I was in prison. Fortunately nothing was taken. I'm inclined to believe it was most likely curiosity seekers more than anything else. At any rate, my lawyer installed an alarm system so there were no further incidents."

I frowned. "Do you think that's wise? Curiosity seekers might return, and I'm guessing the press will be camped out there as well. Have you thought about hiring some security?"

Mariah frowned. "I'm not going to be there alone, at least not for a few days. Elle said she would stay with me. Besides," she added and smiled, "I doubt security is necessary. I'm old news. After all the hoopla this morning, I doubt there's any serious interest in what I do or where I go, although . . ." She paused. "There is this reporter, who's more of a nuisance than anything else. She started bothering me my last days in prison and I have no doubt she'll keep trying, no matter how many times I rebuff her. Can't remember her name. Ginny or Joanie or something like that." Mariah waved her hand. "If she continues to bother me I'm going to call my attorney and get a restraining order. I don't need this added stress." Mariah paused, her hand on the doorknob. "I appreciate your doing this, Nora, more than you know. I'm tired of all the blank spaces. I just want to know the truth."

I looked her square in the eye. "Even if the truth should turn out to be that you did kill your husband?"

She hesitated only slightly before meeting my stare head-on. "Yes. Even then."

Chapter Four

The door had barely closed behind Mariah when my phone rang again, and I saw Hank's name pop up on my Caller ID. I snatched the phone up and depressed the answer button. "Well, well, does this mean you're out of the dead zone?"

"For now, anyway," Hank said. "I've got a few minutes so I thought I'd give you a quick call. Mariah came to see you, right? What did you think?"

Hank's tone was calm, but I could sense the undercurrent of excitement. "She didn't particularly impress me as the murderous type."

"That's because she's not. Mariah could never kill anyone, you can trust me on that. She was framed but good. That damn DA didn't even look at anyone else, and that lawyer of hers, well, Childs isn't a criminal attorney, so I guess I can't blame him too much. He did the best he could, considering the circumstances."

"You mean her amnesia."

"Yes. The prosecution tried their damnedest to prove she was faking it, but all the experts on both sides came to the same conclusion. She wasn't." He paused. "I suppose Mariah told you how we know each other."

"Yes, she mentioned the high school sweetheart thingy. Funny, I've never pictured you as the shy type."

"Hah. I guess I was, back then. Maybe if I hadn't been . . . oh, well, that's all water under the bridge. The important thing now is figuring out who really killed Christian Blackthorne. That person has gotten away with murder, literally, for far too long." He heaved out a long sigh. "I started to make some discreet inquiries at the time, and then . . . Mariah told me to let it go. She'd resigned herself to her fate, even if I hadn't."

"You respected her wishes."

"Yes. She was afraid I'd become too fixated on the investigation, let my other work slide. She told me to destroy any notes I'd made, to move on and forget about her. I complied with her wishes, but I never forgot about it." He paused. "I didn't destroy all of my notes either, and I remember everything as if I'd taken them yesterday. The police dropped the ball, in my opinion. There were a lot of suspects to consider."

"Mariah mentioned her husband's business partner as a possible candidate."

"Paul Lassiter. Yeah." Hank let out a sigh. "He and Blackthorne were partners for years, but toward the end they argued a lot about finances. Lassiter suspected Blackthorne might have been doing a bit of creative bookkeeping to support his lavish lifestyle, and Blackthorne was convinced Lassiter was skimming funds to support a gambling habit."

"Lassiter had a gambling problem?"

"According to Blackthorne, he did. There was never any real evidence to prove it. But the real hot button issue between them was Mariah. He'd made passes at her several times, which she rebuffed. Even the housekeeper testified she heard Lassiter and Blackthorne arguing over Lassiter's flirting with Mariah several times. The prosecution downplayed that, though."

"The housekeeper. She discovered the body, right? What did you think about her? Do you think she could have had a part in Blackthorne's death?"

"Velma Cutter? Not a chance. That woman loved that job. She was brokenhearted when she had to leave it. Wasn't even mad that Blackthorne didn't leave her a cent in his will. Her son, however, is a different story. Jerry Cutter and Blackthorne reportedly went at it several times, and in public, no less. At a party the Blackthornes gave shortly before his death, Cutter accused him of taking advantage of his mother, of overworking and underpaying her. Blackthorne retaliated by accusing the son of being shiftless and lazy. I'm not sure just what Cutter does for a living, but Blackthorne apparently didn't think too much of it. One time he yelled at him that if he were so dissatisfied with the way he treated his mother, he should go get a real job."

"That's all interesting, but it's not what you'd call a real motive for murder, particularly in light of the fact Blackthorne didn't leave the mother anything in his will."

"Oh, there's more. The week before he died, Blackthorne called his attorney. He wanted to press charges against Jerry. Claimed he walked in on the guy helping himself to some small rare jade statues in his living room. Cutter denied it, said he was just looking at the pieces, and Blackthorne was exaggerating because he 'had it in for him,' quote unquote. Anyway, long story short, Blackthorne decided against pressing charges in deference to the mother. She went to bat for the son, pleaded with him to give the boy another chance."

"Hmm. So Blackthorne might have caught Cutter in the act again, only this time Cutter might have had a violent reaction," I said.

"It's a possibility. Personally I think the son was the reason Blackthorne omitted Velma from his will. He probably figured the son would sweet-talk her out of any inheritance he'd leave her."

"What about an alibi? Did he have one?"

"Said he was with a girlfriend on a day trip. She corroborated it, but you know how alibis like that go. It's fifty-fifty they're telling the truth. Then there's Adam Porter. He's a hairdresser, and a friend of Mariah's. He wanted to open his own salon, and Mariah convinced her husband to invest in it. Unfortunately, Porter has no head for business, and the salon tanked. Blackthorne apparently was after him to repay his original investment."

"How much was that?"

"Two hundred thousand dollars."

"Ouch. There's two hundred thousand motives for murder right there."

"I agree, especially since the loan was forgiven upon Blackthorne's death. Porter got off not owing a dime. He had an alibi for the TOD, but it wasn't exactly ironclad. Seems he was at a fantasy hair show, but unfortunately so were five hundred other people. The security guard remembered issuing him an entrance bracelet, but as far as I know, no one could recall actually seeing him there."

"What about the call Mariah overheard? The supposedly pregnant mistress? Did anyone follow up on that?"

"Sure did. Unfortunately, the call was made from an untraceable burner cell. The DA tried like the dickens to shake Mariah on that testimony, but she held fast. She maintained that she heard her husband tell whoever was on the other end of that conversation that if she were pregnant, it was her problem." He let out a small sigh. "Blackthorne was very careful when it came to that part of his life. There's plenty of innuendo regarding his trysts, but no real names, or evidence that any actually happened."

"So no hidden mistresses came forward after his death?"

"Not so far. I doubt we'll ever know that woman's identity."

"Mariah wasn't alone when she came here today," I said. "A woman named Elle Gardner was with her. What do you know about her?"

"Not too much. Her given name is Elspeth and she kept in touch with Mariah while she was incarcerated. Mariah said Elle was the only one of her so-called friends who stuck by her." He paused. "I take it you didn't get a good vibe from her?"

"Nick didn't. As for me, I'm not sure. It's nothing I could come right out and put my finger on. I realize that it's just a first impression on my part, but she seemed to be one of those snooty society types to me. You know, the kind who look down their noses at women who wear orange jumpsuits. At the very least I'd certainly like to know more about her, though, and what her relationship to both Blackthornes was."

Hank let out a sigh. "This case I'm on is a real bear and takes up most of my time. I'm not sure when I'll be able to get back to you. You sound like you have a good handle on things, though. Call or text me if you need anything. It might take awhile, but I'll get back to you."

"I know you will. Oh, and one other thing. There might be a slight complication down the road." I told Hank what Mariah had said about the reporter, and what Carm had told me about the woman in her shop. "If this reporter is after the truth, she might be a big help," I finished. "But if she's from one of those tabloids, well, it could be trouble."

"I'll reach out to some of my contacts, see if they can find out anything. You just keep up the good work. At this rate you'll be a pro PI sooner rather than later."

I chuckled. "Don't tell Ollie that. He's still trying to convince me to turn over Hot Bread to Lacey and join him in the PI business."

Hank chuckled. "Fat chance of that, although truthfully? It's not a bad idea."

"I'd agree with you if I thought Lacey wouldn't run Mom's business into the ground," I said. "As it stands, though, Hot Bread—and my mother's legacy—is my responsibility."

"But you're tempted," Hank persisted. "Admit it, Nora. You'd love to be a full-time PI."

I laughed. "Maybe so, but would you believe I love making sandwiches more?"

"Honestly? No."

Nick let out a yowl and Hank laughed. "Your cat doesn't buy that either."

"If you ask me, Nick's the one who should be a PI. Too bad they don't issue licenses to cats."

"If they did, Nick would be first in line. I've got to get going. We'll talk soon."

Hank rang off and I slid my phone back into my pocket just as the bell above the shop door sounded. I glanced at the woman coming through the door. She was tall and reed-thin, with hair the color of fresh-picked corn on the cob falling in soft ringlets around a heart-shaped face. There was something familiar about her, but I couldn't quite place it. "Hello," I said. "Can I help you?"

Clear blue eyes bored straight into mine. "I hope so. You're Nora Charles, formerly of the *Chicago Tribune*?" She thrust out her hand. "I worked there too, but you probably don't remember me."

I peered at her more closely, and then it hit me. Jennifer Hinkle, or as we used to call her, Pariah Jenn, had leapfrogged over many reporters' backs in her quest for the top. She'd ended up leaving the *Trib* for the bright lights of New York in the form of a popular gossip tabloid. So what was she doing here in Cruz? For the life of me, I couldn't think of why she'd be in town, unless . . . Could she be the reporter that Carm had referred to? The one determined to "get at the whole truth" of Christian Blackthorne's death? If so, that wasn't a good thing.

Nick's head popped out from underneath the rear table, and I thought it seemed he'd been prophetic with his Scrabble tiles earlier.

Trouble was indeed ahead. How much, though, was anyone's guess.

Chapter Five

I arranged my features into what I hoped passed for a pleasant expression and said, "Jennifer Hinkle, right? It's been a long time. You left the *Trib* for a New York paper, right?"

"Yeah, the *Insider*." Her lips twisted into a wry smile. "I'm not with that paper anymore. Actually, calling it a paper is a bit of a stretch. Gossip rag would be more accurate." Her shoulders lifted in a casual shrug. "I've been into freelance work. One has a lot more freedom there. No one to look over your shoulder, telling you what you can and can't do, what is or isn't acceptable. I'm sure I don't have to tell you how confining editors can be sometimes." She gave an appraising glance around my shop. "I see you opted for a drastic career change too."

"Not so drastic. This was my mother's shop. I'm merely carrying on the family tradition." I gestured toward the display case. "Can I get you something?"

She peered at the blackboard menu as she slid onto one of the counter stools. "You have the sandwiches named after famous people. How clever. I think I'd just like a plain old Reuben sandwich, though."

"Sure. Do you prefer a particular type of bread other than the traditional rye?"

She looked at me as if I'd grown an extra head. "It has to be on grilled rye, or it's not a Reuben," she said, her tone serious.

"I totally agree, but I do have some customers who order it on pumpernickel or whole wheat."

"Heathens!" She reached out to touch my elbow. "And can you make it open-faced? It seems like most places out here look at you like you've got three heads when you ask for an open-faced sandwich. You'd think they'd be happy to save an extra slice of bread." She shook her head. "Oh, and a coffee, light and sweet."

"You got it."

I poured hot coffee into one of my oversized mugs, added cream and two sugars and set it in front of her. I reached into my deli case for the corned beef and suddenly realized that Lacey had forgotten to buy sauerkraut. I mentioned it to Jennifer, adding, "I can substitute German coleslaw, unless you'd rather have something else."

She looked up from her phone, which I noted was one of the larger models. The case was striking, a bright pink with white and pink stars emblazoned on it. "What did you say?" she asked.

"I said that I'm out of sauerkraut, but I can substitute German coleslaw."

"Oh, right. Yeah, that'll be fine," she said. She took another look at her phone, then slid it into her jacket pocket. She picked up the mug and took a sip of her coffee, then waved her other hand in the air. "To be honest, I'm not that crazy about sauerkraut anyway. You could leave it off entirely."

I was tempted to say, *"It's not a Reuben without the sauerkraut,"* but decided against it. I prepared the sandwich and slid it inside the broiler. A few minutes later I placed it in front of her. She sniffed, then smiled. "This smells great." She picked up knife and fork, angled off a hunk, popped it into her mouth. "Delicious." She set her fork down, picked up her mug. "So, big doings here in Cruz, huh? I guess you heard about Mariah Blackthorne?"

Uh-oh, I thought. Here it comes. "Hard not to," I said lightly. "It's been all over the news since her release."

"I followed her trial six years ago. I didn't think she was guilty then, and I still don't." She paused and then added, "Let me be frank with you. Mariah Blackthorne is the reason I came here to Cruz. She thinks being back in Cruz might finally unlock her memory, and I tend to agree. And when it does, I plan to be right on the scene. Finding out the real truth about Blackthorne's death would not only be front-page news, but it would make an excellent book."

I stared at her. "You want to do a *book* on Mariah Blackthorne?"

She took another bite of her sandwich, chewed and swallowed before she answered me. "Not on her per se. On this murder. I want to write the real story, not a rehash of what everyone already knows. You know how these types of investigations go. Anything that doesn't fit the scenario gets discarded. The preponderance of evidence pointed to Mariah as the killer, and no one looked very hard at any other suspects because the DA felt he had a slam-dunk case. Trust me, there's more here than meets the eye. A lot more." She leaned forward and said in a conspiratorial whisper, "There were lots of other people with axes to grind against Blackthorne. I have a lot of threads, I just need to piece them together." Jennifer exhaled a deep breath. "I've already gotten an advance from a publisher, not a large one, mind you, but if the book's a hit, why, there's no telling what might come of it. A movie, maybe."

"You sound very optimistic."

"I am. I'm already collecting information for another book. It's amazing how many cold cases are out there." She slid me a look. "I could use some help with this one, if you're interested. I'm sure you've already considered doing an article on this murder for that online magazine you write for. We could team up, maybe solve this together. What do you say?"

I swallowed. I had no desire to work with Jen in any way, shape or form, but on the other hand, I didn't want to alienate her. "I have considered it," I said at last. "But delving into this mystery will be very time-consuming, and right now I'm swamped with my own business."

"O-kay." Jen pushed her plate off to the side, then reached into her jacket pocket and pulled out a card, which she laid on the counter in front of me. She tapped at it with the edge of her nail. "If you change your mind, here's my contact info." Her hand dipped into her tote bag and she pulled out a ten-dollar bill and laid it next to the card. "The sandwich was delicious. Keep the change."

Jennifer slid off the stool and out of my shop. I picked up the money and the card. It was a pale gray background patterned with what appeared to be shooting stars. Printed on it in bright maroon letters was:

Jennifer Hinkle, Freelance Reporter
216-555-0743

On the back of the card she'd scrawled, *Cruz Inn. Room 225.*

Nick wriggled his portly bod out from under the table. He pointed his paw at the card. "Er-owl?"

"Yes, she's persistent. And I'm afraid Mariah is right. She might well prove a hindrance. You remember Blaine Carmichael? She's the female version."

Nick bared his fangs and let out a hiss.

"My thoughts exactly." I sighed. "Maybe I should consider working with her, huh? At least that way I might have a shot at controlling her. She's a loose cannon for sure."

"Who's a loose cannon? That chick I just saw barreling out of here?"

I jumped. I hadn't heard the back door open, or my BFF Chantal Gillard come in. She dropped her quilted Vera Bradley tote on the floor and eased onto one of the stools. "Whatever did you say to her, chérie? She seemed to be in quite a hurry. She was talking to someone on her cell and nearly ran into me." She gave a mock shudder. "I did not get a good vibe from her, not at all."

"Join the club. It's been quite a day," I said with a sigh. I recounted the morning's adventures, beginning with the intern from Hell, Mariah's visit, my conversation with Hank and ending with Jennifer's request. When I finished, Chantal let out a loud sigh.

"It does not pay for me to take a day off," she groaned. "Look at all the excitement I missed."

"Some of this excitement I could do without." I noticed Anna's iPad on the counter and held it up. "With all that went on, I forgot to text Anna that I rescued her phone from Nick's clutches. Which reminds me that I've got to put another ad in the *Cruz Sun* classified section for help."

"That might not be necessary," Chantal piped up.

I looked at my friend. Chantal had a cat ate the canary expression on her face. "And why not?" I asked.

"Marie Monaco came into my shop for a reading this morning. You remember Marie, right?"

I did indeed. Marie was a lovely woman in her seventies who'd been a legal secretary in Cruz for as long as I could remember. She'd been a good customer of mine, but since she'd officially retired about six months ago I'd only seen her a handful of times. She had twin boys, Jim and John, who were about a year older than me, and both were married with families of their own. "I sure do. How is she enjoying her retirement? I remember her talking at her retirement party about how she wasn't going to be one of those women who stays home watching soap operas all day."

"Marie is still very active. She volunteers at the hospital two nights a week, and she's been helping Jim out at his store, running the register, doing light bookkeeping." Jim managed a stationery store over in Wyck, about six towns over. Chantal ran her finger along the edge of the counter. "Marie mentioned that her granddaughter, Michaela, is looking for part-time work. Apparently she has designs on pursuing a culinary career. Marie says Michaela wants to work somewhere where she'll learn something about the restaurant business." Chantal paused. "I asked her to send you Michaela's résumé. I hope you don't mind."

"Not at all. As a matter of fact, she sounds pretty ideal. She will have to pass the Nick Charles smell test, though. And it's not an easy thing to do. Just ask poor Anna."

Chantal looked around. "Where is Nicky, anyway? He usually comes over to greet me."

I frowned. "Why, I don't know. He was lying by the refrigerator when Jennifer was here." I glanced toward the rear of the shop and noticed the back door was slightly ajar. I got up and went over, opened the door all the way and peeped out into my combination garage/storeroom. Sure enough, Nick was there, squatting in the far corner. "Nick," I exclaimed. "What are you doing out here?"

Nick seemed to be occupied with something, so I walked over to him. The minute he caught sight of me, he twisted his body almost all the way around so his back paws were upright. I noticed his front left paw was halfway under the crack in the door, as if he were hiding something.

"Nick," I said. "What's up?"

"Mrr," he said, his golden eyes not meeting mine.

I narrowed my gaze at the cat. "What's with you? You seem guilty to me, Nick. What have you been up to while I've been gone? Are you trying to hide something under there? Or have you lost one of your precious Scrabble tiles?"

He cocked his head, looking at me as if what I'd said made no sense at all to him. At the same time, he kept trying to bat whatever it was further under the door.

"Okay, jig's up. What are you trying to keep from me?"

He gave me a confused kitty stare, but I wasn't buying it. I pushed him gently out of the way, knelt down, and felt underneath the door. A second later I pulled out a thin, jagged scrap of paper. I stood up and smoothed it out. It looked as if it had been torn from a notepad or a book, and the handwriting was cramped and vaguely familiar. I read the words written there:

> There are four main motives for murder: Love, lust, money and revenge. Sometimes it's one, sometimes it's a combination and sometimes it's all of 'em. My first choice: look for a suspect who's got more than one of those as a motive, or maybe all four. Nine times out of ten, that's your killer.

I looked at Nick, who sat with his head cocked. "Where did you get this?"

His whiskers twitched, and then he got up and stalked out of the kitchen.

I turned the paper over in my hand. Light gray with a border. Where had I seen paper like that before? I walked over to the file cabinet in the far corner of the storeroom and jerked open the middle drawer. Yep, they were all still there—the journals of Nick's former owner, PI Nick Atkins. I'd decided to put them in here because Nick had a habit of getting into my locked desk drawer and chewing on the journals. I'd yet to discern whether it was because he missed Atkins, or whether he just liked the taste of the leather covers. I picked up the top one and opened it. Sure enough, the paper in the journal was a pale dove gray with a maroon border, exactly like the sliver I held in my hand. I held the scrap of paper against one of the pages to compare the handwriting. I was no expert, of course, but it certainly looked as if it had been written by the same hand.

I looked at the cat. "Where did you get this, Nick? Did your former human pay a visit here and drop this little piece of advice off?"

Nick stared at me for a minute, then he opened his mouth in a wide yawn and closed his eyes.

I looked at the paper again. Love, lust, money and revenge. I'd remembered them being listed as prime motives in my PI course as well. I glanced over at Nick. "I can think of one suspect who could possibly fit all four of these points," I murmured. "Blackthorne's mystery caller, the supposedly pregnant mistress. And here's a good question for you. How am I supposed to find my prime suspect when I have no idea who she is?"

Chapter Six

It was a quarter to three, and I was considering flipping the sign on the door from *Open* to *Closed* a bit early when who should walk in but Oliver J. Sampson. Ollie, as he likes to be called, with his six-three, two-hundred-ten-pound frame, resembles a bouncer more than a PI. His mocha skin is a bit on the leathery side, from years of alcohol abuse. Ollie and Nick's former human had been partners, and I'd met Ollie when I'd begun searching for Nick the cat's owner. Now Ollie had become one of my closest friends. He slid onto one of the counter stools and touched two fingers to his forehead in a salute.

"Well, well, well," I said. I poured him a steaming mug of black coffee and set it in front of him. "What brings you by?"

"Well, it's not another postcard." He grinned. For a while Ollie and I had received postcards from the MIA Atkins with cryptic messages, but they'd stopped awhile back, and so far we hadn't heard another word. All we knew was that Nick Atkins might—or might not—be a spy, however, all the supporting evidence on that isn't in yet. "To be quite honest, I just felt like a good sandwich."

"Flattery will get you places here," I said and chuckled. "If you like egg sandwiches, I can recommend the Ryan Gosling. It's got everything in it but the kitchen sink. Salami, ham, two kinds of cheese and applewood bacon."

Ollie patted his stomach. "Sounds good. So, what have you been up to? Change your mind about my trying to find Nick Atkins's notes?"

A few months ago I'd learned that Nick Atkins had found Nick the kitten outside a magic shop. I'd originally asked Ollie to see if he could find anything out about the case Atkins had been working on at the time, but I'd since changed my mind, deciding that perhaps it was for the best if feline Nick's past remained a mystery. I gave my head an emphatic shake. "Nope. But I did stumble onto another mystery. Grab a table and I'll tell you all about it."

Ollie nodded, picked up his mug and ambled over to a table near the rear door. I busied myself preparing his sandwich. First I cracked three eggs into a large bowl, added salt, pepper and milk, and whisked it into a frothy concoction. I then moved over to the stove, where I heated up a large frying pan and put in sliced peppers, diced ham, chopped salami, mushrooms, scallions, onion, and crumbled bacon. Once that had cooked for a few minutes I added the egg mixture, then covered the pan. While the egg was cooking I poured fresh coffee into a peppermint-striped mug and set it on the tray. I removed the cover from the frying pan, added shredded cheddar and mozzarella cheese to the omelet, folded it in half, and let it sit for a minute before removing it. I sliced a six-inch roll and slid the omelet between it, then put it on the tray, added a mug of coffee for myself, and carried the whole thing over to Ollie's table. He sniffed the air appreciatively as I set the tray down.

"Wow," he said. "Does that taste as good as it smells?"

"Why don't you be the judge of that," I said as I set the plate in front of him. He picked up the sandwich and took a huge bite.

"It's official," he mumbled around the egg and bread. "You are the best cook in Cruz, or maybe all of Northern California, for that matter."

"What, not the entire state?" I said in a teasing tone.

He grinned. "I wouldn't want you to get a swelled head. How's the catering end of your business coming?"

"I got a few cancellations, which might be a good thing. I really need to hire someone, and soon. I'm sure it's only a matter of time before Anderson steals Lacey away. I've conducted a few interviews, and some of them were pretty promising until Nick decided to conduct his own interview."

Ollie barked out a laugh. "So, he's being picky, eh? Really, would you expect anything less?" He motioned to the empty chair opposite him. "Interview problems aren't all that's bothering you though, is it? You have that preoccupied air about you. You know, the one you get when a mystery's afoot. So, sit down and tell me all about it. What have you gotten yourself involved with now?"

"Since you asked . . ." I eased into the chair across from him, wrapped my fingers around the mug of coffee. "You saw the newscast this morning, right?"

"You mean Mariah Blackthorne? It was impossible not to see it. She was on every channel, and the radio." Ollie's eyes narrowed. "Don't tell me you've gotten involved with her?"

"You remember my friend Hank Prince? Well, as it turns out, Hank and Mariah are old friends. Or, maybe a bit more than that. Apparently they dated in high school, and they've more or less kept up with each other over the years. Long story short, Hank was supposed to come out and try and find out who really killed her husband, but he couldn't make it so he called in a favor."

Ollie let out a low whistle. "Some favor. Seems as if you've got your work cut out for you."

I leaned over and said in a wheedling tone, "I don't suppose you'd care to lend me a hand—if you're not busy with another case, that is?"

Ollie picked up his napkin and dabbed at his lips before answering. "I am supposed to meet with an Adele Brewster later, but it's a relatively simple case. Judgment recovery, identifying assets. Shouldn't take up too much of my time, so . . ." He shrugged. "Why not? It's not as if I've got an extreme caseload. As a matter of fact, at the moment I have an invisible caseload. So, I'm all yours."

A plaintive merow sounded from underneath the table, and a black and white paw jabbed out from beneath the tablecloth. I cleared my throat. "It's always understood that you help too, Nick," I said. "And speaking of Nick's helping . . ." I went over to my drawer and got out the paper feline Nick had been trying to hide earlier and set it on the table in front of Ollie. "Nick was fiddling around with this before. It looks like a page out of his former owner's journals, but I checked and I couldn't find any pages missing."

Both Ollie's shaggy brows rose. "You think it might have been a recent delivery?"

I plopped my chin in my hand. "Your guess is as good as mine," I said.

Ollie studied the paper, then passed it back to me. "It certainly looks like Nick Atkins's handwriting. I can tell you one thing. It's sound advice."

"I agree. The only problem is, the one suspect who fits all the criteria is a big fat mystery. If Nick Atkins is going to drop off advice, you'd think the least he could do is offer some help with finding her." I sighed. "I guess I'm expecting too much."

Feline Nick wriggled out from underneath the table and planted himself beside Ollie's chair. He reached up and put a paw on his leg. Ollie reached down to give the cat a pat behind his ear. "I assume the suspect you refer to is Blackthorne's mystery caller?" At my nod, he said, "I agree, a jilted pregnant mistress should most likely be number one on the list, but at this point I wouldn't discount anyone."

"True." I got up and walked over to my middle counter, opened the drawer, and pulled out a long white sheet of paper. I walked back and set it down in front of Ollie. "I made this up earlier, in between customers. What do you think?"

Ollie bent over the paper. "Ah, a murder board. Nick never liked 'em, but I've always been fond of them. Helps keep everything in perspective."

I was fond of them too. Police call them homicide investigation boards and use them to list all the suspects with motives in a murder case. I'd used this method a time or two in the past and found it to be exceedingly helpful.

On this one, I'd drawn a large square in the center of the page and printed *Christian Blackthorne* in the middle. All around the center square I'd drawn smaller squares, with arrows leading back to Christian's. Some of the other squares had arrows pointing to other ones they had a connection with. For example, above Christian's I'd put a square labeled *Mariah Blackthorne*, and below her name I'd written *caught with murder weapon in hand; cannot remember events.* To the right was a square labeled *Adam Porter.* Underneath his name I'd put *Mariah's friend. Owed Blackthorne six figures?* To the left of Mariah's name was Dr. Paul Lassiter's square. I'd put arrows going to both Mariah and Christian. *Christian's Partner. Suspected CB of skimming funds. In love with Mariah?* There were also squares for Velma and Jerry Cutter, Elspeth Gardner, and one I'd just labeled *Another Mistress?*

"Nice job," Ollie said. He tapped at the square with Lassiter's name. "Why do you have written down that Lassiter suspected Blackthorne of embezzling funds?"

"Mariah said that her husband and Lassiter argued over money. Lassiter thought the business should have been showing more of a profit."

"Odd." Ollie stroked at his chin. "From everything I'd heard, it was the other way around. Blackthorne thought Lassiter was dipping into the till."

"That's what Hank said," I admitted. "He also said there was no proof either one was skimming off the top, but . . ." I looked at the board and then at Ollie. "Think about it. If Blackthorne was right, then Lassiter also fits all of Nick Atkins's criteria. He felt love and lust toward Mariah, and if Blackthorne thought Lassiter was stealing from the business, well, Lassiter might have wanted revenge on both of them." I pointed to Elspeth Gardner's square. "Mariah regards her as a friend, but I get a totally different vibe. It wouldn't surprise me if Elspeth had a fling with the doctor."

"You think she could have been the woman on the phone?"

I tugged at a curl. "That's a toughie. Probably not, but . . . I have a feeling she knows more about Blackthorne's other activities than she lets on. If only I could figure out a way to broach that subject with her. She doesn't appear to be the most approachable person."

"Understandable." Ollie rubbed his hands together. "I'm sure none of these people will be thrilled about being interviewed over something that happened six years ago. You remember what happened the last time, with the Lola Grainger case."

"Yes, that's why I decided to tell them I'm doing an article for *Noir*. Although that might not work either. You know how some people feel about reporters."

Ollie shot me a wide grin. "Yeah, pretty much the way they feel about PIs. We should be seen and not heard, and even then in small doses."

Ollie left shortly afterward after promising to check in with me tomorrow. I locked the door behind him, then went over to my back table and booted up my laptop. Nick lofted onto the table and stretched out in back of the computer, his golden eyes fixed on me. "Yes," I told him. "We're going to attempt some more research on our suspects. Ollie's right, we can't discount anyone just because they might not fit your former master's criteria. People murder for a variety of reasons, after all."

Nick blinked. "Er-owl."

I called up Google and typed in the first name on my list, Adam Porter. Ten minutes later, I'd found out that the name of his defunct salon had been Klip, Kut and Kurl—all spelled with *K*'s. He was currently employed at the Majestica Hair Salon in Gilbert, which was about fifteen minutes away. I grabbed a pad and pen, jotted down the address and phone number. When I was done, I pulled a mirror out of one of the drawers and studied my image. I tugged on an auburn curl. Nick watched me, eyes wide and head cocked.

"It's getting pretty long," I said to him. "I could use a trim, what do you think?"

His paw shot out, jabbed at the air. "Ow-orrr."

"Yeah, me too." I picked up my phone, punched in the salon's number. After about ten rings a bored female voice answered. "Majestica Hair Salon. How can we help you today?"

"Hi, I was wondering if I could get an appointment with Adam Porter for a trim today?"

"No appointment needed, sweetie. You just come right on in anytime. Adam's here till seven tonight, and his schedule is wide open."

I left my name—Nora C—thanked her and hung up, grabbed my jacket off the peg on the wall and shrugged into it. As I turned toward the counter, I felt something crunch underneath my shoe. I glanced down. Six

Scrabble tiles were scattered around the floor at my feet. Nick was nowhere in sight.

"Well, what's this?" I stooped and scooped the tiles up, laid them across the counter. V,O, E, I, L, T. I moved them around, stood back and studied what I'd spelled.

Violet.

Nick's head popped out from underneath my rear table. "Merow."

"Violet, huh? The only Violet I know is Violet Crenshaw, and she hasn't got anything to do with this case." I scooped up the tiles, walked over, and lifted the tablecloth. The velvet pouch was curled up in a corner. I picked it up and deposited the tiles back inside. Nick watched me, eyes wide.

"Sorry, buddy," I said. "Looks like you're slipping this time."

Nick blinked, then abruptly turned his back on me. He flicked his tail and then wriggled back underneath the table. I sighed, although I wasn't particularly surprised.

Most cats can't take criticism, and Nick heads that list. "Get over it, Nick," I called as I walked out the door. "You can't be right all the time."

"Yer-owl!!!"

Chapter Seven

I found the Majestica without too much trouble. It was located in a skinny brick building right in the center of town, across the street from the Town Hall. The wide picture window displayed photographs of models with haircuts ranging from abysmally short to long, flowing locks. I pushed open the door and stepped inside. The interior was well-lit, and there were several haircut stations, most of which were empty. Two female hairdressers, both with short spiky pixie cuts and wearing black smocks that had *Majestica Salon* stitched on the upper corner in bright pink letters, had customers in their chairs. One whose pixie had purple streaks glanced up, saw me, and pointed toward the reception desk. I smiled my thanks and headed in that direction.

The woman sitting behind the black lacquered reception desk had stark white hair cut in a long shag, with streaks of pink, purple and orange running through it. She glanced up as I approached and tapped nails that looked like eagles' talons on top of the counter. Clear blue eyes behind massive red frames looked me up and down. She snapped a wad of gum and said, "Hiya. Can I help ya?"

"Yes. I called about having Adam Porter give me a trim?"

Her gaze skimmed over me again. "Sure. He's the last chair down on the right, next to the shampoo room. Oh, and feel free to help yourself to a cup of coffee. It's complimentary."

I wended my way down the aisle and found the last chair without any trouble. It was sandwiched in between the shampoo station and a large piece of furniture that was most likely a desk but had been turned into a coffee station. Two Keurig coffee makers sat, reservoirs filled with water, waiting for some attention. There were several carousels filled with different types of coffees and teas in between the coffee makers, and the top shelf of the serving area was crowded with boxes of different blends. There was even a French Vanilla Cappuccino that looked appealing. I was just reaching for a pod when the curtains next to the shampoo station parted and a tall thin man with curly black hair and even blacker eyes emerged. He moved toward me and gave me an appraising once-over. "You the chick who called about a trim? Nora C, right?"

I set the cup I'd picked up back down. "That's right." I glanced at the smock, where *Adam* was stitched in the upper right corner. "Adam Porter, I presume?"

"That's me." He reached out a hand, lightly touched my hair. He ran a strand of it between his fingers. "Nice and thick. So, what, you just want a basic dry trim? Bangs and split ends?"

"That sounds fine."

He leaned over to peer more closely at my face. "You've got great skin," he remarked. "I know good skin when I see it." His chest puffed out slightly. "In addition to being a talented hairdresser, I'm also a licensed cosmetologist."

For the first time I noticed an array of jars and bottles on the far side of his station. There were pots of blusher and eyeshadow and another holder with cosmetic brushes of all shapes and sizes. "That sounds like interesting work," I remarked.

"It can be." He was looking at me critically now. "Some dove gray eyeshadow would bring out those gold flecks in your eyes," he murmured. "And your lashes could benefit from a nice coat of mascara. I could give you a quick makeover, if you'd like. Complimentary," he added quickly. "No charge."

"Thanks, but I think the trim will do for now."

He looked disappointed. "Well, if you change your mind, just call back for an appointment. The first sitting and products—I use samples—are complimentary. If you're looking for a specific makeup product that's hard to find, I can help with that too. I've got a lot of contacts in the beauty world."

"That's good to know, but I'll pass for now."

"Okay, suit yourself. But if you change your mind . . ." He shrugged, covered my clothes with a large barber cloth once I'd sat, then picked up a pair of scissors and started snipping away in silence. Either he was unlike most hairdressers I'd met or he was pissed I'd turned down his makeover offer. Well, apparently I was going to have to make the first move. I cleared my throat and said, "You used to own your own salon, right? Klip, Kut and Kurl?"

He paused mid-snip to stare at me in the mirror. "I'm flattered you've even heard of it," he said. "I wasn't in business all that long."

"Actually I remembered you from that trial a few years ago," I said, watching him in the mirror for his reaction. "That doctor's wife. I understand she got released today." When he remained silent, I went on, "Her husband invested in your salon, right?"

He snipped some more off my ends, then stepped around the chair to stand in front of me. He waved the scissors in the air. "You're an inquisitive one, aren't you?" he asked. "All that's old news." He leaned forward, the scissors dangerously close to my cheek. "You wouldn't be a reporter, by any chance?"

I swallowed. I was tempted to lie, then thought better of it. "Actually I'm an ex-crime reporter. I run a sandwich shop in Cruz now, but I occasionally do articles for an online magazine, *Noir*. It's a true crime magazine. I'm doing some articles on cold cases, and what with Mariah Blackthorne being released, this seemed like a good one."

"Uh-huh." He set the scissors down on the counter, eased a hip against it. He reached out, let his fingers roam over my ends. Then he leaned back, crossed his arms over his chest and said, "So you really didn't need this trim, did you? It was just an excuse to pick my brain about Mariah."

I managed a weak smile. "Guilty."

He sighed. "At least you were honest about it. So I'll tell you this. If anyone deserved killing, it was Blackthorne. But Mariah didn't do it."

"You seem pretty positive of her innocence."

He shrugged. "I knew Mariah pretty well. She couldn't kill a fly."

I looked him straight in the eye. "What about you? You and Blackthorne weren't on the best of terms."

He stared at me for a moment, then threw back his head and barked out a laugh. "You don't beat around the bush, do you, Nora C? Since you asked, sure, Blackthorne and I had words. He wanted his investment back, but he knew the risks when he invested. Losing that money was one of the things he and Mariah fought over. Like I said at the trial, I had the money to pay him back, but it was tied up, and he didn't want to wait. He was going to take legal action. I can't deny his death came at an opportune time for me, but I can't take credit for it."

"As I recall, your alibi for the time of death wasn't exactly ironclad."

His lips twisted into a lopsided grin. "True. There were over five hundred people jammed into a small arena. I doubt anyone could swear I was there the entire time, or to an exact time. The police checked all this out when the trial began." He ran his hand through his mop of dark curls. "Look, no one would be happier than me to hear that Mariah was cleared of that murder charge, and to see the real felon suffer, but it's not me." He whipped the bib from around my neck and took a step back. "You're done."

I took a quick look in the mirror. He actually hadn't done a bad job. "Well, thank you for your time," I said.

As I moved past him, he reached out and touched my arm. "I like you," he said. "You're a straight shooter, not like that other reporter."

My ears perked up immediately. "Other reporter?"

"Yeah. She was in here yesterday. Said she wanted a trim too but what she really wanted was to ask questions. And she wasn't half as subtle as you. When I caught on to what she was doing she denied it. And when she realized I wasn't going to budge, she up and stormed out before I could finish her trim." He jabbed a finger at me. "You, on the other hand, didn't try to con me. You were straight from the start. I like that. So I'm going to give you some advice. Take a closer look at that woman."

"The pregnant mistress? That's kind of hard, considering no one knows who she is."

"Ah, I forgot about that. She's a possibility too, but I was actually thinking of Elle Gardner. If you ask me, Elle used her friendship with Mariah as a cover."

"A cover?"

He chuckled. "I doubt you're that naive, Nora C. I'd bet my entire bank account on Elle being a lot closer with the good doctor than his wife." He held up his hand, two fingers pressed tightly together. "Very close. You've heard the saying, 'Keep your friends close, and your enemies closer'?"

I nodded. "Yes."

"Well, then. Think about it. And while you're at it, think about my offer too." He reached into the pocket of his smock, pulled out a card and handed it to me. "My private cell's on there," he said. "I'm serious about that makeover." He closed one eye in a broad wink. "You'd be surprised what I could do for you."

I pocketed Porter's card and went back to Hot Bread, pondering what I'd learned from Adam Porter. I liked the guy. He seemed like a square shooter to me, and I mentally crossed him off my list. Not so much Elle Gardner, though, especially after Adam's cryptic warning.

I let myself in the back door and found my sister sitting at the rear table, pad in hand, drawing. Nick lounged on the rear counter, eyes closed, tail wrapped around forepaws. I shrugged out of my jacket, tossed it across the back of a chair, and stopped to peer over my sister's shoulder. She was doing a charcoal drawing of Nick, and a very good one, I might add.

"Like it?" she asked without looking up. "I think I've really captured his essence."

"It's excellent. What made you decide to do it?"

She set down her charcoal stick and pad and looked up at me. "Actually, I'm practicing. Detective Anderson called me today. I've got an interview tomorrow at four."

"Wow, that's great news," I said. "Dale certainly moved on this quickly."

"She hasn't gotten approval from the city council yet. She told me she's just being proactive, and if they do approve the position, it will only be a part-time one, for now." She grinned at me. "So it appears you won't be losing me all that fast. I can divide my time between both jobs, for now at least."

I gave her a hug. "I'm happy to have you help out part-time, but if I know Anderson she'll move heaven and earth to get that position made full-time. And I know you'd much rather be sketching criminals than making paninis."

Lacey laughed. "Is it that obvious? But really, Nors, getting a full-time position would be great. It would mean that I'd be able to get a place of my own."

"Really?" I furrowed my brow. My sister had never liked living on her own. "What brought that on?"

"We-el, there are times when a gal needs her privacy. You know what I mean, right?" She closed one eye in a broad wink.

Ah, now I realized what she was getting at. "I guess there have been several instances when it might have been nice to have some privacy," I conceded.

"Just *nice?*" Lacey cut me an eye roll. "Ye Gods! Maybe Lee isn't the right guy for you after all."

I ignored her comment and glanced over at the counter. "I see Anne's iPad is gone," I remarked.

"She called and asked about it, said she really needed it tonight, so I told her to come on down. She ran in and out like a scared rabbit." Lacey giggled. "I think she was afraid Nick would pop up out of nowhere, but he behaved himself." She picked up her pad and scraped back her chair. "Oh, and you don't have to worry about me for dinner. I'm going to the diner with Charlaine."

I shot her a look of mock horror. "Charlaine? Not Peter or Hal?"

Lacey giggled. "Nope. This is a girls' night, so we can talk about Peter and Hal. And Charlaine's boyfriend, Sam."

I rolled my eyes. "Okay. Have fun."

She turned, sketch pad under her arm, but paused when she got to the stairway leading upstairs. "I almost forgot. A fax came in for you. I put it on the front counter." She turned and clattered up the stairs to our apartment, and I walked over to the front counter and picked up the two sheets of paper that lay there. The top one was a cover sheet and the message on it was:

Dear Ms. Charles:
Thank you for this opportunity! Attached is my résumé, and I look forward to meeting with you.
Sincerely, Michaela Monaco

I glanced at the attachment. It was neatly typed, albeit pretty sparse. She'd listed as her hobbies cooking and culinary appreciation, and the shelter, her father's store, and a small coffeehouse in Wyck as references. At the bottom she'd written, neatly in ink:

Not much in the way of actual experience in the food service industry, but if enthusiasm counts, then there is an over-abundance!

On anyone else I might have considered the chirpy tone a bit much. Instead I just chuckled, whipped out my cell and dialed her number. When the voicemail kicked in, I left a message asking her to come by the shop tomorrow at three, and if there was any conflict to call back. As I disconnected, I looked at Nick. "Another interview tomorrow," I told him. "Please try not to torture this candidate. I really need to hire someone."

Nick blinked, then padded over to the refrigerator and hunkered down. He stared at me as if to say, *Puny human, I shall decide who's fit to work here.*

I shook my head, then walked over to the stack of mail and started going through it. Bills, bills . . . a postcard from Aunt Prudence I opted to read later, an advertisement for a sale at Krug's Department Store. Nothing from Daniel, although I really hadn't expected anything. I hadn't heard squat from my former FBI boyfriend since he'd taken a dangerous overseas assignment, although it wasn't entirely unexpected. He'd told me before he'd left that he'd be incommunicado for some time, right before he encouraged me to date other men. There were no mysterious postcards from Nick Atkins either, which was probably a good thing. The last envelope in the pile was plain white, no stamp, no return address, just my name printed in block letters across its face. I slit the envelope with the edge of my nail and withdrew a single sheet of paper, on which was printed:

> It is a capital mistake to theorize before you have all
> the evidence. It biases the judgment.

I knew that quote. It was classic Sherlock Holmes. I also knew that Holmes was the detective idol of choice of none other than Nick's former human.

I glanced at Nick. "I think I spoke too soon. This appears to be more advice from your old pal Nick Atkins. Just what is he trying to tell me now? Not to get too fixated on one person, to keep an open mind?"

Nick sat up in front of the refrigerator and raised one paw. "Mer-ooo."

I looked at the note again. One thing I could say: it was certainly sound advice that Nick Atkins, in his own mysterious way, wasn't afraid to dole out.

Chapter Eight

Since Lacey had plans and I really wasn't that hungry, I decided to grab a burger and a brew at the Poker Face. Originally an abandoned firehouse, it was converted into a bar by the original owner. When he decided to move to Arizona he sold it, but the man who purchased it wasn't exactly a genius at business. After less than a year he fell on hard times and was forced to sell. Lance Reynolds, my former high school sweetie and his brother Phil, both tired of the nine-to-five grind, picked it up, and after a few minor alterations the Poker Face had become Cruz's premier watering hole; in fact, Cruz's *only* watering hole.

Since it was such a nice night, Nick and I walked the few blocks over. I pushed open the front door and stood for a moment, letting my eyes get accustomed to the dim light. The focal point of the tavern is its long, cherrywood bar, which takes up one entire side. Lance was usually behind it, mixing up one concoction after another or serving beer on tap. Tonight, though, his second in command, Jose, was behind the bar. I saw at a glance that the tavern was packed. The only seat available was the end stool at the bar. No sooner had I slid onto it than Jose hurried over. He slung his towel over one shoulder and bestowed a wide, toothy grin on me.

"Miss Nora, good to see you."

I returned his smile with one of my own. "You too, Jose. You're certainly busy tonight."

"*Si*. Tonight is Irish Stew night. It always draws a crowd, especially since Miss Alexa makes it. Also, we just started serving sweet potato fries."

I arched a brow. "Also Miss Alexa's idea, I'll bet."

Jose chuckled. "Absolutely. They have been going like hotcakes too."

I glanced around, but didn't see my friend. "Is Lance off tonight?"

"He was supposed to work but Miss Alexa got tickets for *Carmen* tonight at the Rutledge Center, so he asked me to switch."

I raised an eyebrow. "Alexa got Lance to go to an opera? Really? That's one for the books." For Lance, who preferred baseball and football over attending any activity remotely connected to the arts, that spoke volumes about his relationship with Alexa Martin. Alexa was the niece of Violet Crenshaw, the head of the Cruz Museum. She was also a former girlfriend of Nick Atkins, but that's a whole other kettle of fish.

Jose's grin deepened, almost as if he could read my mind. "Miss Alexa, she has him wrapped around this all right." He held up his pinky and wiggled it. "You should have seen him tonight, Miss Nora. All decked out in a suit and tie and his hair slicked back. Mark my words, it won't be long before wedding bells are ringing."

For Lance to put on a suit and tie instead of his customary uniform of Poker Face T-shirt and jeans was another small miracle, so I was inclined to agree with Jose's assessment, and I wondered just how my sister would feel if Lance were to get officially engaged. Even though she maintained she wasn't interested in a long-term relationship with him, I had the distinct impression her feelings for him still ran a lot deeper than she was willing to admit.

Jose held up a mug. "Your usual? A Coors Light?"

"Yes, and I'll take a cheeseburger, medium well, and some of those sweet potato fries to go with it." I felt a sharp tug on my pant leg. "And maybe a saucer of milk for Mr. Nick, here?"

"*Si.*" Jose's smile widened. "We always have milk for Mr. Nick. He can come in the back with me. You know where Mr. Lance keeps your bowl, don't you?" he said to the cat.

Nick's lips parted in what I called his kitty grin. "Yowzer."

Jose filled the mug with Coors Light and set it in front of me, and then he started for the kitchen, Nick eagerly trotting along beside him. I picked up the beer and took a long sip. I saw a couple get up from a booth along the back wall and didn't hesitate. I slid off the stool and made a beeline for it. I sat down, took another sip of my beer, and pulled out my iPhone. I called up Google again and this time I typed in Elspeth Gardner's name. Several different sites came up, but none of them were for the right Elspeth Gardner. They were either too old, too young, or not from Cruz or the surrounding areas. I decided to key in "Elspeth Gardner—Mariah Blackthorne trial." This time I had better luck. I pulled up an article that recounted her testimony at Mariah's trial. I scanned it quickly. "Of course, Mariah complained to me about Christian at times," she was quoted as saying. "What woman doesn't? I complained to her about my husband as well. We've both said on occasion we'd like to murder our husbands, but that doesn't mean we'd actually do it."

Nice. I was pretty certain that testimony hadn't benefitted Mariah. Yet she still regarded the woman as her friend.

I found another small article about a charity fundraiser that Elspeth had hosted a few short weeks before the murder. Elle looked pretty snazzy in a low-cut white gown. She was sandwiched in between two men, one tall, dark and good-looking, the other about an inch shorter than her, on the paunchy side. The caption below the photo read: *Committee chairwoman Elspeth Gardner with her husband, Morris Gardner, and one of the charity supporters, Dr. Christian Blackthorne.*

I studied the photo. Elle's face was turned slightly toward Blackthorne, away from her husband. The expression on her face looked pretty adoring to me. I made a mental note to ask Mariah what Elle's maiden name had been. Perhaps I might find out more information going that route.

I set my phone down and let my gaze wander around the tavern. A woman, her back facing toward me, sat in the booth diagonally across from mine, near the entrance to the restrooms. She was engaged in what looked to be a lively conversation with someone whose face I couldn't see clearly. The conversation was clearly animated, as the woman's hands went up and down several times. As she turned her face slightly, I sucked in a breath.

The woman was Jennifer Hinkle. But who was she with?

I slid my phone into my pocket and picked up my tote. I stole a glance at the bar. Jose was busy serving two men wearing San Francisco Giants T-shirts. I hesitated only briefly, then slung my tote over my arm and started in the direction of the restrooms. As I approached Jennifer's table I made sure to avert my face slightly, just in case she would look up. I needn't have worried. She was much too fixated on arguing with her companion to take notice of anyone or anything around her. She shifted her position slightly, and I caught a glimpse of her companion. Male, high forehead, dark hair slicked back, wire-rimmed glasses, not bad-looking. I paused in the alcove leading to the restrooms and fiddled with the contents of my purse, straining to hear some of their conversation. It wasn't easy, because the two of them were talking in low tones. I caught a word here and there but nothing that made any sense. I snapped my bag shut and was just about to head back to the bar when Jennifer raised her voice.

"I'm not giving you a cent more. I've overpaid already," I heard her say. I twisted my neck just in time to see Jenn take a small envelope from her companion. He mumbled something too low for me to hear. Jennifer responded angrily, "Yeah, yeah. No worries. I'll figure it out for myself. I'm this close to solving it, I tell you. There's only one thing I can't seem to connect . . ."

The rest of her sentence was drowned out in a burst of laughter and the next minute three girls passed me on their way to the restroom, all giggling and laughing. One girl jostled my arm and gave me a murmured "Sorry" before following her companions through the door marked *Ladies*. I shut my bag and walked quickly back to my booth. Once I was seated I chanced a glance at the corner booth.

It was empty. Both Jennifer and her companion had gone.

"Miss Nora."

I glanced up to find Jose hovering over me with a large tray on which rested a fresh mug of beer and my cheeseburger. As he set the tray in front of me, I jerked my thumb in the direction of the now vacant booth. "There was a couple sitting over there," I said.

Jose nodded. "Oh, yes, the blonde and the dark-haired man." He pointed to the rear door. "They just left."

Darn it. "Had you seen either of them in here before?"

Jose shook his head. "Not that I remember. And I would have remembered her," he added with a grin. "Tall, good-looking with legs up to here—" He held his hand just below his chin. "Like a movie star," he added on a sigh.

I took a sip of beer. "How did they pay? By credit card?"

"No, the woman paid cash." His smile widened. "Left a good tip, too."

Jose moved off to wait on another customer and I tapped one nail against the handle of my mug. It had probably been too much to hope for that the man might have used his credit card to pay. Just the fact that they'd taken the most secluded table and exited by the back entrance seemed indicative they wanted their little meeting to remain a secret. I picked up my burger and took a bite, then felt something swish against my ankles. I looked down and saw Nick, half under the table. His upper lip was crested with white.

"Enjoyed your milk, huh?"

"Meower," Nick said, his gaze fixed on my burger.

"What, the saucer of milk wasn't enough for you?"

I broke off a piece of burger and put it on the floor in front of him. He gobbled it down in no time, so I picked up some fries and gave them to him too. A few seconds later I heard the sound of contented slurping. I picked up a sweet potato fry, popped it into my mouth. Crispy, seasoned well. All in all not half bad. A definite improvement over the limp shoestring fries usually offered. I shoved another in my mouth and was just about to take a bite of the burger when Jose hurried over to my booth.

"Miss Nora. I found this on the floor under the table where the blonde lady and the man were sitting." He held out his hand, and I saw a day planner book clutched in it. "I thought perhaps you might want to have a look at it."

I took the planner, turned it over in my hand. "Thanks, Jose. I'll give it right back."

He nodded and hurried back to the bar. I opened the planner and saw several of Jennifer's business cards tucked into a pouch inside the front cover. I flipped through the pages, but they were all blank. Apparently Jennifer hadn't had time to make any notations in it as yet. I was just about to close it when I saw the edge of something gray peeping out from a pocket in the back cover. I pulled it out and saw that it was a business card, done in pale gray with navy blue lettering, and it read:

Dr. Felice McDowd, PhD
Psychiatrist, MD, Psychoanalysis, Hypnotherapy
555-9087

Hypnotherapy. I remembered Mariah's assertion that she'd seen a hypnotist while incarcerated. Could that have been this Dr. McDowd?

I pushed my plate over to one side and whipped out my iPhone, once again called up Google. I plugged in Dr. Felice McDowd's name. Several articles came up, and I clicked on the one that said "Profile." The small photograph there depicted a serious-looking woman, black hair tied back in a severe bun, horn-rimmed glasses and an expression that I imagined was supposed to convey concern. I leaned back and read the accompanying profile:

Dr. Felice McDowd, PhD, MD

I believe in treating the patient as a whole, taking into account the entire person with their psychological, social, and spiritual needs. I treat people going through difficult life circumstances, including relationship difficulties, family problems, anxiety, trauma and job stress. In addition, I treat all psychiatric disorders, including depression, anxiety, bipolar disorder, ADHD, obsessive/compulsive disorder, panic disorder and traumatic memory loss. By integrating psychotherapy, psychopharmacology, and guidance on lifestyle modifications, I strive to significantly improve my patients' general well-being. I work with children, adolescents and adults.

As a physician, I strive to nurture hope and insight, decrease suffering, and assist my patients in achieving their highest level of mental and emotional well-being via personal growth and expression. I conduct video sessions for patients who are traveling or have moved away.

In addition I have pursued advanced psychotherapy training through the prestigious New York Psycho-analytic Society and Institute, and I serve as Staff Psychiatrist at the Central California Women's Facility.

CCWF. That was the same women's facility where Mariah had been incarcerated. Coincidence? I thought not. I hesitated only briefly before switching my iPhone back into call mode and dialing the number. After a few seconds a bored voice said, "Doctor's Service. Is this an emergency?"

I sucked in a breath and then said, "Of sorts. Can you please get a message to Dr. McDowd? My name is Nora Charles, and I need to speak with her as soon as possible regarding Mariah Blackthorne." I gave my number and rang off, then picked up my burger again. I'd hardly taken two bites when my cell buzzed. I saw McDowd's number on the caller ID and I swallowed quickly before depressing the answer button. "Dr. McDowd. Thank you for calling back so quickly."

"You told my service it was an emergency regarding Mariah Blackthorne?" the woman said, in a crisp, no-nonsense tone. "Just who are you and what is your relation to her? I'm warning you, if you are another reporter . . ."

"I am a reporter, or rather, I'm an ex-crime reporter. I'm working with Mrs. Blackthorne to prove her innocence, at her request."

Silence and then: "Hold one moment." The line went dead for several minutes, during which I did a lot of toe tapping. Finally, McDowd came back on the line. "You used to write for the *Chicago Tribune*. Now you run a sandwich shop in Cruz." She paused, and when I made no comment continued, "And, apparently, you are quite a little sleuth." I heard the sound of fingers drumming on the desk and then Dr. McDowd said, "You seem reputable, Ms. Charles. With a high-profile patient like Mariah I must be careful, I'm sure you understand." She hesitated and then added, "My office was broken into a few days ago. Nothing was missing, but some of my files seemed to be out of place."

"Let me guess. One of the files was Mariah's?"

"Yes. I have a feeling that temp who worked here for a week might have been in cahoots with some reporter. I called the agency to complain, and they knew nothing about her." She sighed. "I'll also tell you there was another reporter here last week, and I'll tell you the same thing I told her. I did treat Mariah when she was at CCWF, but I'm limited in what I can talk about due to doctor-patient confidentiality. So, knowing that . . . how can I help you?"

I wondered if the reporter were Jennifer. Most likely that answer was yes. I wouldn't have put it past her, either, to have posed as a temp in order to gain access to Mariah's file. "Let me just ask you this. Do you remember Mariah talking about remembering a sound or a smell? And do you believe she's telling the truth when she says that she can't remember the events of that day?"

McDowd was silent for a few moments. Then she said, "Now, mind you, this isn't a diagnosis, only my opinion. I believe Mariah is telling the truth as she knows it."

"Which means?"

"Which means that whatever happened that afternoon is pushed so far back into her subconscious that she may never retrieve it, no matter how much she may want to." A long pause, and then, "Some people who suffer from traumatic memory loss respond well to hypnotherapy. Mariah was not one of those people. Not only was she devastated by her husband's death, she was much too traumatized by the subsequent trial and its outcome to be successfully hypnotized. And if she should remember, there is a good chance that what she remembers might not be reliable."

"In other words, in your qualified opinion, Mariah's chances of recovering an accurate memory are slim at best?"

"I wish I could say otherwise, but . . . essentially, yes." Another slight hesitation and then, "Tell me, was there any particular reason you asked about Mariah remembering a sound or a smell?"

"She seemed to think that it might be something like that," I said. "Did she remember something like that in one of your sessions?"

"I'm afraid I can't reveal that without breaking doctor-patient confidentiality. However, you seem to have pretty good insights. Remarkable, in fact." Another brief silence and then, "I'm sorry I can't be of more help, Ms. Charles. Good evening."

Dr. McDowd hung up and I sat for a minute, tapping my phone against my chin. I took McDowd's compliment as an affirmation that my theory was correct. I glanced down. Nick had come out from underneath the table and squatted beside the bench, watching me with wide golden eyes.

"You know," I said to the cat, "I think McDowd is the doctor who put Mariah under hypnosis. Apparently that treatment wasn't successful, but that doesn't mean something else couldn't jog her memory and she'd remember."

Nick cocked his head. "Merow."

"I know. Judging from what the doctor said, even if the memory eventually returns, it might not even be reliable or it might not have anything to do with her husband's murder."

I picked up my burger, then set it back down, my appetite gone. There was another possibility as well. Maybe Mariah couldn't put her finger on that memory because deep down she didn't want to. Oh, she said that she did, but in reality she was afraid to remember. And if that were the case, I could think of only one reason.

Mariah was afraid to remember what happened because she had, indeed, murdered Christian Blackthorne.

Chapter Nine

I overslept the next morning, something I rarely do. Nick must have been super-tired too, because he didn't climb on my stomach or lick my face to wake me up to get his breakfast. Instead, when I winked one eye open to look at the alarm clock I'd forgotten to set, he was curled up along my side, front paws in the air, snoring.

I gave him a gentle nudge. "C'mon, Nick. We've got a busy day ahead of us."

One golden eye winked open. Nick stared at me, then closed his eyes and rolled over on his side.

"Fine. You'll come fast enough when you hear the Fancy Feast can open."

I rose, showered and dressed quickly. As I ran a brush through my tumble of auburn locks, I thought about yesterday's events. It was slow going to be sure, but I'd made some progress, and today I hoped to make more. I set down my brush and heard a plaintive meow at my feet.

"Ah, Your Majesty. I see you decided to arise," I said.

Nick stretched out his front forepaws, opened his mouth in a wide yawn.

"Well, shake a tail, buddy. And don't forget, we've got Michaela coming in this afternoon. Try not to torture her, okay? I really need to hire somebody."

Nick widened his eyes as if to say, *Torture? Who, me?*

I reached over to stroke the top of his head. "I love you, Nick, but you make me crazy, you know that? Best behavior today, okay?"

He turned his head sideways and regarded me out of one half-lidded eye. "Merow. Ow-owrr," he said before trotting off. Catspeak, no doubt, which translated into: *Me? I'm always well-behaved.*

Yeah, right.

• • •

There was a line for breakfast when I opened the door at eight, and the customers kept coming in a steady stream until nine thirty. Mollie was off today due to exams and Chantal wasn't due in till one thirty, so Lacey and I were kept busy serving up Tom Cruise Classic Fried Egg Sandwiches and Ryan Gosling omelets. When things finally slowed down, it was just ten o'clock. Lacey finished ringing up a Howard Stern special and then looked over at me.

"Would you mind if I took a ten-minute break?" she asked. "I really need to make a few phone calls."

I figured she wanted to call either Peter or Hal or maybe both, most likely for a pep talk about her interview with Anderson later. "Take twenty," I said. The line had disappeared and our tables were full of customers eating, drinking coffee and watching *The View* on our flat-screen TV. "If we get busy I'll call you."

"Great, thanks." She whipped off her apron and fairly flew up the stairs. I glanced over at Nick, lounging in front of my refrigerator after his morning breakfast of scrambled egg and crumbled bacon. I walked over to stand in front of him. "I mean it, mister," I hissed. "You be good this afternoon. On your best behavior."

Nick glanced up and blinked. Then he raised one hind leg in the air and proceeded to groom himself.

My shop door bell tinkled again, and I turned toward the front counter. Ramona Hickey was just coming through the door, accompanied by a plump woman with a cap of steel-gray hair and bright birdlike eyes. Ramona's gaze fell on me and she raised her arm and waved.

"Yoo-hoo, Nora. I brought along a friend. I've raved about your sandwiches so much she insisted she had to try one for herself. This is Velma Cutter."

I started. Velma? That was a pretty unusual name. What were the odds Ramona's friend was the same Velma Cutter who'd worked for the Blackthornes? I gestured toward my blackboard. "You're still in time for breakfast, or you can have an early lunch. If you're in the mood for hearty I can recommend the Ryan Gosling omelet."

Ramona nudged the other woman in her side. "I bet you'd like Nora's Howard Stern breakfast special. Scrambled egg on a fluffy roll. That's what I'm going to have."

"That does sound good," Velma said. "Make that two. And do you have herbal tea?"

I'd recently started carrying flavored tea because several of my customers had requested them. "Ginger, green tea, Earl Grey and a new one, coconut hibiscus."

"Ginger," Velma responded promptly. She gave her stomach a self-conscious pat. "It's good for the digestion."

"I'll just have my usual coffee," said Ramona. She inclined her head toward the interior of the shop. "Come on, Vel, let's grab that table near the window."

The women moved off and I set about preparing their orders. As I worked, my thoughts were in a whirl. It had to be the same Velma Cutter. What were the odds another person in this area could have that exact name? If she were, that was certainly a lucky break for me, although I wondered how I could get the woman alone long enough to broach the subject of Mariah. I didn't want to discuss it in front of Ramona. She was a good customer but she was also a notorious gossip, and if she got wind of what I was up to, word would spread through Cruz like wildfire.

I put the sandwiches on a tray along with the tea and coffee and carried it over to their table. Ramona was on her cell. She ended the call as I set the tray down and pushed her chair back with an agitated sigh. "I've got to get to the library," she huffed. "You would think they could handle things on my day off, but oh, no. There's always some crisis I have to avert." She looked at me. "I shouldn't be too long. Can you keep my sandwich warm? I should be back in fifteen, twenty minutes tops."

Velma started to rise from her chair. "I'll come with you," she began, but Ramona gave her head a brisk shake and pushed the woman gently back into the chair. "No need for you to come, dear," she said. "Sit and enjoy your sandwich and tea. I'll be back before you're done."

Ramona hurried out, and Velma shifted in her seat. She picked up the sandwich, took a bite, set it back on the plate, then looked up at me. "It is quite good," she said. "I'm just a slow eater."

I gestured toward the empty chair. "Would you mind if I sat down?"

"Not at all." She took another bite of the sandwich. "Very good indeed. Ramona was right, I don't need ketchup. The eggs are lightly seasoned, aren't they? Black pepper?"

"That's one of the spices." I leaned in a bit closer. "I was wondering if I could ask you a few questions?"

She looked at me, her expression puzzled. "Questions? What about?"

"Mariah Blackthorne. You were her housekeeper, right?"

Velma paused, sandwich halfway to her mouth. She set it back on the plate and leaned back in her chair. "Ramona did mention that you consider yourself an amateur detective, and that you write for some online crime magazine, so I guess I shouldn't be surprised you know who I am." She blew out a breath. "I'm glad she's been released from prison. I could never picture her killing Dr. Blackthorne, no matter how mad she might have been at him. I know she loved him."

"You testified at the trial that you heard Mariah threaten her husband more than once, correct?"

Velma shifted in her seat. "Not threaten, exactly. They did have a terrible fight a few nights before his death. She flat out told him that if she caught him screwing around she'd kill him. But that prosecutor cut me off before I could say that it was a typical husband-wife argument. Lots of people say things in the heat of the moment they don't mean."

"So it was an incident similar to the one Elspeth Gardner testified to?"

Velma's nose wrinkled. "I guess. I hate to put myself in the same class as her, though."

I raised a brow at the obvious venom in Velma's tone. "Why do you say that? Elspeth Gardner and Mariah Blackthorne are friends, right?"

"Well . . ." Velma leaned in closer to me. "Mrs. Blackthorne always thought Mrs. Gardner was her friend, but I . . . I had my doubts. I still do. If you ask me, Mrs. Gardner always seemed more interested in Mr. Blackthorne than in Mrs. I can recall a few instances when Mrs. Gardner arrived early for an appointment with Mrs. Blackthorne, and by early I mean she'd arrive before Mrs. Blackthorne was even dressed. So Mrs. Gardner would go and visit with Dr. Blackthorne in his study." Her tongue snaked out, swiped across her lower lip. "Several times I went past the study when she was in there, and I could hear them talking and laughing. Although I guess I shouldn't have been surprised. Mrs. Gardner is a terrible flirt, and Dr. Blackthorne was a very good-looking, very charming man. Women were always throwing themselves at him. He ate it up. My opinion? She was more crazy about him than he was about her." She let out a breath. "I've heard all the rumors about Dr. Blackthorne's womanizing. I never saw any evidence of it at the house, but that doesn't mean it didn't happen."

I nodded. "What about Dr. Blackthorne's partner, Dr. Lassiter? I heard they didn't exactly get along."

"That's true." She pushed a hand through her hair. "He and the doctor argued a lot over business, to be sure. The doctor thought Dr. Lassiter might be, ah, how can I put it delicately? Taking a little extra out of the coffers? And Dr. Lassiter thought Dr. Blackthorne might be doing the same thing."

"So they each suspected the other of embezzling funds?"

"Embezzling! That's the word." Velma leaned in a bit closer and added, "It didn't help that Dr. Lassiter was always sniffing around Mrs. Blackthorne. She had no interest in him, but that didn't stop him. He'd come over, follow her around, watch her with those puppy dog eyes." Velma let out a snort. "The man was in love with her, or maybe in lust is a better phrase. It was so obvious it was pathetic."

"Was it obvious to Dr. Blackthorne?"

"I would think so," she sniffed. "He never came out and directly accused Dr. Lassiter of anything that I heard. Like I said, the only thing I ever heard them argue over was money."

I hesitated, unsure how to broach my next question, then decided to just come right out with it. "What about your son? I've heard that he and the doctor didn't exactly get along?"

Velma's expression darkened. "Dr. Blackthorne thought my son was a bit on the lazy side. Said he spent more time hanging out with his friends from that bicycle club when he should have been helping me. And Jerry thought Dr. Blackthorne took advantage of me. He felt that I should have been paid more for all the work I did for them, and he let the doctor know it on more than one occasion." She blew out a breath. "There was a disagreement a few weeks before the doctor died," she said at last. "It was all a terrible misunderstanding. He thought that Jerry had been trying to steal some valuable figurines from him, but he was wrong! Jerry told me what happened. He was waiting for me, and he saw them there and he picked a few up, just looking at them. My son has always been interested in art, you see, so he was rather curious about them. When the doctor came into the room and saw him holding them, he just jumped to a conclusion."

"So he didn't threaten to press charges against your son?"

"No, he did. That was the misunderstanding." She clasped her hands together so hard the knuckles bled white. "Those figurines were quite rare. He'd just had them appraised at five hundred dollars each. When he saw Jerry holding them, he jumped to the conclusion that my son was about to steal them. It was all a misunderstanding, I tell you. I'm sure it would have been straightened out." She gave her head a brisk shake. "I'm sorry. I'd rather not talk about this anymore. I find the whole episode extremely upsetting. Dr. Blackthorne could be extremely difficult at times, but for the most part I enjoyed working there. I've never found another job that equaled it. Besides, talking about it doesn't change anything. I hope you understand."

"I do, and I thank you for talking with me." I pushed my chair back and stood up. "Please enjoy the rest of your meal. It's on the house."

Velma managed a thin smile. "That's kind of you. Thank you."

Velma turned back to her sandwich and tea, and I walked back behind my counter. I had the distinct feeling that Velma was protesting her son's innocence a little too strongly. If Jerry Cutter had gone back intending to steal the figurines, it was possible that Blackthorne could have caught him in the act. He probably threatened to call the police, and Jerry could have faced a hefty fine and/or prison time. From the little I knew about Blackthorne, I figured he'd have pressed for prison time. And Jerry Cutter most likely would not have wanted to spend time in prison.

But was it a big enough motive for murder? That was the question.

Chapter Ten

Ten minutes later the door to Hot Bread burst open and Ramona sailed through. She hurried over to the counter, placed a hand on her hip and announced, "Well, it looks as if I'm going to have to spend most of the afternoon at that library. I declare, I can't take a day off without some crisis arising. I'll have to take my sandwich to go." She sighed. "It puts the kibosh on my afternoon with Velma, too. I'll have to reschedule."

As Ramona hurried off to share her news with Velma, I wrapped her sandwich and put her coffee in a to-go container. When she appeared back at the counter a few minutes later, I said, "No need to pay today, Ramona. Your sandwiches are on the house." I glanced at Velma, who stood uncertainly behind Ramona. "Consider it a reward for introducing a new customer."

"How nice of you, Nora," purred Ramona. "Sorry, but we've really got to get going." She grabbed Velma's arm and propelled her out of my store. I found myself feeling sorry for Velma Cutter. It was evident to me that she was unaware of her son's true nature.

There were a few people in the shop, but they were all busy eating and watching the TV. I glanced over at Nick, sprawled on his back in front of the refrigerator, hind legs spread out, paws in the air, looking quite . . . comfortable. He twisted his head, fixed me with his golden stare.

"What do you think, Nick? If you're not too tired, maybe you'd like to help me with another Google search?"

He flopped over, struggled to his feet, whisked his tail in the air. "Merow."

I sat down at my rear table, pulled the laptop in front of me. Nick lofted himself into the chair next to mine and sat erect, his eyes riveted to the screen as I called up Google. "Velma Cutter didn't seem too fond of Paul Lassiter, did she? Let's see what else we can find on him."

I'd barely typed in Lassiter's name, though, when the bell above the door jangled. Without looking up I called out, "I'll be right there. The butternut squash soup is excellent, if you're interested, and I think I have one bowlful left."

"Sounds great," said a deep voice. "I'll take a big bowl, along with a Thin Man tuna melt."

I let out a squeal and pushed my chair back, startling Nick, who jumped to the floor. I hurried over to the counter and beamed at the tall, good-looking man who stood on the other side. "Samms! I thought you were at Quantico taking that special training course!"

Leroy Samms brushed an errant curl of ink-black hair out of his eyes and leaned over to give me a kiss on the cheek. "Got called back," he said. "Rick and I have a debriefing on another matter today, but I'll be taking the red-eye back to Quantico tonight. I just had to swing by and see you."

"Aww," I said. "You missed me."

"Believe it or not, Red, I did. Plus, I'm hungry." He grinned.

Leroy Samms had been my senior year college crush, and we'd shared a few steamy moments when we worked together on the college paper. We'd lost touch after graduation, but reconnected when he arrested my sister Lacey for murder last year. Shortly after that he'd relocated to Cruz as the new head of Homicide. It wasn't long before the FBI recruited him, and he now worked out of their small satellite office in Cruz. Chantal and Lacey had been pressuring me for months now to give my relationship with Samms another chance, and since Daniel had given me his blessing, sort of, before he'd gone off to England, we'd recently begun dating. So far it was going well, except for Samms's annoying habit of calling me by the nickname he'd given me in college, Red. To retaliate, I refused to call him Lee. However, my calling him by his last name didn't seem to bother him.

"No problem, as long as you don't mind waiting while I make up some fresh tuna salad," I said as I pulled a bowl out of the cupboard. "Nick had the last of it for a snack."

"Of course not." He made a show of smacking his lips. "Your tuna salad is well worth waiting for."

I opened the refrigerator and removed the prechopped onion and celery I always kept on hand. "Flattery will get you everywhere."

He grinned. "So, what's new? Did you hire your new part-timer yet?"

"Nope." I cast my gaze in Nick's direction. "My store mascot has rejected every possible applicant so far."

"That's not too surprising. Your store mascot, as you put it, is very protective of you."

"It's more like he hasn't yet found one he could wrap around his paw. However, I do have a very promising interview scheduled for this afternoon." I added mayonnaise to the onion and celery, started to stir. "How about you? How is the training going?"

"Pretty good. I feel out of touch with reality, though. We've been sequestered all week. When we weren't in classes, we were studying." His nose wrinkled. "Almost reminds me of cramming for finals in college. Remember those days? Gulping down NoDoz to pull an all-nighter."

"I wouldn't know about that, being the A student that I was," I said and chuckled. I waved my spoon in the air. "I guess you haven't heard the news about Cruz's newest resident, then?"

Samms rested his chin in his palm. "If you're referring to Mariah Blackthorne, I managed to catch most of her release. That was quite a speech she gave. It seems she's determined to prove her innocence."

I finished mixing the mayonnaise into the tuna, onion and celery, pushed the bowl to one side and started to pull out bread and cheese. "She was here yesterday," I said.

Samms's eyes widened. "Mariah Blackthorne was here? In your shop? Don't tell me she came in to have a sandwich?"

"Not exactly," I said. "She happens to be an old friend of Hank Prince's. Apparently Hank promised her he'd try and find her husband's real killer and prove her innocent but he couldn't get away from Chicago right now, so . . ." I spread my hands. "He called in a favor."

Samms let out a snort. "He volunteered you, you mean."

"In a word—yes." I finished spreading tuna on the bread, added cheese and a slice of tomato, and slid the sandwich onto the grill. "To be honest, I'd already considered digging into it for an article for *Noir*. Her case has always fascinated me. I never thought she was guilty."

"As long as we're being honest, I never did either." Samms tapped at his stomach. "It's just a gut feeling, but she didn't strike me as the type to commit a cold-blooded murder under any circumstances. Overhearing that conversation between her husband and that mystery caller is what saved her from a life sentence."

"She's hopeful that reestablishing herself here will help get her memory back."

Samms frowned. "That might not be in her best interests. Think about it, Red. If the real murderer is still out there, and thinks there's a chance Mariah might recall what happened that day, she could be putting herself in real danger."

"I pointed that out, but she's determined to go ahead anyhow."

He looked me straight in the eye. "If you're helping her, you could be in danger too."

Impulsively I covered his hand with my own. "Don't worry, I don't intend to take any unnecessary chances."

He barked out a laugh. "You never *intend* to take them, Red. It just always seems to work out that way. Probably because you're determined to be a combination Nancy Drew and Lois Lane." He pulled his hand free and chucked me under the chin. "Look, Lois, I'll be in Quantico another couple of days. I won't be around to throw on my blue tights and red cape and rescue you if you get into trouble."

While I was digesting the sight of Samms in blue tights and cape, a loud "Er-ew" sounded from somewhere near my feet. The next second Nick leapt up and onto the counter, and arranged himself, tail curled around his front paws. "Er-ew" he said again, cocking his head to one side, his golden gaze focused on Samms.

I laughed. "Hey, Superman, he's telling you not to worry. Super Kitty has my back."

"So he does," Samms mused. "Super Kitty might actually be a good nickname for him. That cat has rescued you more than once. I have to admit, you and he do make a good team. And I know how pointless it can be to try and dissuade you when you've already made up your mind." His lips twisted into a rueful grin. "At least this time, there are no dead bodies for you and Nick to find. Just promise me you'll be careful. And if you should find anything that indicates someone else was responsible, you'll tell Dale Anderson right away."

I scrunched up my nose. Dale Anderson wasn't exactly my biggest fan, or Nick's either, but she and Samms had known each other a long time. I was convinced part of the reason for Dale's ambivalence toward me was because she herself nursed a mega crush on Samms and was jealous of his attentions toward me. When I'd mentioned it to him though, he'd pooh-poohed it, insisting he and Dale were just friends. Men could be so obtuse sometimes. "Yeah, okay. Sure," I said. "I'll call her first thing."

He gave me a look that clearly said he didn't believe me. I lifted the sandwich off the grill, transferred it to a plate, then got out a soup bowl. "Speaking of Dale, Lacey has an interview with her this afternoon for a sketch artist job."

Samms smiled. "I know. Dale called me. I gave Lacey a good recommendation."

The fact that Dale had called Samms and not me really didn't surprise me. It did annoy me, though. It all went back to that "men could be so obtuse" thing. I decided to change the subject. "So, you mentioned you followed Mariah's original trial. Did anyone in particular stand out as a suspect for you?"

His brows drew together as he thought. "Well," he said at last, "I didn't much care for Blackthorne's partner. I thought he seemed a bit overconfident on the stand."

"I've heard each one suspected the other of embezzling company funds."

"I don't doubt it. Blackthorne probably spent a bundle on women, and Lassiter was rumored to be known to run up quite a tab at the blackjack tables. The one I would have watched more closely, though, was the housekeeper's son."

I pushed the plate with the sandwich and the soup bowl filled with steaming squash soup in front of him. "Jerry Cutter. I was thinking about him as well."

"Yep. He hung around with some pretty shady types. As a matter of fact, one of my men in St. Leo arrested him once on suspicion of breaking and entering. Unfortunately, we couldn't make the charges stick. But Blackthorne supposedly had caught him red-handed and was this close to having him thrown in the slammer." He picked up his spoon, took a big spoonful of soup. "Wow. Hot. Good, but real . . . hot."

"Not according to his mother," I said thoughtfully. "She said that was all a big misunderstanding."

Samms dabbed at his lips with a napkin. "Of course she'd say that. She's his mother." He let out a sigh and reached into his jacket pocket, pulled out his cell. He glanced at it and frowned. "Gotta go," he said, rising. "That text was from Rick. The debriefing got pushed up. Apparently they want to get it over with so we can hurry back to Quantico."

"Lucky you." I slid the sandwich off the plate, wrapped it in wax paper and slid it into a paper bag. "One sandwich to go." I dumped the contents of the soup bowl into a container and handed it to him. "Soup too."

"Thanks. It's too good to waste." He gave my arm a squeeze. "Say, we'll be back late Friday. How would you feel about having dinner at Felipe's Saturday night?"

My eyebrow rose. Felipe's was an upscale French restaurant in nearby Pebble Beach. It was not only elegant, it was pricey, and had gotten the nickname "the proposal palace" because many women had received engagement rings there. "Felipe's, huh? Is it some sort of special occasion? Oh my gosh!" I raised both hands. "Don't tell me it's your birthday?"

"My birthday isn't for another month and no, it's not a special occasion. I just heard the food is great there and I thought it would be nice, instead of our usual burgers at the Poker Face."

I goggled at him. "Felipe's is pretty pricey. There are places just as nice that have more reasonable prices. Give me ten minutes and I'll get you a whole list."

He huffed out a breath. "You sure are stubborn, Red. Most women wouldn't worry about price. They'd just go out shopping for a new dress, or a new lipstick, or something."

I gave him a saucy smile. "Well, as you know, I'm not most women."

"Boy, do I ever." He leaned over and gave me a swift kiss on the lips. "I'll take a rain check on a more satisfactory goodbye later. And we're going to Felipe's. End of discussion." With a quick wave, he was out the door. Nick cocked his head at me. I reached out, stroked him absently on the head.

"So, what do you think, Nick? Is there more to this dinner than meets the eye? It's a bit too soon for Samms to want to take our relationship to the next level, don't you think? I mean, we've only been on a handful of dates." I paused. "And there is still Daniel, although I have to admit that prospect grows dimmer with each passing day. I know he said he'd be in deep cover for awhile, but you'd think he'd manage to at least send a postcard. Your former human seems to manage that just fine."

Nick's golden eyes narrowed and he let out a deep, rumbling purr.

I stroked his soft fur. "You're right. I'm probably jumping the gun. Anyway, we've got to put first things first. Our priority right now is zeroing in on who else had a motive for killing Christian Blackthorne. All this other stuff . . . it'll work itself out, right?" I paused. "Including delving into your past. You understand why I put that on hold, right? I mean, it's bad enough wondering if your former owners will ever return and claim you. I'm not sure I can deal with the possibility of you being something other than . . . just an ordinary cat."

"Ow-owrr," said Nick. He looked at me as if to say, *"Ordinary? Me?"* Then he turned his back, jumped down from the counter and ambled over to the back table, where my laptop still sat open. He hopped up on the chair, looked pointedly at the laptop, then at me.

"You're right. Before Samms came in, we were going to do some more research, weren't we?"

I walked over and slid into the chair. Instead of checking out what my search of Paul Lassiter had produced, though, I typed in "Jerry Cutter, suspicion of robbery, St. Leo," and hit enter. I was rewarded by one very brief article in the Police Blotter section of the *St. Leo Sun:*

> Jerome Cutter, 27, held on suspicion of robbery, Greco's Fine Arts. Accused of making off with several ivory statuettes. Suspect was apprehended six blocks from store, but none of the statuettes were found in his possession. Suspect did have a large bankroll of over two thousand dollars in fifties and hundreds on him. Cutter made bail and the charges were summarily dismissed for lack of evidence.

Well, it certainly seemed like Jerome, aka Jerry, had a penchant for lifting valuable figurines. Coincidence? Impulsively, I typed in "Jerome Cutter—Police Mugshot St. Leo, CA—Images" into Google and hit the enter button. A few seconds later I was looking at a not-too-flattering shot of a guy with a high forehead, dark hair and eyes, a weak chin, an arrogant tilt to his mouth. And even though he wasn't wearing glasses, I was ninety-nine-point-nine percent positive that Jerry Cutter was the man I'd seen in the Poker Face—Jennifer Hinkle's mysterious companion.

Now, what were the two of them doing together? I recalled the envelope Jerry had handed Jennifer, and Jennifer's words. She'd paid him for something. What could it be? As I pondered that question, I felt my cell vibrate in my pocket. I whipped it out and glanced at the number, but it said Private Caller and was one I didn't recognize. I was tempted to let it go to voicemail, but Nick padded over and started pawing the air, pointing at my phone.

"You want me to answer? Okay. But if it's a telemarketer, no catnip for you." I hit the receive button. "Nora Charles."

"Ms. Charles?" The male voice on the other end was smooth. "This is Dr. Paul Lassiter. I understand you're making inquiries about Mariah Blackthorne. If that's true, I'd like to see you." He paused and then added, "As soon as possible."

Chapter Eleven

Lacey and I had just finished with the bulk of the lunch crowd when my cell rang again. I answered, hoping that it wasn't Chantal saying she'd be late. I'd already told Paul Lassiter I'd be at his office at two. An eager voice asked, "Mrs. Charles? This is Michaela Monaco. My class finished early, so I wondered if I could come in now for that interview? I'm about ten minutes away."

I glanced at the clock, which read twelve twenty-five. I did a quick computation in my head. Lassiter's office was about a fifteen=minute drive. Barring any Nick complications, I should be fine time-wise. "Sure, that would be fine."

"Great. See you in a few."

I disconnected and stole a glance at Nick, who was chowing down on his new favorite food item, my lobster salad. "Michaela will be here soon for her interview, Nick," I said to the cat. "Please try and behave, okay?"

Nick paused in his slurping to glance over his shoulder and give me the equivalent of a kitty death-stare before he resumed eating. Oh, well, I thought. I tried.

At twelve forty a tall, gangly girl with dirty blonde hair done in two pigtails hurried into the shop. She strode right over to the counter and thrust out her hand. "Ms. Charles? I'm Michaela Monaco."

"Nice to meet you. Why don't you come on back here?" I motioned her to step behind the counter. "We can chat at my rear table."

I noted that Nick was no longer sprawled in front of the refrigerator. I had a feeling he'd ducked underneath the table (the better to hear the interview there, my dear), but I was loath to peek under the tablecloth to find out. We sat down and Michaela unzipped the black case she was holding and handed me another copy of her résumé, this one with several other letters attached. I skimmed them quickly, saw they were letters of reference. I admit, I was impressed. Not even the fastidious Anna had thought to bring references.

"These are good," I said after I'd looked at them. "Why don't you tell me why you'd like to work in a deli slash food catering environment rather than some other sort of part-time job?"

Michaela clasped her hands in front of her. "Well, to be honest, I could probably get a job at Trent's. Or with my dad. But working in retail stores won't help me prepare for my future career. I'd like to be a professional chef someday. I think working my way up, starting with a small food shop, learning the business from the ground up, is a smart idea."

I nodded. "You realize that sometimes, when I have a catering job, I might ask you to put in some long hours. How would you feel about that?"

Michaela shook her head. "Honestly? It wouldn't bother me at all. I'm looking forward to working with food and with people. For example, I'd love to see just how you get your ideas for different sandwiches, and how you determine what sells and what doesn't. I'm also hoping on your catering jobs that we could possibly explore different types of recipes. I love to try out the ones I see on the cooking shows." She chuckled. "My dad's my best guinea pig. I don't think my mom appreciates the extra weight he's put on, though—oh! What was that?" She paused as a loud "Ow-owrrr" emanated from beneath the table.

Ah, the moment of truth had arrived. "I forgot to mention there's another staff member here whose smell test you have to pass," I said.

The startled expression vanished from her face, replaced by a wide smile. "Oh, you mean your cat, Nick. My grandma mentioned him. He sounds like a real smart fellow."

The smart fellow in question chose that moment to thrust his head out from underneath the table. "Ow-owrrr," he said again.

Michaela leaned over and peered at Nick. "Wow, he's sure a handsome one. Is that a white streak behind his ear? He's so cute," she squealed.

Nick wriggled all the way out from under the table and squatted by Michaela's chair. He cocked his head to one side, his golden eyes slitted.

Michaela looked at me. "Chantal told my aunt that Nick used to belong to a private investigator, and Nick learned a lot from him."

I chuckled. "At times it certainly appears that way."

"Chantal said that Nick likes to spell out words with Scrabble tiles. I think that's pretty cool. I never met a cat who could spell before."

"Nick has many talents," I said carefully. I looked at the cat. He was sitting quietly, just watching Michaela, looking pretty much the way he looked before he decided to pounce on something. The calm before the storm.

Michaela bent over, held out her hand. Nick leaned forward, gave her fingers a sniff. I held my breath, hoping that he wouldn't decide to take a nip. Michaela leaned over further and lightly touched Nick's head. "Hey, Nick. I've got a recipe for cookies that are special for cats. If you like, I can bake you some and bring them back when—I mean if—Ms. Charles hires me. What do you think of that?"

Nick sat back on his haunches and pawed the air. Then he dropped back to all fours and positioned himself beside the girl's ankles.

I looked at Nick, then at Michaela. "Do you really have a recipe for cat cookies?"

She nodded. "It was on one of the food shows. There's one for dogs, too. I baked a batch for the shelter and the animals just loved them, so I'm hoping your Nick will, too. If not, well, I do a pretty good Crab Louie and" —she cast a glance downward at Nick—"I whip up a mean lobster salad. Chantal told my aunt that's Nick's new favorite food."

I was definitely impressed. No doubt Chantal had told Marie about Nick's attitude toward the other applicants, and Marie had passed on the info. Michaela had done her homework to learn just what would get her in good with my finicky feline. "Plus," Michaela dropped her voice to a whisper, "Chantal always tells me in advance when she's got a finished batch of collars in case I want to bring some to the shelter, so I can give Nick some advance warning. I know she likes to try them out on him, but . . . if he's like a lot of the cats at the shelter, I bet he doesn't like wearing 'em."

With that, Nick jumped right on Michaela's lap and let out a big, rumbling purr.

I couldn't help it—I started to laugh. "Well, Michaela, it would appear you've passed the biggest test of all. You've gotten Nick's approval."

She let out a squeal. "Oh, golly. You mean I've got the job?"

Nick waved one large paw in the air. "Yowr." Catspeak for *Absolutely*.

I grinned at the girl. "You heard it, straight from the cat's mouth. You're hired."

• • •

I managed to pry Nick away from his new buddy Michaela and gave her some papers to take home to fill out. When Chantal came in, I told her the happy news: Michaela had met Nick's stringent requirements. I promised to tell her all about it as soon as I got back (leaving out the part about the collars, naturally) and departed shortly thereafter to keep my appointment with Paul Lassiter. I drove to downtown Cruz and located the building without any trouble. It was a two-story, rather modern brick building. The entrance doors, as well as one entire side of the building, was glass. I stepped into the lobby, which had a definite art deco feel, what with the black and white checkerboard square rug and cushy white leather furniture. I walked right up to the sleek black desk and smiled at the equally sleek receptionist sitting behind it. Her eyes widened a bit as I gave Lassiter's name, and she turned her head and spoke softly into her headset. A moment later she looked up at me, her smile a mile wide, and told me I could go on up, corner office, second floor. I rode up in the black and white elevator, *Beethoven's Fifth* playing in the background, and in seconds stepped out onto the second floor. This one was done in tones of beige and pink, and as my feet sank into the plush pink carpeting I had visions of beaches in Bermuda. I half wished I were there now as I walked to the end of the hall to stand before a dark paneled door with a plaque that read *Dr. Paul Lassiter, MD, PhD*. I opened the door and walked in. Another sleek receptionist sat behind a cherrywood desk. She looked up with a smile, not as wide as the first receptionist's, as I approached. "Nora Charles?" she asked before I could speak. "Dr. Lassiter is expecting you. Go right on in."

"Thanks," I said, and squared my shoulders. I took a deep breath, turned the knob, and walked into the sanctum sanctorum.

The man sitting behind the massive oak desk had his back to me, looking out the picture window. As the door clicked shut behind me, he whirled around in his chair, and I had my first good look at Paul Lassiter. Even behind a desk he was a formidable-looking man, broad-shouldered with heavy features. His hair, which at one time had probably been thick and wavy, was now thinning at the sides. Thick eyebrows over pale blue eyes seemed to enhance the aura of authority the man conveyed.

Lassiter didn't rise, merely nodded at me. He raised his hand and pointed to one of the leather chairs in front of his desk. I walked over and sat down. Not surprisingly, the leather was supple, butter-soft. Expensive, like the rest of the office trappings. I took a quick glance around. A bookcase off to the right held several hardcover volumes, medical journals mostly. The wall to my left held several framed diplomas from prestigious universities.

"Ms. Charles."

He spoke my name softly, but with a commanding air. I dragged my gaze away from the diplomas and looked straight into his eyes. "Dr. Lassiter."

"Thank you for coming. Pardon me if I don't mince words. I believe in getting straight to the point, I've no time for niceties. I hear you're conducting an investigation into Christian's death?"

I wondered briefly who might have tipped off Lassiter—Elle, perhaps? I raised my chin and said, "I wouldn't call it an investigation. As you may or may not know, I'm an ex-true crime reporter and I do occasionally write articles for an online crime magazine, *Noir*. Mariah's return to Cruz has sparked a lot of interest, and my editor suggested I do an article on her."

He nodded. "I'm familiar with the magazine, and with your work, Ms. Charles. It is a six-year-old cold case, but then again, so was the Grainger case." He leaned back a bit. "I thought perhaps Mariah might have persuaded you to quiz people on her behalf."

"I won't lie to you, Dr. Lassiter. I have spoken with Mrs. Blackthorne. She's fully in favor of my doing this article. I think she hopes it might give her some sort of closure as to what happened the day her husband died."

"I see." Lassiter leaned back in his chair and steepled his long fingers beneath his chin. "Mariah was never convinced that she could have murdered Chris."

I crossed my legs at the ankles and leaned forward in my chair. "Apparently you were, though."

Lassiter leaned across the desk. "I was under oath. I couldn't lie. Have you read the trial transcript?" I shook my head and he continued, "You should if you want to do a comprehensive article, but right now let me fill you in. I was in Chris's den, waiting for him, when I overheard them arguing just outside the door. Mariah was in a fit. She accused Chris of playing around, and he was telling her to grow up. She screamed at him, said that if she couldn't have him, no one else would."

There was a brief silence and then I said, "I also understand you testified she went after him with a knife."

One shaggy eyebrow rose. "That's true. It happened about a week before he died. I was once again waiting for Chris in his study, but Mariah cornered him on the stairway. They were arguing over some bill she'd found in one of his dresser drawers, either a hotel bill or a floral bill, I'm not sure which. It went on for a while, and I could hear it was getting pretty heated, at least on Mariah's part, so I decided I'd try and calm her down. When I opened the study door all the way I saw Mariah pointing a knife at her husband, threatening to cut him into little pieces if she ever caught him cheating on her. She had a wild look in her eyes, so I stepped in and shouted at her. She stopped immediately and dropped the knife. It was almost as if she didn't realize what she was doing." Lassiter pushed back his chair and rose. "The prosecution asked me if I thought Mariah capable of murder, and I said at that moment, yes. Mariah appears sweet and demure, but she's got a devil of a temper."

"So you think that's what happened? They had another argument that day and she lost her temper?"

"It's possible. In a rage, she might have just picked up the first available weapon, that bust, and smacked him over the head. She was probably so shocked afterward she just blanked it out of her memory." He picked up a pencil, twirled it between his fingers. "So, what's the point of this story? Trying to ferret out the truth? You said Mariah is in full agreement, so I imagine that means trying to pin the crime on someone else?"

I shifted in my seat. "I'm not looking to pin anything on anyone. Mrs. Blackthorne, as I'm sure you're aware, still has amnesia regarding that day. She just wants to know the truth."

"I imagine she does," he said softly. "People often have different ideas about what the real truth entails. Reporters, for example. No offense, but some of them say all they want is the truth, but it's a lie. What they really want is a front-page, career-changing story."

"You seem to be familiar with what some reporters want." I laced my hands in front of me. "Have you been approached by another reporter?"

His brow arched slightly and he tapped the pencil against the desk blotter. "As a matter of fact, I have been. I will say, though, she gave off a much different vibe than you. More desperate for information. So, she's after the sensationalism, and you're after the truth. The truth as I see it is whether it was intentional or not, Mariah murdered Chris. But let's say for the sake of argument she didn't." He barked out a laugh. "Lots of people had motive or reason to want my partner dead—including me." He drummed his fingers lightly on the desk. "Let me save you the trouble of inquiring around, Ms. Charles. Chris and I hadn't been seeing eye to eye on lots of things months before he died. We were in complete disagreement over the direction our practice was taking. He wanted to expand, I didn't. I'd mentioned going out on my own several times, which annoyed Chris to no end."

"Interesting," I said. "I've also heard the two of you clashed over money problems."

"That's true. I thought, and still do, that Christian was, how can I put it? Borrowing funds when he got short. He accused me of doing the same to cover his own tracks, I'm sure." He tented his fingers in front of him. "Gossip had it that I had a gambling problem. I admit to frequenting the blackjack tables at some of the casinos, and I do indulge in a monthly poker game, but I pride myself on gambling responsibly. I certainly never lost enough to justify dipping into the company till, so to speak." He paused and then added, "I believe Christian's looking to place blame had more to do with the fact that he thought I was in love with his wife."

I raised a brow. "Were you?"

The smile he offered me seemed enigmatic. "Let's just say Mariah's a beautiful woman, and I'm a red-blooded male. I knew that Christian wasn't treating her as well as she deserved." He spread his hands. "I confess I was enamored of Mariah. However, when I made my feelings known, she wasted no time in setting me straight. Christian might not have been faithful, but Mariah was determined to be."

"So it didn't annoy or anger you that she rebuffed your advances?"

He settled back more comfortably in his chair. "I did not kill Chris over my frustration with our business, or over his wife. As I told the police, I was playing poker in Santa Barbara with three other doctors."

"That would be the poker game you mentioned?"

He nodded. "We get together once a month, and as fate would have it, there was a game scheduled for that very day. I was with them from three in the afternoon until midnight. As far as I know, the police never thought it necessary to verify my alibi, but if you want to, feel free." He picked up a pen, scribbled something on a nearby pad of paper and then pushed it across the desk to me. "There you are. Dr. Christopher Winkler, Dr. Thomas Spurlock, and Dr. Donald Roberts. They operate out of their offices in Santa Barbara. Call them. I'm sure they'll be happy to vouch for me."

I scribbled down the names, then slid the paper into my pocket and laid his pen back on the desk. "You mentioned others who might want to see Blackthorne dead?"

"Gosh, where should I begin?" He started to tick off on his fingers. "There's the Cutter fellow, the housekeeper's son. Chris disliked him intensely, claimed he was lazy and shiftless. The kid hated Chris even more, thought he took advantage of his mother's work ethic and didn't pay her what she was worth. He complained but he never made a move to get a job to help out, either. He contributed nothing to his or his mother's support, other than possibly getting his hands on what wasn't nailed down."

"You're saying Jerry Cutter's a thief?"

"To put it delicately, the boy had sticky fingers and probably still does. Two days before his death, Chris came into my office and sat right where you're sitting and told me he'd just had one heck of an argument with the kid. Seems he'd caught him in the act of lifting some small art objects from his house. He'd had some small jade pieces vanish a few months before, and he wondered if Velma might have taken them. He knew they were having financial troubles. He also suspected Mariah might have sold or pawned them and given the Cutter woman the money—that was something else they argued about. He thought Mariah was too soft with the help. Anyway, he told me he had proof Cutter was a thief and he wanted to press charges but was holding off on account of the mother. He confided to me that unless Jerry made restitution for what he'd taken previously, he was going to go through with it, make the kid serve time. 'Someone has to show that kid tough love, Paul,' he said to me."

"What about Mariah's friend, the hairdresser? Adam Porter? I understand he owed Dr. Blackthorne a lot of money."

Lassiter drummed his fingers on the desk. "Ah, yes, Porter. An excellent hairdresser but a lousy businessman. Mariah talked Chris into fronting the money for his salon. A very great deal of money, I might add. Six figures. The salon tanked in less than six months."

"And Dr. Blackthorne wanted his investment back."

"Of course. Wouldn't you? Chris was rather emphatic on it, and no amount of pleading on Mariah's part could change his stand. That was another of their arguments."

"I understood Porter had the funds to repay Dr. Blackthorne, they just weren't liquid enough."

"That is true. But Christian was very impatient. He felt he'd been much too lenient with Porter and didn't want to wait."

"I see. That leaves Elspeth Gardner."

"Elspeth?" He looked at me blankly and then his expression cleared. "Oh, you mean Elle? Mariah's friend?" He tented his fingers, pressed them against his chin before he answered, "Now that's an angle I hadn't thought about. It could be possible, I suppose, although . . ."

"Yes?" I prompted as he hesitated.

Lassiter shifted in his chair before he answered. "Those last few weeks before he died, Chris was a bit upset over a woman. She was making noises about wanting a more permanent relationship, which of course Chris wasn't willing to give her. He seemed quite agitated over it."

"Do you mean the mysterious pregnant mistress?"

Lassiter rubbed his hand over his chin. "I suppose I do. I did mention all this to the police at the time, but they didn't appear too interested. They did check out the phone call, but it came from a burner phone."

"And you had no idea who it could have been?"

He was silent for a long moment before he finally said, "I got the distinct impression that she might have been a patient of Christian's at one time. Of course, he couldn't confirm or deny it—ethics, you know—but it was a definite vibe." He glanced at his watch. "And now I really must terminate this interview. I've a patient due in about twenty minutes, and I need to review my notes from our last session." He paused and then added, "Good luck, Ms. Charles. I think you're going to need it. And when you see Mariah, tell her in spite of everything, I wish her well."

* * *

Back out on the street, I glanced at my watch. Oddly, I'd found the interview very enlightening, particularly Lassiter's remarks about the mystery woman. Being involved with a patient, either current of former, would be a serious breach of ethics and would definitely explain the air of secrecy, and I found myself wondering if Elle Gardner had ever sought out the good doctor's services. Possibly Mariah might know the answer to that. I dialed her number, but the call went straight to voicemail. Undaunted, I pulled up Google on my cell and got Mariah's address. I programmed the directions into my Garmin, and about twenty minutes later found myself piloting my SUV down the winding driveway that led to the Blackthorne estate. The mansion was built in the style of grand European castles that I'd seen on travel sites on the Internet. It was good-sized without being overly enormous, and sported a large tower turret on the front and smaller ones sticking off the sides. There was a wraparound porch that extended almost the entire length of the building, and the windows glowed a muted shade of gold in the late afternoon sun. If Mariah were so inclined, it was the type of place that could easily be converted into an upscale B&B. I parked, hurried up the short flight of steps and then hesitated. Perhaps Mariah wasn't at home, or if she was, maybe she didn't want company. As I debated what to do, the door was suddenly flung open and a wild-eyed Mariah stood on the threshold. She grabbed my arm and pulled me into the foyer.

"Nora, thank God you're here," she cried, placing a hand over her heart. "I think someone just tried to kill me."

Chapter Twelve

"What!" I cried, but Mariah let out a moan and swayed toward me. I caught her arm and led her into the living room. My shoes sunk into the plush mauve carpeting as I guided her over to the long, brocaded sofa, positioned directly in front of the fireplace. She sank into the deep cushions and lay her head back against its brocaded back. Her hand fluttered toward an end table on which rested an enormous ceramic pitcher and two crystal goblets. "Water," she croaked.

I picked up the pitcher, poured some water into one of the glasses and handed it to her. She downed the contents in one large gulp, held out the glass. "More," she whispered.

I poured her some more, and this time she took a few sips, then carefully set the glass on a wicker coaster on the oak mission-style coffee table in front of the sofa. She leaned back and passed a hand over her eyes. "Thank you," she said.

I eased myself onto the cushion next to her. "What happened, Mariah?" I asked. "You said you thought someone was trying to kill you?"

She pulled her hand away from her eyes and looked at me with a vacant stare. "I was napping," she said. "I guess . . . I guess it was a dream. But it seemed so real! I could swear someone was next to my bed, looking down at me, eyes so hate-filled—oh!" She gave a shudder and squeezed her eyes shut.

I patted her arm. "Do you want me to call the police?"

Her eyes snapped wide open. "Oh, no! Please don't. I-I'm not even certain there was a break-in." She brought her arms up to hug herself. "I must have had a bad dream, but it just seemed, oh, I don't know. So vivid. So real."

"Dreams can be like that. Do you want to tell me about it?"

Mariah's hand went up to lightly massage her temples. "I felt a headache coming on, so I took an aspirin and stretched out on my bed. I was just drifting off when suddenly I had this sensation of being watched. The room was dark, I had the shades drawn, but I thought I saw a shadowy figure next to my bed, and I had an impression of eyes blazing with hatred . . . I ~~laid back down and~~ closed my eyes, and that was when I felt something soft and silky brush against my neck. I reached up with my hands and tried to grab it, but someone jerked it out of my grasp." She let out a soft sigh. "I fell back against the pillows. I was still half asleep, I think. That's why I—I'm not sure if it was even real."

I touched her shoulder and said gently, "Do you think that perhaps what you experienced might have been a memory?"

Her eyes widened, but then her shoulders hunched in a shudder. "No. It had nothing to do with that afternoon. I'm certain of it. This was . . . something else."

I glanced around sharply. "Are you here alone? I thought your friend Elle was staying with you?"

"She was, but . . . she had to go home, take care of some business. I thought I'd be all right here but . . ." She pushed her hair back and let out a shaky laugh. "Apparently not."

I stood up. "Where is your bedroom?"

"Second floor, first door on the left."

"Wait here. I'm going to run upstairs and have a quick look around."

"Oh, Nora." Mariah's hand shot out, grasped mine. "Do you think that's wise? What if—what if there really was someone? What if they're still there?"

I reached into my pocket and held up my phone. "I'll have it in my hand the whole time. If I see or hear anything suspicious, I've got the Cruz police on speed dial." She started to protest, but I gave her a gentle push back against the soft cushions. "I'll only call the police if I find an intruder. You stay put. I'll be right back."

Mariah closed her eyes and I hurried out of the living room and up the staircase. At the landing I paused, listening, but I heard nothing. I moved quickly down the hall to the first door on the left, twisted the knob and stepped inside. A massive, canopied king-sized bed covered with a pale yellow down comforter took up most of the room. It was flanked on either side by maple end tables, on which reposed delicate antique brass lamps. A book lay next to the clock radio on the table nearest the big bay window. I leaned over and peered at the title: *Psychoanalysis in the Twenty-First Century*. Even more interesting was the name of the author: Dr. Felice McDowd.

I turned my attention to the window, which was open about a quarter of the way. I walked over to it, pushed it all the way up and looked outside. It was a good drop from the ledge to the ground, and there was no tree or drainpipe anywhere near the window, so it was a good bet if someone had gotten in, they hadn't been using this route. I shut the window and started to turn away, when something tangled in the edge of the comforter caught my eye. I bent down for a closer look. It was barely visible against the soft pink background, but it was there—a single thin pink thread. I plucked it up and tucked it in my pocket, then exited the bedroom. I walked swiftly down the hall and peeped into the rest of the rooms. When I was satisfied no one was lurking about, I made my way back to the living room. Mariah had moved to one of the Queen Anne chairs and had paid a visit to the bar. She was sitting with a glass of what appeared to be white wine, and she looked at me with an anxious expression. "Find anything?"

"Just this." I reached into my pocket and pulled out the pink thread. "I found it tangled in the edge of your comforter. Is it yours?"

Mariah squinted at the thread. "I do have a pink-and-white-striped sweater," she admitted. She looked at the thread more closely, then shook her head. "No. My sweater is a baby pink. This is a deeper shade. It's not mine." She shifted her gaze to me. "It was good you showed up on my doorstep. What brought you here, anyway?"

Before I could mention my session with Lassiter, the doorbell pealed. Mariah grabbed my wrist. "Oh, who can that be? No one other than you and Elle knows I'm here, unless . . ." She lowered her voice to a whisper. "You don't think it could be that horrid reporter?"

I slid the thread back into my pocket and patted Mariah's hand. "If it is, don't worry. I'll get rid of her."

I hurried out into the hallway and over to the front door. I went over to the side window, parted the curtain just about a quarter of an inch, and peered out. Elle Gardner stood there, tapping her foot impatiently. She glanced up, caught sight of me and made an impatient gesture toward the door. I opened it and she pushed through, eyes flashing. "I forgot the key Mariah gave me," she said. Her gaze raked me up and down. "What are you doing here?" she snapped.

"Nora is visiting me." We both turned as Mariah approached. She walked over to me, linked her arm through mine. "It's a good thing she stopped by. I thought that someone was in the house, that they tried to attack me."

"What! Who was it?" Elle cried. She pushed me aside and went to envelop Mariah in a bear hug. "Are you all right?"

"Yes. It was just a bad dream, but it really frightened me."

Elle grasped Mariah's arm. "You've cooped yourself up in this house and now you're imagining all sorts of things. What you need is to get out, get some fresh air. I think we should take a little field trip."

Mariah extricated herself from Elle's grasp and took a step backward. "Oh, I'm not sure I feel like going out," she demurred.

"Nonsense." Elle clapped her hands. "I think going out will be good for you. After all, you've paid your debt to society, Mariah. You can't live here like a hermit. You've got to get out, face people, enjoy the rest of your life. Come on, let's go shopping. There're some shops in Cruz you simply have to see. One in particular I know you will love."

"Well . . . all right." Mariah hesitated, then waved her hand in my direction. "But only if Nora comes too."

A shadow crossed Elle's face, but it was gone in an instant. She smiled at me, a bit too widely. "Of course she can," she purred. "If she wants to."

"Sure," I said quickly. "A shopping expedition sounds like fun." Out of the corner of my eye I saw Elle's smile falter just a bit. Tough. I'd planned on tagging along even if I hadn't been invited.

Especially since I noticed that underneath her smart black and white houndstooth blazer, Elle had on a pink cashmere vest, the same shade of pink as the thread I'd found in Mariah's bedroom.

Mariah got a light jacket out of the hall closet and then we all trooped outside to Elle's car, an olive-green Mercedes S-class sedan. Elle opened the front passenger door and motioned for Mariah to enter; I opened the rear passenger door and slid in behind Mariah. I sank into the rich leather seats, thinking that Elle certainly wasn't hurting for money. I'd gone out with a guy in Chicago who'd owned one of these and I knew the base cost was about the total of Hot Bread's receipts for at least three years, maybe more. I remembered Mariah saying Elle was devoted to her husband. Judging from this I thought it was very possible Elle's love affair were with her husband's money and not the man.

Elle slid in behind the steering wheel and a moment later the engine purred to life. She backed the car around and headed down the driveway and out onto the main road. Mariah let out a deep sigh and turned to gaze out the window. "I think you were right," she said. "Maybe getting out for a bit is just exactly what I need."

"Of course it is," Elle answered. "You can't be cooped up in that house twenty-four-seven."

Mariah turned her head to look at me. "Isn't she sweet. Always looking out for me. Elle is one of the best friends I have." She paused. "And the funny thing is, if it weren't for Christian, we might have never met."

I felt my pulse quicken at those words, and I leaned forward. "Really?

How so?"

Mariah glanced at Elle. "It's all right to say, isn't it?" she asked. "After all, Christian's dead so . . ."

"We met at Christian's office," Elle said shortly. "I was a patient of his, very briefly. Stan and I were having some problems, and I'd heard good things about Christian. I decided to go for one session and ended up being his patient for six months." She let out a low chuckle. "The only reason I stayed that long was because I met Mariah. She dropped by one evening just as my session was ending, and we got to talking. We've been friends ever since."

Mariah nodded vigorously. "Elle is the closest thing I've ever had to a sister."

I leaned back against the seat cushion. Lassiter had mentioned he'd gotten the impression the woman Blackthorne was involved with might have been a former patient. Elle's admission that she had been one solidified her position in my top suspect category. I slid my phone out of my pocket and sent a quick text to Hank: *Investigation proceeding. Can U verify alibis for Paul Lassiter and Elle Gardner?*

I added the names of the three doctors Lassiter had given me, hit send and slid my phone back into my pocket. I was relatively certain Lassiter's alibi would check out, but now I was extremely curious as to where Elle Gardner might have been the day of Blackthorne's death.

Cruz's business district loomed ahead, and Elle made a sharp turn onto Main Street. "Is anyone hungry?" she asked.

"I could go for something to eat," Mariah admitted. "I skipped lunch and only had a piece of toast for breakfast."

"Good," Elle said, "because there's a lovely little tearoom here that opened a few weeks ago. We can have some tea and sandwiches, and then there's a store right across from the high school I think you'd love, Mariah. It's primarily a beauty supply store, but she has the most divine collection of perfumes, lotions and bath products I've seen in a long time. I've been in there at least a dozen times since it opened, and the smells are divine every time."

My head snapped up. Was she talking about Carm's store? "You mean Skin and Scents?"

Elle met my gaze in the rearview mirror. "I think that's the name. Anyway, I was in there the other day and bought a bottle of Joy. She had an excellent price on it."

I sunk down a bit lower in my seat so Elle couldn't see me worrying my lower lip. After what Carm had said about Mariah the other day, I knew she wouldn't be happy to see her come into her store. I decided to offer up an alternative. "There's a very nice thrift shop near there," I suggested. "They have a wide selection of perfumes too, and they'll probably be more reasonably priced than Skin and Scents."

I caught a glimpse of Elle's nose wrinkling in the rearview mirror. "Thanks, but we're not on a budget—not yet, anyway," she said. She angled a glance at Mariah. "I noticed a whole shelf of lavender-scented products when I was in there. You're still fond of that scent, right?"

"Oh, yes. I would like to see what they have. Who knows, maybe they will have something similar to my Midnight Lace." Mariah twisted in her seat so she could look at me. "I loved that perfume. Whenever I'd run out, Christian would turn up with a new bottle." Her tone turned dreamlike. "It was a light, clean scent. Notes of lavender, jasmine and bergamot. It evoked images of birds chirping, grass growing. I loved it so."

"I tried to get some for Mariah while she was in prison," put in Elle, "but they discontinued the scent."

Mariah shook her head. "Such a shame. Now I shall have to find another, and it won't be easy to top Midnight Lace."

"Well, maybe that store will have something similar," Elle suggested. "It's worth a look, right?"

Mariah sighed. "I guess."

I settled back in my seat. Well, I'd tried. Maybe we'd get lucky and Carm wouldn't be working today.

Elle managed to find a parking spot across from the tea shop, aptly titled Take Tea and C, and we trooped inside. The tiny shop was packed and every table appeared to be filled. I recognized the owner, Marianne Ferrante, as she bustled about, teapot in hand, flitting from table to table. She noticed us standing by the door and hurried forward. "I'm so sorry," she said. "We had a big rush today. Apparently there are big sales all along Main Street. A table should free up soon, though, if you care to wait?"

Elle tapped her foot impatiently on the parquet floor. "How long of a wait?"

Marianne brushed a strand of salt-and-pepper hair out of her eyes and scanned the quaint little room. Every table was filled with customers, mostly women, chattering and sipping tea and eating what appeared to be either delicious finger sandwiches or mouthwatering scones. "I just seated five tables a few minutes ago, so . . . maybe a half hour?"

Elle raised both eyebrows, then turned to us. "Skin and Scents isn't far from here. We could go look in there and then come back."

"You could do that," Marianne said. "Skin and Scents is a lovely shop. Tell you what, tonight's our dinner night. We're serving Yankee Pot Roast. If you're interested, it'll be my treat."

"That's very kind of you," murmured Mariah. She looked at us. "What do you think? I haven't had a good pot roast in years. Velma used to make an excellent one."

"I'm in. What about you, Nora?" Elle asked.

"Sure. Pot roast sounds good." If it were tasty, I'd get a small take-out portion for Nick.

"Wonderful," Marianne said. "I'll expect you back in about a half hour, forty-five minutes then?"

"We'll be here," Elle sang out. She waved her arm. "Okay, ladies. It's off to Skin and Scents."

• • •

I was decidedly impressed as I followed Elle and Mariah into Skin and Scents. It was the first time I'd set foot in Carm's shop, and I had to admit Elle's assessment was correct: the aromas were indeed fragrant and spicy, even more so than those from Marianne's tea shop. I paused and gave a quick glance around. The shop seemed to be divided into two sections: The right side was chock-full of beauty supplies—makeup, hair care products and the like—and was rather Spartan in nature. The other half, the fragrance half, however, reminded me of an upscale jewelry store. Long glass cases held bottles of all shapes, sizes and colors, gleaming bottles that sparkled like gems. The whole left side of the section was mirrored, with glass shelves that held a selection of scented soaps, lotions, even candles and essential oils. A small sign behind one of the glass counters read, *Let us create your own personal scent*. It appeared that Carm was catering to the upscale with the fragrance portion of the store, and more to the general public with the beauty end. I idly wondered which half made the most profit.

Elle's sharp eyes noticed the sign and she touched Mariah's arm. "Look over there. They have a perfumer who crafts personal scents. I bet they could make you up something even better than Midnight Lace."

"Maybe," murmured Mariah. "I suppose we could inquire."

Elle took Mariah's arm and steered her toward the sign. I glanced idly around the shop. Over on the beauty side, a cluster of teenaged girls were giggling over a hairspray display. Two women, their backs to me, were idly checking out various brands of hair color. The perfume side appeared deserted, except for us and for one man standing at the black marble counter. I noticed that Carm didn't appear to be anywhere around, and some of the earlier tension I'd felt dissipated.

The curtain behind the counter parted and a woman holding a small wrapped package came out. She seemed familiar, and a few seconds later I realized why—it was Gillian, Carm's round-faced friend. I almost hadn't recognized her. Today she wore her hair up in a French twist rather than loose around her shoulders, and her apparel—a crisp white shirt and navy cardigan—was a definite improvement over her usual threadbare one. I figured Carm had made good on her promise to hire her.

Gillian smiled at her customer. "There you go, Mr. Murray. That will be fifty-seven ninety-five."

As Mr. Murray fumbled in his wallet for his credit card, Gillian glanced up and saw me. She flashed me a quick smile, and then her gaze shifted to the small counter where Mariah and Elle stood. Her eyes widened, and the credit card slipped from her hand. "Oh, goodness me," she murmured. "I'm really clumsy today." She bent to retrieve the card and quickly rang up the order. She handed him the slip along with the package. "Thank you for shopping at Skin and Scents," she said. Murray left and then Gillian turned to vanish into the back room again, but not without a final glance in Mariah's direction.

Mariah hadn't failed to notice how her presence seemed to bother Gillian. She and Elle walked over to where I stood and Mariah sighed, plucking nervously at the sleeve of her jacket. "Maybe we should go," she murmured. "Seeing me upset that woman, I'm sure of it."

"Well, then, that's her problem," Elle snapped. "Honestly, Mariah, are you going to let some goggle-eyed store clerk get the better of you? Get used to it. People will stare at first, but then . . . they'll get over it. That woman did, and pretty quickly too, I might add."

"I hope you're right," Mariah said. She didn't sound convinced.

I smiled at Mariah. "How did you make out with the personal scents?" I asked.

"The perfumer isn't in today," Elle answered. "I took his card, though. We'll come back." She turned to Mariah. "Over there is the display of lavender I was talking about." She took her hand and I followed them as Elle led Mariah down the middle aisle. She paused before a shelf and made a sweeping gesture. "See, there's a hand lotion, a bath lotion, a shampoo, a spritz, a cologne . . . lavender was in Midnight Lace, right?" Elle snatched up the deep-purple bottle with one hand, grabbed Mariah's wrist with the other. Before the other woman could protest, she'd spritzed her wrist with the cologne. "That smells nice," she announced. "I think you should treat yourself to a new signature scent. Recreating Midnight Lace is too much like dipping into the past."

Mariah frowned. "Maybe you're right," she said slowly.

"Of course I am." Elle tossed her head. "You've got to let go of the old and embrace the new. I think you should try something totally different." She reached for a bottle on another shelf. "Here. This scent is pine, cherry and sandalwood. Try this." She uncapped the bottle and spritzed a good amount onto Mariah's wrist.

Mariah bent her head and sniffed. "Not bad," she said. She held out her wrist to me. "What do you think, Nora?"

I took a sniff. "Very pine-ey. It reminds me of Christmas."

"Christmas," Mariah murmured. "My favorite holiday. Wouldn't it be wonderful to have that lovely feeling all year round." She set the bottle back on the shelf and said, "I saw more bath salts one aisle over. I'm just going to have a quick look."

"I'll go with you," Elle said. "I could use some new bath salts."

The two moved into the adjacent aisle but I lingered a moment looking over the various offerings. Then I decided to take a closer look at the display for the customized fragrances. As I moved in that direction, I saw Gillian walk into the aisle opposite the display. I hurried over, saw her straightening a display of French perfume. She glanced up, saw me, and her face split into a wide smile. "Hey, Nora," she said. "I see you finally made it down here. How do you like it?"

"It's great," I said. "Carm certainly has put a lot of work into it." I gestured at her smock. "You're working here now?"

Gillian pulled a face. "Yes, Irene made good on her threat and cut my hours, so Carm hired me to work two days a week so I wouldn't lose any income." She lowered her voice and added, "Don't ever tell her, but I so prefer the bookstore. It's not half as busy as this place, although I suppose I shouldn't complain. Busy means my hours won't be cut, right? And I do need the money." She moved closer so her face was only inches from mine.

"Plus, there are some added perks. I get a fifteen percent discount on all the scents, and twenty on makeup."

I was close enough so that now I could see what Carm had been talking about the other day. Gillian's foundation was pretty thick. I imagined she'd probably welcome the discounts. I took a swift glance around the shop and added, "I take it Carm's not working today?"

Gillian's laugh tinkled out. "Oh, Carm works every day. You just missed her, actually. Her son has an event at school and Carm had to run a quick errand before it started. She'll be back soon, though. Tonight the shop's open till nine and I go home at seven."

That surprised me. "I didn't know Carm had a child," I said.

"Kenny's hardly a child. I think he'll be six or seven in a few weeks. But to tell you the truth, I'm glad she's not here right now. If Carm knew Mariah Blackthorne was in her store, she'd have ten fits." She pulled her sweater more tightly around her. "I hope she leaves before Carm gets back. I'm not in the mood for all the drama."

"I don't believe we'll be staying much longer," I assured Gillian. I figured a change of subject was in order so I gestured toward the sign on the wall. "I didn't realize you could have a personal scent made?"

"Yeah, it's something Carm's trying out. She hooked up with some guy who's a perfumer—I think that's the right term. He comes in two days a week to blend special scents. You have to make an appointment. I think the guy's booked for this entire month already."

I goggled at her. "You're kidding."

"Nope. You'd be surprised how many people want their own personal scent. They don't want something that half the population has. They want to be unique." She cocked her head at me. "You should try one of those special blends, Nora. Yours would probably have an air of mystery. Maybe something like . . . this?" She reached for a bottle on a nearby shelf, pulled out the stopper. She held it under my nose and I breathed in deeply—and almost choked. The perfume was definitely strong, I'd give it that.

"Citrus, lemon, patchouli and just the barest hint of tobacco," said Gillian. "It's very earthy and mysterious."

I smiled and shook my head. "I think that might be a little too much mystery for me." I sniffed at the air. "Your scent is nice, though. Nice and light. Did you have it blended?"

Gillian shook her head. "Oh, no. I couldn't afford to do that." She made a little face, lifted her wrist and sniffed at it. "Actually I just spritzed this on. I ran out of my current one the other day, so I'm trying some others out. So far I haven't found one I really like."

Elle appeared in the aisle just then, two large glass containers clutched in each hand. She spotted Gillian and strode right up to her. "I was looking for bath salts in a lime and ginger scent," she said. "Do you carry anything like that?"

"Lime and ginger? I don't think so, but I'm sure we could order it for you," Gillian said.

Elle made a little noise in her throat. "Don't bother. I'll just take these."

"Okay," Gillian said. "I can ring you up now."

"Wait, my friend is buying some bath salts too. I want everything put on my bill—ah, there she is now."

Mariah came around the corner just then, a glass container of bath salts in one hand. Her head down, she butted right into Gillian's back. "Oh, I'm so sorry," Mariah murmured. "I wasn't watching where I was going, I'm afraid."

Gillian hesitated, then reached out and gave Mariah a tentative pat on the shoulder. "No harm done," she said. She looked at Elle. "Are you ready now?"

"Yes." Elle reached out and plucked the jar from Mariah's hand. "This is my treat, and don't bother to protest. I insist."

As Elle and Gillian moved off toward the counter Mariah and I went over to stand by the front door. Mariah glanced casually around the shop. "This really is a very nice store," she said. "I think I would like to come back and talk to the perfumer. Maybe I should try something new—oh my God!" She stopped speaking, and her back stiffened. Her eyes flashed, and her lips compressed into a thin line as she pointed down the aisle opposite where we stood. "What is *she* doing here?" she rasped.

I followed Mariah's pointing finger, and my own heart skipped a beat as I saw who had caught Mariah's attention: Jennifer Hinkle.

Chapter Thirteen

Before I could say a word, Mariah started down the aisle toward Jennifer. "What are you doing here? You're following me, aren't you?" she screamed at the reporter.

Jennifer appeared startled, but she held up both hands in a gesture of surrender as Mariah approached her. "Mrs. Blackthorne, I'm not following you," she said. "I just came in here to look around."

"A likely story," Mariah spat. She walked right up to Jennifer and shook her finger in her face. "Didn't I warn you to leave me alone and to stop dogging me? If I catch you around me again, I swear I'll . . . I won't be responsible for what I might do to you. I—ooh."

Mariah's eyes closed and she swayed uncertainly on her feet. I hurried forward and slipped my arm around Mariah's shoulders to support her. Jennifer took a step back, and as she did so I caught a glimpse of a soft, pink scarf sticking out of the edge of the voluminous tote bag slung over one arm. Unless I missed my guess, it was the exact shade of pink as the thread I'd found in Mariah's room.

Jennifer turned on her heel and made a beeline for the door, vanishing through it just as Elle hurried over to us. "What happened?" she asked me, then without waiting for me to answer, she nudged me aside and pulled Mariah close to her. "Dear, are you all right?"

"I'm fine," Mariah spat. "It was that horrid reporter. She's following me!"

"I'll be right back," I said and hurried out the front door after Jennifer. I spotted her halfway down the block. "Jennifer," I yelled. "Stop."

Jennifer stopped, turned and saw me. For a minute I thought she was going to bolt, but she stood there, tapping her foot and waiting for me to approach. As I drew close to her, she lifted her chin and growled, "What do you want? To accuse me too?"

I folded my arms across my chest. "I don't know. Have you done something that I should be accusing you of?"

"Of course not." Jennifer shifted her tote bag from one hand to the other. "It's not a crime to shop, is it? I happen to have been in that store before and I like their products."

I tapped my foot against the sidewalk. "So you weren't spying on Mariah?"

"Spying? Heck, no!" Jennifer put a hand on her hip. "For your information, I was already in the store when the three of you came in. I was very careful not to let you see me because I figured my presence would be upsetting to Mrs. Blackthorne, and I was right."

"If you were so concerned about upsetting her, you could have left when you saw us come in," I said.

Jennifer shrugged. "I guess I could have, but I didn't think that was necessary." She glanced at her watch. "Sorry to cut this short, but I've got to get going."

I wasn't about to let her get away so easily. "Just a sec." I gestured toward her tote bag, where the pale pink scarf peeped out. "Nice scarf. Is it new?"

She shot me a puzzled look. "Yeah, I just bought it yesterday. So?"

"It's very pretty. I just wonder why you've got it stuck in your tote and not wearing it."

She stared at me. "Who are you," she growled, "the Fashion Police? What is it of your business what I wear?"

I got right up in her face. "I'll tell you why it's my business. Mariah Blackthorne had a dream earlier about someone sneaking into her bedroom and trying to strangle her. When I investigated I found a pink thread tangled up in the comforter, the same color as that scarf."

Jennifer's eyes popped. "You're serious? Someone broke into her house? That is interesting," she murmured. A second later her head jerked up. "You think it was me, don't you? Well, you're wrong. Why on earth would I do that?" she screeched, waving her arms back and forth.

I held up my hand and said in a soothing tone, "Calm down, Jenn. Of course I don't think you were trying to kill her. Mariah was having a dream. But I think it's possible that you might have broken into her house looking for some sort of evidence, and you snagged the scarf on something."

Jenn's arms dropped to her side and she tilted her head. "Ah, so now I'm a housebreaker in addition to being a troublemaker? Sorry, Nora, you're way off on that." She reached into the tote and whipped out the scarf, dangled it under my nose. "See for yourself. No loose threads. If someone left a trail of pink behind, it wasn't me."

The scarf was indeed intact. I watched as Jennifer stuffed it back into her tote bag and decided to try another tack. "Well, then, maybe you can tell me why you were all cozy with Jerry Cutter?"

Her head snapped up. "Who?"

"Don't play dumb. I'm sure you know who I mean. I saw the two of you together at the Poker Face."

Jennifer thrust her jaw forward. "You used to be an investigative reporter, Nora. You know darn well why I was with him. I was interrogating a witness."

"Yeah, well, I'd be careful if I were you, Jennifer. From what I hear, Jerry's more of a suspect than a witness."

Her brow wrinkled and her lips pressed flat. "From what you hear, eh?" she said. "And just what are you doing, hanging out with her? I thought you were too busy with your business to do any investigating? Or was that just for my benefit?"

"No, not entirely," I said. "I am busy, but Mariah happens to be a friend of a good friend of mine who asked me to look out for her."

She gave me a long, searching look. "So you *are* investigating," she said at last.

"Let's just say I'm making a few discreet inquiries."

"On behalf of this friend of hers. Does this friend have a name?"

"I'd rather not say."

Both her brows went up. "Right. And I'm sure in the course of making these 'discreet inquiries' you're planning a nice feature for that online magazine. Admit it, Nora. You want to solve the mystery yourself and you don't want to share the glory."

"Trust me, I'm not in competition with you, Jennifer. If you can prove Mariah didn't murder her husband, then I'm all for it. I just don't want to see you put yourself in danger doing it."

"Yeah, well, thanks for the concern, but it's totally unwarranted. Jerry Cutter makes a good suspect on paper, that I'll admit, but he's not Blackthorne's killer."

The conviction in her tone surprised me, so much so that for a moment I couldn't think what to say. Finally I got out, "Just what makes you so sure of that?"

She shrugged. "Just my gut feeling, after talking to him. He told me— oh, no!" She stopped speaking and waggled her fingers in the air. "You're not going to trick me that easily, Nora Charles."

"Jennifer, I'm not trying to trick you. I'm just telling you to exercise a bit of caution. It's been my experience that sometimes those gut feelings don't work out."

"Yeah, well, mine have always paid off. Anyway, it's all moot, or it will be soon enough." She leaned into me and said in a low tone, "This much I will tell you, so you can eat your heart out. I'm this close to uncovering the real killer." She held up her hand, both middle fingers touching. "And getting closer by the second."

I felt a chill race up my spine at her words. "What do you mean by that?"

Her lips curved in a cat ate the canary smile. "Wouldn't you like to know? Sorry, Nora. You had your chance. Now you can just read about it in the paper along with everyone else."

With that, she plopped her tote bag on her shoulder, turned on her heel, and walked swiftly away. I debated going after her but figured it wouldn't do any good. Knowing Jennifer, her boast about being close to exposing the killer was nothing more than false bravado. At least I hoped that were the case.

I retraced my steps back to Skin and Scents. Mariah sat in a chair near the register, sipping a cup of water, while Elle hovered solicitously about her. Gillian was behind the register, looking decidedly ill at ease, but her thin features arranged themselves into a smile when she caught sight of me. She hurried out from behind the counter and down the main aisle toward me.

"Nora, thank goodness," she breathed. She glanced over her shoulder toward the counter and then whispered, "Mrs. Blackthorne seems to be much better now, but . . ." She lifted her shoulders in a helpless shrug.

I knew what she was thinking and I reached out to pat her arm. "I know. We'll be leaving now." I walked over to where Mariah sat, Elle hovering over her like a guard dog. She glanced up, saw me, and for an instant something flashed across her face—annoyance? I ignored her and bent to take Mariah's hand. "How are you feeling?"

"Much better. I do feel foolish, though," Mariah said. "I didn't mean to cause a scene."

"Nonsense," Elle said briskly. "From what you've told me about that woman, I thought you showed considerable restraint." Her gaze softened somewhat as she turned to me. "You went after her, didn't you. What did she have to say for herself?"

"Not too much, actually," I hedged. "She denied spying on Mariah, and then she made an excuse and took off."

Elle tossed her head. "She belongs behind bars, if you ask me. The woman's a nuisance. Mariah, can't you charge her with harassment or something?"

"She hasn't really done anything that's against the law," I said. "It would be very difficult to make any charges stick."

Elle's lips puckered. "Yeah, freedom of the press, right? Morrie, my husband, always says laws are in place to protect the criminals, not the innocent. I'm starting to agree with him." She took Mariah's arm, helped her out of the chair. "Why don't we stop by the tea shop and get our dinners to go. We can eat them back at your house, and then I think you should get into some pj's and we'll watch an old movie, what do you say?"

"That sounds nice." Mariah looked hopefully at me. "Would you like to stay for dinner, Nora?"

"Thanks, but I have some prep work that I need to do for tomorrow's lunch menu back at Hot Bread," I said. "I'll ride back with you and get my car, though."

"Okay." Mariah looked disappointed. "Some other time."

"Yes," Elle purred. "Some other time. Definitely."

She took Mariah by the arm and the two of them started for the door. After a moment I followed, thinking that I wasn't going to hold my breath for *that* invitation.

• • •

Nick greeted me when I walked into the shop. I bent down to give him a scratch on the white streak behind his ear. "Miss me?" I asked the cat.

"Meower," Nick said as he rubbed his portly body against my ankles.

I sighed. "Well, it certainly has been an eventful afternoon." I tossed my bag on the counter and sank into one of the high-backed stools. "My interview with Paul Lassiter went well, and he seemed sincere, but I'm not ready to take him off the list of suspects just yet. He seems to have Mariah's best interests at heart, but that could be a cover. He did point a finger at Jerry Cutter, though. And after talking to Jennifer Hinkle, I'm convinced he definitely bears further investigation. She might think he's innocent, but I'm not all that sure."

Nick blinked twice, laid his head on his paws.

"Mariah had a dream that someone tried to kill her, but no one was in the house when I had a look around. I did find a pink thread in her bedroom, though, that an intruder could have dropped." I frowned as I realized that I'd never checked out Elle's pink and white sweater. Elle had a key, she could easily have let herself in. As fast as I thought of that, though,

I rejected the theory. I didn't trust Elle, but she was staying with Mariah. She had a pretty fair run of the place. There would be no reason for her to sneak into the house.

Or was there?

"I'm not too sure about Elle either," I said. "She claims to have Mariah's best interests at heart, and Mariah trusts her, but there's just something about her that rubs me the wrong way. Of course, it could just be her snooty attitude, but somehow I think there's more to it than that." Suddenly I snapped my fingers. "Oh, darn. I forgot to ask Mariah if she knew Elle's maiden name. Maybe Hank can find it out for me."

I pulled out my phone and checked my texts. Nothing from Hank. Well, he'd said he was going to be pretty much incommunicado. I knew that he'd get back to me when he could. I sent another text asking if he knew Elle's maiden name and set the phone back on the counter. I looked at Nick. "So, what do you think, Nick? Lobster salad for you for dinner?"

The cat's head jerked up. He licked his lips. "Yowzer."

I got up, went over to the refrigerator to get the bowl of lobster salad. As I carried it back to the counter, my phone rang. I picked it up, glanced at the screen and frowned.

Unknown Caller.

I hesitated, tempted to let it go to voicemail, but Nick let out a sharp meow. I frowned. Maybe it was Hank. Maybe something had happened to his other phone and he was calling me from a burner phone with some news. I hit the answer icon. "Nora Charles."

The voice that floated back to me sounded as if it were speaking through one of those mechanical devices specifically designed to disguise one's voice. "Nora Charles," it rasped. "If you know what's good for you, you'll stop looking into Christian Blackthorne's murder. No good will come of it. Mariah Blackthorne is guilty as sin."

Then there was silence.

Chapter Fourteen

"Someone apparently thinks you're getting close to something."

I topped off Ollie's second cup of coffee and set the pot back on the stove. It was a little after two the following day, and we had Hot Bread all to ourselves. Since I'd skipped lunch I prepared grilled cheese sandwiches for both of us, and as we ate I recounted the events of yesterday, topping it off with the mysterious phone call.

"Apparently," I said dryly. "I just wish I knew what it was I was getting close to, exactly. Because so far I've come up with nothing concrete that proves Mariah's innocence, just a group of people who all might have had good reason to want Blackthorne dead."

Ollie tapped his spoon against the rim of his mug. "Do you think maybe your mystery caller could have been that reporter?"

"Jennifer?" I rubbed absently at my brow. "Her feathers did seem a bit ruffled when I admitted to making inquiries," I said. "From what I remember of her, though, making anonymous threats wasn't exactly her style."

"Her style could have changed, particularly if she feels threatened by you." He took a bite of his sandwich, dabbed at his lips with his napkin. "I just think you should consider the possibility. In her eyes you're a foe, not a friend. You didn't want to work with her, so now you're on the opposite side, even though you're both after the same thing."

I couldn't suppress a chuckle. "Sounds a bit like an oxymoron, doesn't it? Opposite yet similar."

"Are you going to tell Detective Anderson about the call?"

"Dale?" I cut Ollie an eye roll. "Oh, gosh, no. I don't want to get her involved unless it's absolutely necessary. After all, I wasn't threatened—not outright, anyway. I was just advised to halt looking into Mariah's case." I tapped my finger on the counter. "That's another thing that makes me think the caller wasn't Jennifer. The person said that Mariah was guilty as sin. Jennifer definitely feels the opposite way."

"She could just have said that to throw you off the track."

"I think you're giving her too much credit."

"Ow-rrrr!"

Nick jumped onto the far end of the counter, cocked his head. "Ow-rrr," he said again.

I chuckled. "Nick apparently thinks so too."

Ollie held up both hands. "Far be it from me to disagree with little Nick. He's been right far too often."

Nick looked at Ollie, then at me, and then let out a low, rumbling purr.

I turned back to Ollie. "I do admit that I am a bit concerned for Jennifer, though. I think her desire to solve this and make a name for herself is making her careless."

"In what way?"

I told Ollie about seeing the girl with Jerry Cutter, and the snatches of conversation I'd overheard. "She doesn't think that Jerry could be guilty," I said, "but on paper he's one of my top three suspects. Lassiter wasn't too fond of him, and even Samms said that Jerry used to hang around with some pretty shady characters."

"The company one keeps is always telling," remarked Ollie. "I wonder why Jennifer discounted him so quickly as a suspect?"

"Perhaps he convinced her that it was all a big misunderstanding. That's what his mother said. Jerry was just fingering the statues while he was waiting for her, and Blackthorne jumped to a conclusion, probably based upon Jerry's past."

"It's possible." Ollie leaned back a bit on the stool. "How are the other suspects on your board shaping up?"

"Good question. Maybe it's time for a review." I got up, got the paper from the drawer where I'd stashed it, and laid it on the counter in front of Ollie. Before we could look at it, though, the bell above the door jangled and Louis came in. He walked right up to me and embraced me in a giant bear hug.

"Wow," I said when he released me. "What was that for?"

He grinned. "I hear through the grapevine that you're working to prove Mariah Blackthorne's innocence. I hope this means you plan to write everything up for *Noir*! Circulation will triple with that article."

I sighed. "Yes, it's true and yes, I plan to write it up—regardless of the outcome."

Louis looked shocked. "You mean you think she's guilty?"

"I'm not making any assumptions one way or the other yet. But if I had to hazard a guess, I'd say there are a lot more people who had better motives to off Christian Blackthorne than his wife."

"We were just about to go over them," said Ollie. He motioned to the stool beside him. "Want to join us?"

"I will indeed," said Louis. "And I'll have a grilled ham and Swiss on rye too."

While I prepared Louis's sandwich, he and Ollie went over the suspects on my murder board. Louis, of course, was familiar with all of them. I set the sandwich in front of him, refilled everyone's coffee cups, and then plunked myself down on the stool on the other side of Ollie. I put the murder board in the middle of the counter and tapped at one square with my nail. "I definitely do not have a good feeling about Elle Gardner," I said. "She admitted to being Blackthorne's patient. Said that was how she and Mariah met." I paused. "Lassiter mentioned that Blackthorne was having trouble with a woman wanting a more permanent relationship from him. He thought she might have been a patient."

Louis tapped at the square labeled *Another Mistress?* "So you think this person could have been Elle?"

"It's possible. Why, you don't?"

Ollie frowned. "From what I hear, Elle Gardner's marriage might not be one made in heaven, but it keeps her in fancy cars and jewels. I doubt she'd endanger it."

"She might if she were really in love with Blackthorne," I persisted. "After all, he wasn't exactly a pauper. He could have supported her in the lifestyle she loved."

"True, but his financial status couldn't hold a candle to Morris Gardner's." Louis paused. "Besides, according to the conversation Mariah herself overheard, that woman was pregnant, true? And Elle Gardner has no children."

"That we know of," I said. "She could have had an abortion, or had the child and put it up for adoption. She has enough money so that it wouldn't take much for her to cover her tracks."

Louis took another bite of his sandwich. "I've got to agree with Ollie on this one. I don't know for certain, but I'll bet that Gardner had an ironclad prenup drawn up before he married Elle. He also has an excellent team of investigators on his payroll. If he had the slightest suspicion that she cheated on him, they'd waste no time getting the goods on Elle. Then Gardner would divorce her so fast her head would spin, and he'd make certain that she never got a cent of his money. She's too fond of the good life, so I doubt she'd risk it."

"Maybe," I said. I picked up a pen. "Maybe I should add another square and put Morris Gardner's name in it. For all we know, perhaps he found out about his wife's affair and eliminated the competition."

"If you ask me that's a real long shot," Ollie chimed in. "I'd concentrate on the suspects we already have. What about Lassiter? He was always high on my list."

"The man does possess a certain amount of charm," I admitted. "He was very forthcoming at our interview—possibly a bit too forthcoming. He offered names of doctors who could vouch for his whereabouts the day Blackthorne was killed. Apparently the police didn't delve into it too deeply at the time. I sent Hank a text and asked him to look into it."

"A wise move," Ollie agreed. "What about the hairdresser? Adam Porter?"

"I'm inclined to dismiss him. He was forthcoming about his alibi being difficult to prove. He just didn't give off a murderous vibe to me. He did, however, point a finger at Elle Gardner. He intimated that she was only friends with Mariah in order to be close to Blackthorne. I suppose he could have said all that to direct suspicion away from himself, but I don't think so."

"Okay," said Louis. "I'm inclined to agree. I didn't think Porter had it in him to kill anyone either. We'll eliminate him for now." He drew an X through Porter's name. "Who else?"

I tapped the square with Velma Cutter's name. "After speaking with her, I've eliminated Velma too. I doubt the woman could kill a fly. Her son, though, could be another story. Jennifer might have eliminated him as a suspect, but I'm not so sure. I think it could be very possible Blackthorne caught him in the act of stealing, and the guy lashed out at him with the bust."

Louis frowned. "Maybe."

Ollie and I both looked at him. "You don't agree," I said.

Louis shook his head. "Jerry Cutter is a shady figure, all right, but he is pretty devoted to that mother of his. I don't think he would have killed Blackthorne for the simple reason that he wouldn't want it to have any impact whatsoever on his mother. He wouldn't want her to be thought of as having sired a killer."

"People with the best of intentions can get carried away in the heat of the moment," said Ollie. "I disagree. I wouldn't be so quick to discount him." He looked at me. "What do you think, Nora?"

"He's one of my top suspects," I admitted. "But Jennifer didn't agree. She said he made a good suspect on paper but he wasn't the killer. She sounded pretty convinced, too." I pushed the paper aside. "I am definitely going to have to find a way to talk to Jerry Cutter. He's next on my list."

"And on that note, I have to get going." Ollie pushed back his stool and stood up. "Just let me know if you need my services. For instance, if you arrange an interview with Jerry Cutter, I will be happy to rearrange my schedule to accompany you."

"As my bodyguard?" I asked teasingly.

"If the situation warrants, then yes."

"I'd be glad to go along too," said Louis. He flexed his arm. "I can be pretty competent in the bodyguard department as well."

Nick poked his head out from underneath the back table. "Ow-rrr."

Both Louis and Ollie exchanged a look, and then Ollie grinned. "And if either of us is unavailable, there's always little Nick. Let's face it, that cat is an excellent bodyguard who has saved your hide more than once. If push comes to shove, my money's on him."

• • •

Ollie left and Louis lingered a bit longer, finishing his sandwich and coffee. "Keep me informed of your progress," he said, flipping a ten-dollar bill on the counter. "And if you need me to use my hacking skills, you have but to ask."

I grinned at that offer. Louis was, oddly enough, a whiz when it came to computer systems and had helped me get valuable information on more than one occasion. I had a feeling that he enjoyed it. I assured him that I would definitely let him know. He left a few minutes after three and I made sure the sign was flipped to *Closed* before I locked the door. Then I went in the back and fired up my laptop. Nick padded over and arranged himself comfortably at my feet as I called up my favorite search engine. I typed in each of the doctors' names that Lassiter had given me. They all had a practice together in Santa Barbara, a very lucrative one by all accounts. Spurlock and Winkler specialized in marital counseling, while Roberts's practice targeted adults with severe mental pathology. I also noted that all of them—Lassiter included—had graduated from USC in the top half of their classes. Lassiter and Spurlock had been in the same class, Roberts and Winkler a year ahead. They'd also all been in the same fraternity. Blood brothers, no doubt. But were they brothers who would lie for one another?

It was a distinct possibility.

I had just cleared my screen when I heard a furious pounding at the door. Geez, could no one read a sign? "Sorry, it's after three. We're closed," I yelled, but the pounding continued. Nick put his paws over his ears and slunk further under the table. Finally I pushed my chair back and walked over to the door and snapped the lock back. I opened the door a crack and said loudly, "We're closed."

"I don't care. I want to talk to you, Nora Charles."

Before I could answer, the door was pushed back and Carm stood there, glaring at me. "Carm," I said. "What's the matter?"

She pushed past me without a word and walked over to my counter. She eased a hip against it and shook her fist in the air. "I've got a bone to pick with you. How dare you bring that woman into my shop!"

I swallowed. "By that woman, I imagine you mean Mariah Blackthorne?"

Carm's eyes flashed. "Of course I mean Mariah Blackthorne. Who else would I mean? Honestly, Nora, I told you how I felt about that woman. And to bring her into my shop, where I understand she caused a scene, no less! Unacceptable!"

I swallowed. Apparently Gillian had spilled the beans about my being there with Mariah. "Okay, if you'll just calm down for a minute, I'll explain," I said.

Carm let out a loud Hmpf, then clamped her lips together and crossed her arms over her chest. "Fine," she said in a tight voice. "Explain."

"In the first place, it wasn't my idea to bring her to your shop. It was her friend Elle's. She wanted to show her some beauty products she thought she might like. As for creating a scene, there was no one in the shop when that happened other than us and Gillian. Mariah was a bit overwrought. About an hour before, she'd thought that someone had broken into her house and tried to kill her."

Both of Carm's eyebrows went up. "Someone broke into her house? Really?"

"Well, no. It was just a vivid dream. But she was quite upset, and that reporter had been bothering her, so when she saw her in your shop, she just lost it."

"Swell," Carm muttered. "I knew that woman was a reporter. She's definitely trouble. Do you know I saw her rooting through my dumpster the other day? I yelled at her and she left, but obviously not for good if she was there today too." She let out a giant sigh. "Like I said, no good can come of any of this. She's after a sensational story, and she won't stop until she gets it. And God only knows who else might come sniffing around. Mariah should have cut her losses and moved away."

I took a step forward and said in a soft tone, "Think about it, Carm. Suppose it had happened to you. You were accused of killing your husband, but you couldn't remember anything of what happened. Wouldn't you like to find out the truth?"

Carm's lips tightened, and then she gave a grudging nod. "Maybe. Then again, if I'd done the deed, maybe I wouldn't want to remember. Who wants to carry that load of guilt around with them for the rest of their life?"

I bit the inside of my cheek. It seemed nothing I said placated Carm where Mariah was concerned. "Why are you so against her?" I asked. "It's not as if she ever did anything to you personally, is it?"

Carm flushed and averted her gaze as she answered. "She's giving Cruz a bad rep, which is something we don't need, especially when you're trying to get a business off the ground. How do I know that her being in my shop won't dissuade others from coming in?" She paused, took a breath and then went on, "You weren't here in Cruz when all this happened, Nora. Public opinion was heavy against Mariah, and I'm pretty sure it still is. I bet if you start asking around, I'm not the only one who thinks she should leave town for good."

"People are innocent until proven guilty, and her guilt was never conclusively proven," I interjected.

"No, because she copped a plea and took a deal. If you ask me, deep down she knew she was guilty, and that's why she did that." She hesitated a moment and then said, "Look, I'm sorry I snapped at you. When Gillian told me what happened, I . . . I got upset."

"Frankly, I'm surprised Gillian mentioned it to you at all," I said. "She was so afraid that you'd return before Mariah left."

"Yeah, well, she didn't want to tell me, but I saw she was upset and I wormed it out of her," Carm said. "Anyway, I'm sorry I came in here like a tornado. I should have known you'd have enough sense not to let Mariah anywhere near my shop if you could help it."

I hesitated, unsure just how to broach what was on my mind. Finally I decided to just come out and say it. "No offense, Carm, but you seem to have a very passionate dislike of Mariah, and I can't help but think that maybe there's more to it than just her presence being bad for business."

Carm's tongue snaked out, licked at her lower lip. She barked out a stiff laugh. "Oh, really, what else could there be? You don't know me all that well, Nora. If you did you'd realize that being passionate is one of my character traits. I'm not saying it's a particularly good one, but . . . it's just the way I am. I'm sorry if my strong feelings upset you, but I won't apologize for them." She gave her long hair a toss and then added, "You know, I'm not the only shopkeeper who would like to see Mariah leave town. Maybe you should ask around before you jump to conclusions."

And with that, Carm turned on her heel and marched out of my shop.

Chapter Fifteen

Despite my feeling that Carm was lying, I still couldn't help but ponder her parting words. Were other shopkeepers upset by Mariah's presence here? I hadn't heard anyone else complain, but then again. I hadn't gone around asking. I decided that I'd ask Louis about that at the next opportunity. He'd mentioned public opinion was high against Mariah, so if any of the shopkeepers were against her return, he'd probably know. I just couldn't shake the feeling, though, that there might be more to Carm's dislike of Mariah than met the eye. For now, though, it would have to wait while I concentrated instead on Jerry Cutter.

I fired up my laptop and then paused, thinking. Something Velma Cutter had mentioned when she'd been in Hot Bread was niggling, but I just couldn't put my finger on it. I glanced over at Nick, who was lying on his back in front of the refrigerator, paws in the air. He started to wiggle his back paws in a circular motion, and that's when the lightbulb went off in my head.

"Velma said Blackthorne thought Jerry spent too much time at his bicycle club," I cried. "That could be a good lead." I typed in "Bicycle Clubs—Cruz" and hit enter. When the screen shifted I bit back an annoyed cry. There had to be at least thirty names listed. Who knew there were so many bicycle enthusiasts in Cruz? I nibbled at my lower lip, trying to think how best to narrow the list down. Of course, I could contact Velma Cutter. She might know what club her son belonged to, but I wanted to avoid that avenue if at all possible. I sighed and flexed my fingers. "Well, I guess I'd better get started," I said to Nick. The cat had abandoned his position by the fridge and was now squatting beside my chair. "Maybe we'll get lucky and I'll find something quick."

I clicked on the first name, Cruz California Bicycle Club, and was directed to a very sparse website that actually looked more like a blog. It just related information regarding the club's last trip, and there was a notice about the date and time of the next meeting at the bottom. "This one's a bust," I told Nick.

I clicked on the next name, Bikers Cycle and Fitness, and was directed to a more elaborate site. This appeared, however, to be more of a bike sales site. One of the tabs was labeled "Photos" and I clicked on that one. A page with a ton of photographs appeared, showing folks in shorts, standing beside shiny bicycles apparently purchased from Bikers Cycle. I scrolled down, and one photo in the far corner caught my eye. It depicted a small group of people with bikes. Some wore helmets, some didn't. One guy in the far corner, leaning over a shiny red bike, grabbed my attention. True, the photo wasn't a very clear one, but he did resemble the man I'd seen in the Poker Face with Jenn. I looked at the caption beneath the photo: *Tuesday Night Riders: Jan, Buddy, Alma, Fred, Justin, Harley, Aimee and Jerrold.*

Jerrold. Could that be Jerry?

I looked at the other photos, but none of the others had this Jerrold in them. There was no information on the last names of the people in the photos either. I clicked on the tab for contact info. The cycle shop was near here, and it was open tonight till seven. I closed the laptop and pushed back my chair. "Well, nothing ventured, nothing gained, Nick. Wish me luck. I'm going to check out some bicycles, and if I'm real lucky, get some info on Jerry Cutter."

• • •

Since it was such a pleasant afternoon, I decided the walk to Bikers Cycle would do me good. I walked straight down Main Street, turned left at Dayton, and three storefronts in arrived at my destination. I pushed open the door and walked into the shop as a cheery set of jingling bells announced my arrival.

The shop's ceiling hung low, but my initial feeling of claustrophobia dissipated as I noticed the bright lights shining on what had to be at least a hundred bicycles. Sparkling rays of light danced across the walls, the floors, and me. I tore my fascinated gaze away from the display and looked around the shop. Over in the far corner a large man in a Cruz Buccaneer sweatshirt was examining a purple bike. My gaze traveled to the counter near the large picture window. A lone man was behind the counter, poking at a computer. He glanced up, saw me looking at him, and managed a small smile. "Hey. How's it goin'?" he asked.

I smiled back. "Not bad."

He cut me an appraising glance. "You interested in a cycle?"

"Truthfully? It's been years since I've ridden. Lately, though, I've thought about getting back into it. I could definitely use more exercise."

He grinned, revealing teeth yellow with nicotine stains. "Couldn't we all?" he said.

I held out my hand. "I'm Nora Charles. I own Hot Bread. It's a sandwich shop about fifteen minutes from here."

"Alden Mather." He took my hand, and I noticed that he had a firm grip. "I'm the owner, sales director, PR man, janitor, and whatever else here at Bikers Cycle and Fitness."

"Pleased to meet you. I admit I did check out your shop online. I found your photo section particularly interesting. It looks as if you have a varied clientele."

He smiled. "Yeah, we sponsor bike trips once a month. Usually get a good crowd. You'd be surprised how many people like biking for exercise."

"I see. So you run those trips yourself?"

"The part-timers help. Aimee is a real cycle nut. She rarely misses a trip. Jerry, on the other hand . . ." He shook his head. "That guy's a winner. If he weren't so knowledgeable about bikes, I'd probably have fired him months ago."

I felt my heart skip a beat. "Jerry? That would be the Jerrold in the photo?"

"That's the one." He glanced at his watch. "He'd be the ideal one to help you pick out a bike, if he shows up. He's due here any minute for his shift, and he better show up. My wife'll kill me if I have to work late again and miss her pot roast dinner."

As if on cue, the bells above the door jingled again and a dark-haired man wearing a black leather jacket and distressed denim jeans walked in. I recognized the high forehead and cruel mouth immediately from the photos I'd seen. He walked right up to the counter, slanted me a curious look, and then turned to Alden. He shot the man a maddening grin. "Bet you thought I wasn't gonna show up tonight," he said.

"Where you're concerned, Jerry, I never know what to expect." Alden hooked a thumb in my direction. "This is Ms. Charles. She's interested in a bike. Help her out, won't you?" Alden shot me a smile, walked around the counter and out the door.

I turned to Jerry. "I'm actually considering getting back into biking," I said quickly. "I haven't been on one in years."

Jerry gave me an assessing look. "I'm sure we can find something to suit you," he said with an ingratiating smile. He puffed out his chest a bit. "Biking is my specialty. So . . . what sort of bike have you ridden?"

I looked at him blankly. "Type? Just a regular bike, I guess. I didn't know there were types."

"Oh, sure." He lifted his hand, started to tick off on his fingers. "There's road bikes, touring bikes, hybrids, city bikes, trekking bikes, utility bikes, mountain—"

I held up my hand. "Whoa! All those? You're kidding."

Jerry grinned and I saw he had a set of perfect white teeth, no nicotine stains. "Nope. Trust me, there are a lot of categories. I'm thinking you'd be a road bike. You know, the regular, everyday kind."

"I saw your photo on the website. What type of bike do you ride?"

"I've ridden pretty much all of 'em. Right now I'm into mountain biking. Those babies have sturdy, highly durable frames and wide-gauge treaded tires to help the rider resist sudden jolts. Some riders like the single-speed, but I like the ones with twenty gears. You get more traction. The Freeride bikes have a shorter wheelbase and you don't have to worry about weight. They're good on gaps and drops. Fatbikes are good for snow and sand, but what I really want to get into are the IceBikes. You ride 'em on ice, just like the name implies."

"I'm impressed," I said, and I really was. "You do know a lot about bikes."

"Yeah, well, at one time I wanted to open my own cycle shop. Instead I work here," he said, pulling a face.

"Running your own business is very ambitious and a lot of hard work," I said. "Believe me, I ought to know."

"Yeah, well, that dream died. I tried to raise enough capital, but I just couldn't. I had a rather wild, shall we say, youth. It went against me when I applied for a loan." He scrubbed his hand across his chin. "They said they'd consider it with a cosigner, but there's just me and my mom, and she would never have qualified. She doesn't have much money at all."

"That's too bad," I said. "There was no one else you could have asked?"

He shook his head. "Nope. My mom did hint around to her employer, but that was a definite dead end." He hesitated and then said, "I had what you'd call a wild youth. Got in some scrapes. I straightened out, but Blackthorne didn't approve. The guy hated me."

"Hated? He doesn't anymore?"

"Not exactly." He ran his hand through his hair, mussing up the sides. "He's dead," Jerry said flatly. "The guy was murdered a few years ago."

"Murdered!" I let my eyes widen and my jaw slack slightly. "Oh my goodness! That's terrible."

"You'd think so, wouldn't you," Jerry said, his tone musing. "But the world's a better place without him in it, trust me. Christian Blackthorne was an evil, mean-spirited man."

I twisted my lips into a little O of surprise. "Christian Blackthorne? Oh, I remember hearing about that case. They said the wife did it."

Jerry frowned. "She went to prison for it. She couldn't remember what happened. It was never proven that she was the one." He made a little grunt of frustration. "The guy was loaded, and he didn't leave my mother one red cent in his will, not after all the years of service or all the crap she took from him. I always told her he took advantage of her and guess what? I was right."

"You mentioned that it was never proven the wife did it," I said. "It sounds to me as if you think she might be innocent."

He was silent for a few moments and then said in a low tone, "Mrs. Blackthorne is one very classy woman. I can't picture her killing the doc, but then again, people sometimes get pushed beyond their limits. How she ever married a heel like Blackthorne is a mystery to me."

It sounded to me as if Jerry might also have had a bit of a crush on Mariah. Aloud I said, "But the case seemed so open and shut. There were no other suspects, right?"

"Oh, there were plenty of suspects. They just never bothered to look," said Jerry. He hesitated and then said, "They questioned me though."

I widened my eyes. "They did? Why?"

He shifted his weight from one foot to the other. "Blackthorne and I had a big argument right before he was killed. He accused me of stealing some figurines from his home."

"Why would he do that?"

Jerry looked down at the toe of his shoe. "It all goes back to that wild youth I mentioned. I have a sort of . . . history of doing things like that. But that's all behind me. Like I said, I turned over a new leaf, that's why I was trying to start up the shop. Fresh start and all that. But Blackthorne never really trusted me. He thought I spent too much time hanging around here, when I should have been out looking for a job. He didn't consider this work." He raised his gaze to meet mine. "I wouldn't have stolen anything from him, on account of my mother. He'd have held it against her forever, made her work even harder. As it is, he cut her off with nothing. Anyway, I had an alibi for the time of death. I was out mountain biking with my friend Rhoda. As if I'd waste my time killing the likes of him. It wouldn't be worth going to prison for, although I do think whoever did do it deserves a medal."

I leaned my elbow on the counter. "So, if you had to take a guess, who do you think might have killed him?"

He cocked his head, pursed his lips, considering. Finally he said, "If you ask me, I think the police should have tried harder to find that woman. I saw her at the house a few times."

"Woman? Do you mean Elle Gardner?"

He barked out a laugh. "I almost forgot about her. She's another piece of work. She and the doc were tight, but that's not who I'm thinking of. It's another woman. I saw her hanging around the house a few times when I was there, and once, not long before the murder, I saw her and the doc arguing in the driveway. At least it looked like they were arguing. I was too far away to hear anything. They were flapping their arms at each other, and then she hopped in this beat-up old Ford and drove off, and not a moment too soon. Mrs. Blackthorne came home not ten minutes later."

My heart was beating so loudly I was certain he had to hear it. "Did you tell all this to the police?" I asked.

"Yeah, but they didn't seem too interested. Like I said, they had their perfect suspect. They didn't want to look elsewhere."

"Could you describe this woman?"

His lips scrunched up for a moment and then he said, "To be honest, I didn't pay all that much attention to her. She had light brown hair—I think. I only saw her from a distance, but there was nothing outstanding that stuck in my mind." He shrugged. "She looked like hundreds of other women, you know, the ones who just sort of blend into the background. What's that word? Non-something?"

"Nondescript?"

"That's the one. She was nondescript." He flashed me a smile and rubbed his hands in front of him. "But enough about the past. We've got other, better things to talk about." He gestured toward a bright pink bicycle. "How do you like this baby?"

• • •

It was a few minutes past five when I let myself in the back door of my shop. As I pushed through into the kitchen, Nick rose from his position by the refrigerator to amble over and wind himself around my ankles. I bent down and gave him a scratch behind one ear. "Miss me?" I asked.

He looked up at me, blinked. "Yow-rrr."

"I'll take that as a yes." I went over to the table and flopped into a chair. "It was a very interesting interview," I said. "And I almost became the proud owner of a shiny pink bike. Fortunately two teenage girls came in just as Jerry was getting ready to write up a sales slip. I managed to get away by telling him I had to get back here and I'd definitely think about the bike."

Nick blinked, then opened his mouth in a large yawn.

"Yes, I know you're not interested in that. You want to know what I think of Jerry Cutter." I leaned back in the chair. "He's bitter, to be sure, but he also seems honestly devoted to his mother. He definitely thought Blackthorne took advantage of her. He denied taking those figurines, but he didn't try to hide the fact he has a past. I have to admit, I think I agree with Jennifer's opinion of him. I don't think he stole those figurines, and I don't think he killed Blackthorne either. I would like to know more about that mystery woman he mentioned, though. I've got a feeling that she could be this mysterious mistress, and who knows? Maybe Blackthorne's killer too."

Nick waved one paw in the air. It looked as if he were pointing toward the storeroom. "What's up, Nick?" I asked the cat. "Do you think I should look through your former owner's journals for more pearls of wisdom?"

The cat looked at me, then blinked. His head swiveled again toward the storeroom. "Okay," I said. "Let's have a look. Can't do any harm."

We entered the storeroom, and just as I started for the file cabinet Nick let out a soft meow. A second later there was a loud knock on the back door. I frowned. "Now who could this be? Chantal's working at Poppies tonight, and Samms is at that debriefing—unless Lacey forgot her key again."

I got up and walked over to the door, parted the curtain, and peered out. I let out a gasp and flung the door wide. "You," I cried. "What are you doing here?"

Chapter Sixteen

The tall man standing on my back stoop shot me a mischievous grin. "Is this how you greet all your visitors?" he asked. "Or just the ones you've known for a hundred years?"

I flung my arms around him. "Hank Prince, you are a sight for sore eyes. What are you doing here? I thought you were working a big case in Chicago?"

"I got lucky and wrapped it up early. I told my boss I was taking a week vacation and coming down here. I drove pretty much all day and night." He hugged me back and then said, "So, are you going to invite me in, or are we just going to give your neighbors a show all night?"

I grabbed his arm and pulled him inside. Hank is a tall man, six-three easily, with a stocky build. He has reddish brown hair that he wears a bit longish on the sides and the nape of the neck, deep blue eyes that peer out from behind massive tortoiseshell glasses, and a killer smile. No one ever takes him for a private investigator, which is partly the reason he's so successful. And I lost count of the number of cases he helped me with when I worked in Chicago. He was a master at ferreting out information, the more elusive the better. There's nothing Hank likes better than a good challenge.

Which might well account for the attraction between him and Mariah, I thought.

Hank pulled out a chair and eased his large frame into it. He thrust his long legs out in front of him. Nick came forward, sat next to Hank's chair, and looked up at him. He cocked his head to one side and regarded the detective with wide golden eyes.

Hank leaned forward. "And this, I take it, is the famous Nick Charles? Your partner in crime solving?" He extended his hand toward the cat. "I'm pleased to meet you at last, Mr. Charles. I've heard a lot about you. All good, no worries."

Nick took a step closer, sniffed at Hank's fingers. His pink tongue snaked out, gave them a lick. "Merow," he said. Then he turned around, walked back to the refrigerator, and lay down.

I grinned. "Looks as if you've passed muster. Believe me, if he didn't like you, you'd know it. He's tortured more of my part-time applicants than I care to think about. Fortunately, he approved of the most recent applicant. She starts here tomorrow."

He chuckled. "I don't doubt that he was fussy. He seems to be a very discerning fellow." Hank whipped his gaze to me. "So, how are things progressing with Mariah?"

"Slow but steady. She seems like a very nice person and definitely not the type to murder her husband. I do think, though, that she's still haunted by the experience." I quickly filled Hank in on the recent happenings. "I'm not entirely certain that returning to her house was a wise move," I finished. "Although I'm pretty sure she's doing it in the hopes that it will jog her memory about what happened that night."

Hank's lips had compressed into a straight line when I was telling my story. Now he leaned forward. In a voice tinged with concern he asked, "I was afraid that her coming back here could make her a target. You're certain that there was no one in the house?"

I hesitated, then shrugged. "No, I'm not certain. As I said, I did find that pink thread. Jennifer Hinkle had a scarf that matched the color exactly, but there were no pulls or loose threads on it. I forgot to get a better look at Elle Gardner's vest, though. It was the same color pink."

"You mentioned Elle was staying there, though," said Hank. "I'm sure Mariah would have given her a key, so why would she sneak into the house, or for that matter, invade Mariah's bedroom?"

"A good question. I guess I didn't really think that through," I admitted. "I suppose that since I took a dislike to the woman, I'm too eager to think the worst."

"Well, if it'll make you feel better, I share your opinion about Elle. I've always thought that she cozied up to Mariah so she could get closer to Blackthorne. Proving that, though, is a different matter."

"Louis said that he doubted Elle would have cheated on her husband. According to him, Morris Gardner's money makes Blackthorne's look like chickenfeed, and Elle wouldn't take a chance on losing it."

"That's probably very true," Hank agreed. "But love can make people do some very strange things."

"Love or lust," I said reflectively. "According to Nick Atkins, that's a prime motive for murder. Did you manage to find out Elle's alibi for the time of Blackthorne's murder?"

"Yep." Hank pulled a notebook out of his pocket, flipped some pages. "She said that she was at her spa the entire afternoon. Records show that she did check into the spa around noon, but no one can actually remember seeing her there during the day. She supposedly checked out after six that evening and went directly home. Her maid corroborated the fact that she arrived at six thirty, went and dressed for a dinner she was attending that evening at the country club with her husband."

"And how about Lassiter's alibi? Did that high-stakes poker game check out?"

Hank rubbed absently at his forehead. "Those doctors corroborated it, but I'm not entirely sure I buy it. After all, they're fraternity brothers. It wouldn't surprise me if they all lied to give Lassiter his alibi. However, it would be pretty tough to prove." He was silent for a moment and then added, "Blackthorne's death was very convenient for Lassiter. I understand that Blackthorne threatened calling in an accountant to go over the business financials, but that halted upon his death."

"That's funny," I said. "Lassiter told me that he suspected Blackthorne of skimming off the top. And if Blackthorne were guilty of that, no doubt he'd have called in an accountant who would have been prejudiced toward his side."

"Ah, so it's a case of the pot calling the kettle black, eh? Maybe both of them were dipping into the till. At any rate, I believe Lassiter's testimony against Mariah was colored by her rejection of his advances. There were some instances that Mariah told me about that she didn't even tell her lawyer. The guy was an absolute heel."

I saw how upset Hank was so I didn't press for details. Instead I just said, "I went to the hair salon and spoke with Adam Porter. I have to say, I believed him, even though his alibi is a lot like Elle's. No one could actually verify seeing him at that fashion show."

"I believed him too, and I know he made a good impression on the DA. Then again, the DA was fixated on Mariah and didn't really want to look elsewhere. That's why that phone call was so important." Hank sighed and stretched his long legs out in front of him. "I still think her lawyer made a mistake not letting the case go to trial. She might have gotten off entirely."

"Maybe not. It seems that public opinion is pretty high against her, even today." I told Hank about Carm. "Her dislike for Mariah does seem a bit over the top, but what if that opinion is shared by other merchants in Cruz? If it's this bad today, it must have been worse six years ago."

"It was," admitted Hank. "There were lots of people jealous of Mariah. She was a beautiful ex-actress who married a rich guy who many thought was way out of her league. The unfavorable public sentiment against her came mostly from females. And there were seven women on that jury. If you want my opinion, I think this Carmela's feelings toward Mariah are probably justifiable, at least in her mind." He paused. "You said she has a son?"

"Yes. Gillian said he was around six years old—oh!" My eyes widened and I looked at Hank. "Are you thinking what I'm thinking?"

"That if Carm had Blackthorne's baby, he or she would be about that age. Yep." He made a notation in his book. "I'll have the dates checked out."

I pursed my lips. Carm the mysterious pregnant mistress? If that were true, it would definitely account for her attitude toward Mariah. I turned to Hank and said, "I interviewed another suspect today, Jerry Cutter. I was a bit leery, but now I have to admit I can see why Jennifer said he was no killer. He didn't give that vibe off at all. I don't think I'd trust him around any valuables, but commit murder? I doubt it. Especially not Blackthorne. He was too concerned about the fallout it would have on his mother."

Hank shook his head. "So Cutter's a mama's boy, eh?"

"I don't think I'd go that far, but he did seem devoted to her. And Louis said pretty much the same thing."

"It could be an act."

"He didn't strike me as being that good an actor." I paused and then added, "He mentioned seeing a woman arguing with Blackthorne. He couldn't offer much in the way of a description, though, other than she struck him as plain-featured with mousy hair."

"Interesting. That description could fit thousands of women around here." He paused and then asked, "What about this Carmela? Would that description fit her?"

My brow wrinkled as I digested that, and then I slowly shook my head. "There's nothing about Carmela that's nondescript, so offhand I'd have to say no. Of course, I have no idea what she might have looked like six years ago."

Hank made another notation. "Something else to check out. Did Cutter mention this woman to the police at the time?"

"Yes, but he said they didn't seem too interested in her. They were already fixating on Mariah." I jumped up. "Where are my manners? You must be hungry if you drove straight here from Chicago. Can I make you something?"

He patted his stomach. "I stopped at a few fast-food drive-in stops and loaded up on burgers and fries, so I'm good for now. What I'd like to do is see Mariah." He pulled his cell out of his jacket pocket. "I tried several times to reach her, but each time my call went straight to voicemail."

"If she went to take a nap it's possible she might have shut her phone off. Why not try her again?"

While Hank made his call, I decided to check my own phone, which I'd put on silent while I was in the bike shop. To my surprise, I had two missed calls, both from Jennifer Hinkle. I noted she'd left two voicemails. I played the first: "Nora, it's Jennifer Hinkle. Please call me as soon as you get this." The second one was a bit longer. "Nora, as much as it pains me to ask you, I could use your input. I'd like to talk to you about that woman in the perfume shop, Skin and Scents. You seem to have a knack for figuring out things. Call me as soon as you get this."

I frowned. It sounded as if Jenn wanted to talk to me about Carmela. But why? I hit the redial number and the call went straight to voicemail. After the beep sounded I left a brief message asking her to call me and then looked up to see Hank frowning at his phone. "Something wrong?" I asked.

He tapped the phone against his palm. "Still no answer. I confess, I'm a bit worried. Perhaps someone might have really broken into her house."

I told Hank about Jennifer's voicemails. "I tried calling her back and my call went straight to voicemail also," I finished.

Hank's frown deepened. "Do you think Jennifer could have gone over to Mariah's?"

I was already shrugging into my jacket. "It's very possible," I said. "And judging from Mariah's reaction the last time she saw Jennifer, there could be fireworks. We'd better get over there now."

The three of us piled into my SUV and headed out. Hank dialed Mariah twice more and each time the call went straight to voicemail. The sun was just dipping below the horizon when I made the turn that led to Mariah's house. As we proceeded down the winding driveway, I saw the first floor was ablaze with lights. I pulled up and parked right in front of the house. Hank had the passenger door open before I cut the engine and was halfway up the steps by the time Nick and I exited the SUV. As I turned to follow him, I caught a movement out of the corner of my eye. I swung my gaze toward the garden and blinked. Was that a dark shadow I saw flitting across the lawn?

The shadow vanished almost as soon as I saw it, and I frowned. Had I imagined it? Or was it just an animal, maybe a raccoon or a deer? At my feet, Nick gave a low growl, tail bristling. "Uh-oh," I murmured. "You saw something too, didn't you, Nick?" I glanced toward the house, but Hank was nowhere to be seen. "Come on, Nick," I whispered. "Let's take a quick look."

The evening shadows were beginning to lengthen. I took out my phone and switched on the flashlight app, then Nick and I started across the expanse of yard. Most likely it had been an animal I'd seen, but I just had to be sure. I flashed the light around. Under other circumstances, I would have found Mariah's garden fascinating. It was situated in the backyard just beyond a brick patio, slightly raised above the level of the yard. It was circular, with a three-tiered concrete fountain square in the center. Twin cupids played with a stream of water that shot out from the mouth of a large fish at the top. The outer pathways had been squared off on all sides. Graveled paths divided the pathways into pie pieces of closely planted beds of peonies, geraniums, Angelonia and Astrantia. Dotted in between were stone figures in the shapes of various animals—owls, birds, deer. I noticed there was a gaping hole beside some of the Astrantia. To the rear of the garden proper was a tall stone wall that separated it from the rest of the backyard. A narrow opening in the center led to a couple of steps that made the elevation change to the yard easy to manage. As I stood for a moment to get my bearings, Nick let out a loud yowl and started to race toward the opening.

I'd heard that yowl before, and it was never good. I swung my light in that direction and my blood ran cold. A pair of long, khaki-covered legs protruded from the opening.

I raced forward, terrified at what I might find. I heard footsteps behind me and gave a quick glance over my shoulder and saw Hank hurrying toward us. I kept going, though, and when I reached the opening I just stood for a moment, staring, my mouth agape at the tableaux before me.

Nick sat on one of the stone steps, looking down at the khaki-clad Jennifer Hinkle. Red blood oozed from the back of her head, forming a round red circle on the concrete. A little blood dribbled down the front of the white blouse she wore. About ten feet away from Jennifer lay a stone owl, its base smeared with bright red. Beside it, hand outstretched toward its base, lay the inert form of Mariah Blackthorne.

Chapter Seventeen

"Nora, what's wrong—oh my God! Mariah!"

I turned and saw Hank's face blanch as he took in the macabre scene before us. He immediately went over and knelt beside her. His hand moved up her arm, to her shoulder and then her neck. "There's a pulse," he breathed. "She's alive, but very weak."

I'd pulled out my cell and dialed 911 while Hank was examining Mariah. When the dispatcher answered I said, "We need an ambulance. Someone's been hurt."

"I need your information, ma'am," the dispatcher said. I gave it to her. After she informed me the ambulance was on it's way, I added, "Better also notify the police," I added. "There . . . there's another body." I glanced over at Hank, who'd moved over to Jennifer and was feeling her pulse. He looked at me and shook his head. "I think she might be dead."

I disconnected and went over to join Hank. I knelt beside Jennifer and touched two fingers to the side of her neck. "No pulse, but the body's still warm," I said. I remembered the dark shadow I'd seen and added, "Nick and I saw a shadow flit across the lawn. Whoever did this might still be lurking somewhere near," I whispered.

Hank rose. "I'll take a look around." Seeing my worried expression, he patted his side and added, "Don't worry, I'm armed. You and Nick stay here."

Hank glided off toward the other end of the garden, and I turned to look again at Jennifer's body. Nick squatted beside her. He glanced up, saw me, then raised his paw and pointed at Jennifer's jacket pocket, where something white peeped over the edge. I also noted there was a faint tan smudge on the edge of the jacket sleeve. "Merow," said Nick. He waved his paw at the object. "Merow."

I figured he wanted me to remove whatever it was, and I shook my head. "Sorry, Nick. I admit I'm tempted, but you know how Anderson feels about tampering with a crime scene."

Nick looked at me with his big golden eyes. Then he leaned over and hooked his claw into the object and gave a tug. He removed his paw and I saw a small slip of white paper dangling from it.

"I guess you don't care how Anderson feels," I remarked. I leaned over and removed the paper from his paw. I looked at it and frowned. Written there were the words *Insolence, Ethereal, Amaranth.*

"This makes no sense," I murmured. I knew *insolence* meant rude and disrespectful behavior, and an *ethereal* meant celestial or heavenly. I had no idea what *amaranth* meant.

Nick rubbed against my ankles. "Merow," he said again. I looked at the paper and then at the cat. "You think I should take this, don't you?" I shook my head. "You're a bad influence, Nick."

He looked up at me and blinked. "Merow."

I pulled out my phone, snapped a photo of the paper, and then slipped it back in Jenn's pocket while Nick made little grumbling sounds. "Sorry, pal, but that will have to do," I said. "I know you don't think there's anything wrong with tampering with a crime scene, but I bet you'd sing a different tune if Anderson hit us with an obstruction of justice charge, which I've no doubt she's dying to do."

Nick's answering yowl was drowned out by the wail of an approaching siren. A moment later an ambulance pulled up right in front of my SUV, followed by a dark blue sedan. The driver's door opened immediately and Dale Anderson emerged. A few seconds later a young officer exited the passenger side. I let out a breath and turned to Nick. "Looks like I put that back just in time. I think, Nick, that later you and I are going to have to have a little discussion about proper crime scene protocol."

Nick flicked his tail, a sure sign of kitty annoyance. I sighed and turned my attention back to the driveway. Anderson and the younger officer were nowhere in sight, but two EMTs had exited the ambulance and were now headed in my direction, pushing a gurney loaded with resuscitation equipment. I recognized one of them, Harold Dugan, a medical student who came in Hot Bread at least four times a week. The other was a short middle-aged woman I had never seen before, with graying hair cut in a pixie style. They paused in front of me, and the woman, whose name tag read *Barbara,* said in a clipped tone, "Where are they?"

I pointed. "Over there. The older woman is still alive. She's got a pulse, but it's very faint. The other—" I choked up and couldn't go on, just shook my head. Barbara gave a brisk nod and she and Harold piloted the gurney in the direction I'd pointed. I started to follow when I heard someone behind me clear their throat. "Nora Charles. Well, fancy meeting you here."

I whirled around and met Dale Anderson's dark and stormy gaze. "Detective Anderson," I said. "How nice to see you."

One corner of her lips twitched upward as she responded, "Yeah, I bet. So it was you who found the body?"

"Actually the two of us did."

"The two—oh." Her gaze fell upon Nick at my feet and her lips twitched. "Ah, so both of Cruz's favorite body magnets are on the job tonight."

I flushed at her use of Samms's nickname for Nick and myself. Dale Anderson is what I've sometimes referred to as a female Samms. She had a no-nonsense attitude that was, at times, as frustrating as it was satisfying. Actually, I've always thought that if circumstances were different, she and I might have gotten to be actual friends. As it was, we were more like frenemies. I had the feeling that she grudgingly respected my flair for detection, although I was also certain wild horses would never drag that admission out of her. "Jennifer's body was still warm, so we thought maybe the culprit was still around somewhere. Hank went to take a quick look around the garden."

Dale's eyebrows rose. "Hank? Who's Hank?"

"A friend of mine—and Mariah's. He's a PI."

Dale blew out a breath. "Swell. Just what I need. A PI running around my crime scene." The young officer stood right behind her, and now Dale waved her arm at him and barked, "Rogers! Take a look around the perimeter. See if you find anyone snooping around. If you do, bring him right over to me."

"Yes, Detective," the officer said. He hurried off quickly, and Dale pulled her notebook and pen out of her pocket, started to jot something down. As she did so, I gave her a quick once-over. The long coat she wore flapped open and I caught a glimpse of a tight-fitting coral dress and nude nylons. Her hair, which she usually wore pulled back from her face in a severe bun, hung loose and flowed across her shoulders. I also noted that her lips tonight were stained with a bright red gloss, not her usual clear pink shade. Sudden realization hit me and I cried out, "Oh, gosh! You were on a date, weren't you?"

Her eyes darkened even more. "*Were* being the operative word," she said. She tapped her pen against the pad and motioned over to where the EMTs had pulled a sheet over Jennifer's body and slanted me a glance. "You called the victim Jennifer, so I'm taking a wild guess you know her?"

"Sort of. Her name is Jennifer Hinkle. We worked on the *Trib* in Chicago years ago. She came into Hot Bread a few days ago. She wanted to enlist my help in proving that Mariah Blackthorne had nothing to do with the murder of her husband."

Anderson raised one eyebrow but didn't look at me. She scribbled something on her pad and then said, "Did she now? And did you agree to help her?"

"No, mainly because I'd already promised Hank that I'd look into the matter."

"Hank. That's this PI Hank?" Her frown deepened. "Does he have a last name?"

"Prince. As I said, he and Mariah are old friends. He was going to help out, but he got jammed up with a case and asked me to look into it."

"I see. And, of course, you wanted a chance to hone your newly minted PI skills."

"No, not really," I began, but then a voice called out, "Detective Anderson!" We both turned and saw Rogers hurrying toward us. "I found this in the bushes." He held out his hand and I gasped as I saw what he had clutched in it. Anderson gave me a sharp look. "You recognize that?" she asked.

I looked again at the pink case with stars on it. "I think so. Jennifer's phone was in a case like that."

Anderson took the case from Rogers, flipped it open. It was empty. She handed it back to Rogers. "Bag this, and look around, see if you can find the phone. And keep looking for that PI."

"Yes, Detective."

He hurried off and Dale turned to me. "Care to show me just where you found them?"

I nodded, and we walked the short distance to where the EMTs were huddled over Mariah. Anderson lifted the sheet covering Jennifer, then knelt beside the body. A few seconds later she straightened. "Looks like she got a bad blow to the head. The ME will verify the exact cause of death." Her gaze fell on the bloody owl figurine, still laying there. "I'm guessing that's most likely the murder weapon." She tapped at her chin with the edge of one bright red nail, then slid her glance to me. "You didn't touch anything, did you?"

I hesitated. "I touched her to make sure she was dead," I said finally. "And there was a paper falling out of her jacket pocket. I tucked it back in."

Behind me, Nick let out a loud "Pfft."

Anderson was scribbling in her notebook. "So this is exactly how you found them," she muttered. "You didn't touch that owl figurine, correct?" I shook my head no and she added, "What about Mrs. Blackthorne?"

"Hank went over, felt her pulse. That's how we knew she was still alive."

"He didn't move her?"

I shook my head. "No."

Anderson nodded. I could tell what she was thinking. Once again Mariah Blackthorne had been found with a dead body, inches from what appeared to be the murder weapon. A chilling coincidence?

Rogers reappeared. I thought he seemed slightly out of breath. "I checked the vicinity, Detective. No sign of a phone."

"Perhaps the killer took the phone with him or her," I suggested.

Anderson gave me a sharp look, then turned back to Rogers. She pointed to the owl. "Bag that. Possible murder weapon. I take it you didn't find Mr. Prince?"

"No, ma'am. There was no one around that I could see." He looked over at where the EMTs were loading Mariah onto the gurney and shook his head. "Boy, talk about history repeating itself! I mean, six years ago she was found lying not far from her husband, with a bloody bust, and now—"

"Yes, yes, Rogers, I'm familiar with the case," Anderson snapped. "Just do what I told you and keep your opinions to yourself."

"Yes, ma'am," Rogers muttered. I saw his cheeks flame a bright red as he hurried away. Dale turned back to me. "Where do you think your friend has gone off to, Nora?" she asked.

"I'm right here."

We both turned as Hank approached. He walked right up to Anderson and held out his hand. "You must be Detective Anderson. I've heard a lot about you. I'm Hank Prince. I'm a private investigator and an old friend of both Nora's and Mariah's."

Dale's gaze sharpened as she took Hank's proffered hand. "So I understand. Nora mentioned you went to check the grounds?"

"Yes. The body was still warm so we thought perhaps the killer might still be around. Unfortunately, it looks as though we were too late. I searched the entire perimeter but didn't see anyone."

"We'll have a look around as well." Her brows drew together in a frown. "Okay then, there's no need for you to further contaminate these premises. The two of you are free to go."

"*Ma-row!*"

Dale glanced down, pinned Nick with her gaze. "Pardon me. The three of you are free to go. If I need any more information, I'll contact you." She looked directly at Hank. "Where can I reach you, Mr. Prince?"

Hank gave Dale his cell phone number. "Anything I can do to help find out who did this to Mariah, please call me at once," he said. He started to turn away, then paused. "I almost forgot. I found this in the bushes. It might be evidence."

Hank pulled an iPhone from his jacket pocket and extended it to Anderson. Both her eyebrows went up, and then she took the phone and slid it into her pocket. "Thank you, Mr. Prince. Like I said, if I need to ask you anything further, I'll be in touch."

She turned and walked back over to the crime scene. I looked at Hank. "Oh my gosh," I cried. "Was that Jenn's phone?"

Hank put a finger to his lips. "Not here," he murmured. He took my arm and guided me back down the driveway. The EMTs were just about to load Mariah into the ambulance, and we hurried over to them. "Where are you taking Mrs. Blackthorne?" Hank asked.

"County Hospital," Barbara said promptly. "It's the closest one."

Hank reached out, took Mariah's hand. Her face was pale beneath the oxygen mask. "She's still unconscious?" he murmured.

Barbara nodded. "Her blood pressure is a bit high, and she might have a concussion. It looks like she got a pretty bad blow to the side of her head. Do you know the name of her physician?"

"It used to be Dr. Emmanuel Stringer," Hank replied.

"That's good. I think Dr. Stringer might be on duty tonight," said Barbara. "We'll notify him we're bringing in Mrs. Blackthorne."

"Good. I'd like to give you my name and number. Mrs. Blackthorne and I are old friends, and I'd appreciate being notified of her condition."

Harold finished loading Mariah into the ambulance while Barbara took Hank's cell number. Then they jumped into the vehicle and pealed away, sirens blaring. Once the ambulance disappeared from view, I turned to Hank. "You know, when Mariah wakes up, there's a possibility she might be able to identify who did this," I said. "If so, she could be in danger. I'm pretty sure that whoever did this thought they were leaving behind two dead bodies."

"I've considered that," Hank said. His lips compressed into a thin line. "A police guard would be a prudent idea."

We reached my SUV. I unlocked it and we climbed in. This time Hank slid into the passenger seat, while Nick sprawled across the backseat. Once we were all settled I turned to Hank and said sternly, "Okay, spill. That was Jennifer's phone you found?"

He nodded. "I started to look at it, but then that young officer started scouring the area. He was sniffing around like a bloodhound puppy. I figured if I hung around looking at the phone I'd get caught, so I did the next best thing." His hand dipped into his pocket and he held up a small flash drive. "I downloaded the contents. We can go back to Hot Bread and examine them. I noticed that she did have a few files on there."

"I doubt she had anything of any consequence," I said. "Jenn was always very cagey and careful with her information. Any pertinent files would most likely be stored on her laptop, or maybe an iPad."

"Okay. And they would probably be in her hotel room. I don't suppose you know where she was staying."

"As a matter of fact, I do. When she came into Hot Bread she gave me her contact info in case I changed my mind about helping her. I put the card in my wallet." I reached for my bag on the floor, found my wallet and extracted Jenn's card. "She was staying at the Cruz Inn, room 225."

Hank grinned. "Tell me, how do you feel about a little B&E?"

I pressed the start button and the engine roared to life. "I confess, Ollie and I have done our share in the past." Behind me, Nick let out a soft *grr*. "We'll have to be extra careful not to get caught, though, seeing as I just lectured Nick on proper crime scene protocol."

Hank's grin widened. "And just why did you do that, may I ask?"

"He found a paper in Jenn's pocket he wanted me to take. I didn't, but I did take a photo of it." I pulled out my phone and called the picture up. "It's three words, but none of them make any sense."

Hank frowned as he looked at the photo. "Especially that last one. It sounds like a disease."

He handed me back the phone, and I slid it back into my pocket. "We can tackle this later, along with the phone download. Right now I think that we should hightail it to the Cruz Inn. I'm sure that Detective Anderson will want to look through her room as well, and I'd just as soon not run into her there."

<u>Chapter Eighteen</u>

The Cruz Inn is situated just north of the business district, a quaint vine-covered edifice that might have looked out of place in a different town, but not Cruz. I pulled into the almost full parking lot and found an empty spot in the back. Anderson knew my vehicle, so I didn't want to park too close on the off chance she'd arrive before we left. Hank eyed Nick as he jumped out of the passenger seat and onto the concrete, then looked at me. "He's coming?"

I pointed to a large sign on the hotel's veranda: *Pets Welcome.* "It's part of the reason the hotel is so popular," I said. "Nick will just blend in."

Hank shook his head. "Somehow I doubt that. That cat doesn't just blend in." He bent and gave Nick a quick flick under his chin. "You know what I mean, buddy. It's plain to see you're no ordinary cat. You've got charisma, in spades."

Nick blinked and rubbed his body against Hank's ankles. "Merow."

"If you're done sucking up to my cat, we should get going," I said tartly. Hank chuckled, but Nick hissed. I ignored him and led the way across the parking lot, up the front steps and into the lobby, which was clean and cozy as always. Some might find the lobby's raspberry shag carpeting a bit much, but I thought it was the perfect offset to the dark paneled walls. A separate alcove, off to one side, advertised a buffet breakfast from six a.m. to nine. A display rack nearby offered a selection of brochures of local businesses and nearby attractions. I made a mental note to come back sometime and put some Hot Bread flyers out.

The marble fireplace, clearly the focal point of the lobby, had a glowing fire burning and several people sat around it in the comfortable, high-backed chairs. At the other end of the lobby behind the mahogany reception desk, a tall blonde with a cheerful smile waited on a family that consisted of father, mother, a whining toddler and a screaming baby. I wondered how she managed to keep that smile in place. My patience would have worn thin long ago.

"Nice place," Hank observed. "Perhaps I should have checked in here instead of the Motel 6 on the highway."

"You can always switch tomorrow," I said. "I'd say you could stay with me, but Lacey is in my spare room right now."

"No worries. I think I'll stay where I am. The thought of dogs and cats running around a hotel is a little disconcerting to me. After all, not every animal is as intelligent as Nick."

We went over to the bank of elevators and Hank hit the up button. The elevator doors opened and we stepped inside. I hit the button for the second floor. When the doors opened, a large sign directed us to room 225, at the end of the corridor near the stairs. I paused in front of the door and looked at Hank. "Okay. You're on. Let's see how your B&E skills compare to Ollie's."

Hank pulled another pair of vinyl gloves from the inner pocket of his jacket, handed them to me. "You certainly come prepared," I remarked. "Flash drives, gloves."

He chuckled. "After so many years doing this, you learn what to have handy. One day when you're a pro PI, you'll see."

"That's a long way off, my friend." I put the gloves on, then fished my wallet out of my tote bag. "Ollie usually uses my American Express card," I said. "Which one works for you?"

"None," he said bluntly. "Normally I'd use my picklock, but with this type of lock, that's no good. And neither is your credit card."

"Rats!" I hadn't thought about the fact it was a different type of lock. "Can you get inside?"

He shot me a deprecating look. "Is the sky blue?" Hank reached into his inner pocket and pulled out a Magic Marker. I stared at it. "What are you going to do, write on the lock?" I asked.

"No. This is a special kind of marker. There's a device inside that will unlock any hotel room door."

I looked at the marker with interest. "Really? What sort of device?"

He closed one eye in a broad wink. "Now, Nora, if I told you that I'd have to kill you. Stand aside."

Hank fiddled with the lock for all of five seconds before the light on the handle turned green. He pushed the door open, slid the marker back into his pocket, and made a sweeping gesture. "After you."

"Showoff." I resisted the urge to stick my tongue out at him as I sailed inside, Nick at my heels.

The room wasn't overly large, but it wasn't small either. A large, queen-sized bed took up most of the space. A low dresser done in French Provincial white occupied one wall. A twenty-four-inch flat-screen TV sat atop it. There was a suitcase propped up against the wall to our left, near a closet. The closet doors were open, and I walked over to take a look. Two pair of black jeans hung there, and a green and white flowered shirtwaist dress. A pair of heels was placed neatly beside what appeared to be a brand-new and very expensive pair of Nikes. I recognized the heels as being a designer brand that easily cost a couple hundred, at least. Two shoeboxes lay in the corner of the closet.

Hank was going through the dresser drawers on the other side of the room. "Not much here," he announced. "Some blouses and underwear, that's it, and only two pair of each. She doesn't seem to be much of a clotheshorse."

"No, she never was," I remarked. "Her wardrobe, as I remember, consisted mainly of jeans and faded T-shirts. I remember she had a thing for shoes, though," I added. "She always used to keep her shoes in the boxes. I wonder why she didn't do that with these?"

"Maybe she forgot."

"She wouldn't forget. She was anal that way." I bent over, selected the top box. I sat on the edge of the bed and whipped off the lid. A thick mound of fluffy white tissue paper greeted me. I dove my hand inside, touched something hard. I pulled it out. "Well, I'll be," I murmured.

Hank was at my side in an instant. "What did you find?"

I held up a pyramid-shaped glass bottle. "It looks like a perfume bottle. A very expensive one. Genuine crystal, unless I miss my guess." I removed the large stopper and sniffed. "Woodsy," I said. "It's got a definite woodsy aroma." I ran my hand across the bottle. "The label's been peeled off, so you can't tell the scent."

"I don't know much about perfume," Hank admitted. "Could this be Midnight Lace?"

I shook my head. "I don't think so. Mariah said Midnight Lace had a soft, clean scent with notes of lavender and jasmine." I took another sniff. "This one is stronger, more . . . exotic. Definitely not a clean innocent vibe. If I had to describe it in a word, it would be . . . sexy."

Hank took the bottle from my hand, took a sniff, then handed it back. "Why would Jennifer have an empty perfume bottle in this box? And where did she get it?"

I squinted at the bottle. "It's not totally empty," I said. "I think there's a drop or two left in here. Hand me my purse, please." Hank did so, and I rummaged around, finally pulled out a white handkerchief. "It was my mother's," I said. "I always carry it around for luck." I tipped the bottle and a few drops fell out onto the hankie. I stuffed the handkerchief back in my bag, replaced the stopper on the bottle and set it down on the bed beside me.

"Anything else in that box?" asked Hank.

I was already sifting through the tissue paper. My fingers touched something hard and I pulled out a small teakwood box. I lifted the lid and there, nestled on a bed of black velvet, lay a key. I picked it up, turned it over in my hand and then held it out to Hank. It was long and thin, with three loops on top. "It looks like it could be a safe deposit key, what do you think?" I asked.

Hank held out his hand and I dropped the key into it. He studied it for a few moments and then said, "It could be a safe deposit key. I've also seen keys like this made for strongboxes." He held it out and pointed. "There's a number on it, 582, and a stamp. Locksmiths can usually tell from that what type of key it is."

"I'm tempted to take it with us, but I suppose that isn't a good idea. Even though this isn't an official crime scene, I'm sure Anderson would consider it as tampering with evidence."

"I see why you got high marks in PI class," said Hank with a grin. "We can't remove anything, but we can do this." He pulled out his cell, switched to camera mode and took two quick photographs of the front and back of the key. I pulled out my cell as well and took photos of the perfume bottle. I replaced the items in the box and then selected the second box. A folded piece of paper lay inside. I picked it up and opened it. It was a photocopy of an article from the *Ohio Star*, dated seven years ago. I scanned it quickly. It was about an Anne Gillespi, who police suspected of murdering her husband. The murder weapon, believed to be a Smith & Wesson .38 revolver, had never been found. There was a photograph of Anne with the article, but it was too grainy to make out anything other than she was thin and had long, light-colored hair.

"I vaguely remember that incident." Hank had finished his photography and was now leaning over my shoulder. "The DA liked Anne for the crime, but the evidence against her was mostly circumstantial. In the end he decided not to prosecute. I think he felt there was enough reasonable doubt so that a jury might acquit her."

"Interesting," I said. "I wonder why Jenn had this hidden, though. It can't have anything to do with Mariah's case. Oh, wait." I snapped my fingers. "She said she was collecting information for another book after she finished with Mariah's case. I'll bet she intended to start investigating this

Anne Gillespi."

"That would have been quite an enterprise. As far as I know, Anne dropped out of sight right after the trial. Can't blame her, I guess. In spite of the fact she was never arrested, there was still that cloud of doubt around her, and the media branded her a pariah. I figure she changed her name and maybe her appearance too, in order to make a fresh start."

"If she was truly innocent, who could blame her," I remarked. "Anyway, Jennifer would have looked upon finding her as a challenge." I took a photo of the article, then shoved it back in the box. I replaced the boxes in the closet just as I'd found them and shut the door. "Now what?" I asked. "So far we haven't turned up her laptop or an iPad." I moved to the far corner of the room and opened the highboy. "Maybe it's in this room safe."

"Worth a look," said Hank. He walked over and examined the safe. "Piece of cake," he said. He reached into his pocket for a screwdriver, and about ten minutes later swung the safe door open.

"How did you do that?" I marveled, and as soon as I said it, waved my hand. "Never mind. I know. You can't tell me till I become a professional PI."

"Please, I'm like a magician. Allow me some secrets." Hank reached inside the safe and withdrew a laptop. He booted it up, pulled out another flash drive, and hunkered in front of the computer. "She's got a lot of files," he grumbled.

I'd been looking out the window, and now I turned to Hank. "Better hurry up," I said. "I think Anderson's car just pulled into the parking lot."

Hank frowned, then fiddled with the computer again. "There's a folder marked MB. I'm copying that one." Five minute later he had the flash drive in his pocket and the laptop back in the safe. "Okay, let's get out of here."

I started for the door and then stopped. "Where's Nick?"

I spied my cat lying next to the dresser. He had something white stuck on one paw and was trying to remove it with his hind legs. "Honestly, Nick. What have you gotten into now?" I walked over to the cat and could see that the offending article was a white Post-it. I reached down and flicked it off his paw. The Post-it stuck to my finger, and I saw there was writing on it.

Photo AG?

I looked at the cat. "Where did you get this, Nick?" I asked.

Nick sat up straight, his eyes wide. "Merow?"

I squinted at the note. It looked like Jennifer's handwriting, but I wasn't one hundred percent sure. What photo, I wondered. Did she mean the one in the article? The initials *AG* could surely stand for Anne Gillespi. Had she already started to research her?

Nick meowed loudly again. I hesitated, then shoved the Post-it into my pocket. Then we exited the room. Once in the hall, we decided to play it safe and go down the stairs. When we reached the main floor, we opened the door and peeped out. Anderson was flashing her badge at the girl behind the reception desk. The girl said something to Anderson, who shook her head and held up the plastic room key. Then Anderson and Rogers started for the bank of elevators.

"Thank goodness," I whispered. "Once they get on that elevator, that's our exit cue."

My heart skipped a beat, though, when Rogers paused and said to Anderson, "Maybe we should take the stairs, Detective? Bettina said that room is right next to them."

I sucked in a breath, then expelled it a moment later when I heard a soft ding and Anderson said, "The elevator's here, Rogers. Let's just get in. It's not that much of a walk from the elevator to that room. Besides, I think we could both use the exercise."

"Yes, ma'am," Rogers mumbled as he followed Anderson into the elevator. We waited until the doors closed, and then we slipped out and across the lobby. Neither of us spoke until we'd crossed the parking lot and were once again in my SUV, Hank beside me, Nick in the back. I wasted no time in backing out and pealing out of the lot. Once we were safely on the main road, I said to Hank, "I could give Ollie and Louis Blondell a call. They might be able to help us with Jenn's files."

"Sure, the more the merrier," said Hank. His hand dipped into his pocket and he pulled out his own phone. He looked at the number, then at me. "It's County Hospital." He flicked the answer icon. "Hello, Hank Prince." He listened for a few moments, then said, "Thank you for calling me. We'll be right there." He closed the phone and slid me a look. "Change of plans. We've got to get to County Hospital right away. Mariah is awake."

• • •

I've never been a big fan of hospitals. There's just something about their stark whiteness and the antiseptic smell that never fails to make me nauseous. I bit back the feeling, though, as I pulled into the hospital parking lot. Nick rose and stretched, but I wagged my finger at the cat. "Sorry, Nick. They don't allow cats in hospitals." Nick's eyes widened a bit, and his tail fluffed out. "Don't worry," I said soothingly. "You aren't missing much, trust me. We won't be long."

We left my unhappy kitty washing his face in the backseat and hurried up the steps and into the main lobby of the hospital. Hank went right over to the desk. "I received a call about a patient," he said. "Mrs. Mariah Blackthorne. My name is Hank Prince."

The nurse behind the desk tapped on her keyboard a few times, squinted at the monitor and then looked at us. "Oh, yes. You left a request to be notified about her condition. I've paged Dr. Stringer and he'll be with you in just a moment."

Hank drummed his fingers impatiently on the counter. "Is there anything you can tell me in the meantime?"

The nurse clucked her tongue sympathetically. "Other than that she's conscious, no, I'm sorry. That's up to Dr. Stringer. Ah, here he comes now."

A tall man in a white coat with a shock of thick gray hair approached us. The expression on his face was bland and he pushed his wire-rimmed glasses a bit farther up on his beak-shaped nose as he regarded us. "You must be Mr. Prince," he said. "I'm Dr. Stringer, Mrs. Blackthorne's physician. Fortunately, I was on duty tonight and was notified immediately upon her arrival."

Hank nodded and gestured to me. "This is my friend Nora Charles. She is the one who found Mrs. Blackthorne tonight."

Dr. Stringer gave me a nod. "It's a good thing you found her when you did. She sustained quite a blow to the side of the head. If she'd lain there for very long without medical attention, things could have been much worse. As it is, she appears to have a bit of cerebral confusion."

Hank and I exchanged a glance. "Cerebral confusion? That sounds serious," Hank said.

"As I said, it could have been. Mariah seems to have a mild case. Upon awakening she complained of being dizzy, of a ringing in her ears and slight nausea, all of which are symptoms. I'm going to keep her at least overnight here for observation to see if she experiences any other symptoms."

"I see," said Hank. "Would you mind telling us what these other symptoms might be?"

"Not at all," began Stringer, when a nurse hurried over to him. "Doctor, please come. It's Mrs. Blackthorne."

Stringer turned and hurried down the corridor, and Hank and I followed right behind. We stopped at the doorway to Mariah's room. Mariah lay on the bed, her face pale against the white sheets. She looked up as Stringer approached. "Dr. Stringer, thank goodness," she said. Her hand went to her forehead and she began rubbing at it. "My head is pounding. I feel as if it's trapped in a vise."

"Just stay calm, Mariah," Stringer said soothingly. "I thought something like this might happen. That was quite a blow to the head you took."

Mariah's face clouded. "A blow to the head?" she said blankly. Her gaze traveled to the doorway, and her expression brightened when she caught sight of us standing there. "Hank," she cried joyfully. "I'm not dreaming? You're really here?"

Hank looked at Stringer, who nodded. Then Hank hurried over to the bed, bent over and gave Mariah a hug. "Yes, it's really me," he said. "My case wrapped up early so I decided to come here." He pulled back, looked down at her solicitously. "How are you feeling?"

Her lips screwed into a pouty expression. "Like I was run over by a Mack truck. I have a killer headache." She looked over Hank's shoulder at me. "Oh, and Nora came with you. How nice."

"Ms. Charles is the one who found you, Mariah," said Dr. Stringer.

Mariah looked over at the doctor. "Found me?" she repeated.

I stepped over to the bed and looked down at Mariah. In a gentle tone I said, "Yes, Mariah. You were lying in your garden, unconscious." I deliberately refrained from mentioning Jennifer. "Do you remember how you sustained that blow to your head?"

"A blow to the head?" Her hand shot up and she touched the side of her head gingerly. "Why . . . I have no idea," she said. She looked at us, and her voice took on a note of panic. "The last thing I remember was lying on the sofa in my living room. My cell rang, and I got up and started to cross the room to answer it. After that, it's all a complete blank. I don't remember a thing."

Chapter Nineteen

Hank and I exchanged a look, then he took Mariah's hand and squeezed it gently. "So you don't remember answering your cell?"

Mariah let out a deep sigh. "No. I know I got up and started across the room. Then I felt a bit woozy, and after that nothing, until I woke up here."

"What about earlier in the day?" I asked. "Do you remember anything about that?"

Mariah frowned. "Yes. I thought I might try and get some rest. I was alone in the house. Elle's husband returned from his business trip, so she went back home, and I just felt so darn tired. Wiped out. I thought maybe a nap would do me good, but I didn't feel like climbing the stairs to my bedroom, so I put a CD in the Bose, Beethoven's Symphonies, one of my favorites. I was just starting to drift off when I heard my cell go off. I remember feeling irritated, because I'd tossed it on the desk and that was across the room, and I really didn't feel like getting up, but I did. So I forced myself to get up, and halfway across the room I started to feel a bit wobbly, and then . . . I woke up here."

Mariah's free hand clutched at her blanket. Hank gave her other hand another squeeze. "Do you remember eating or drinking anything before you went to lie down?"

She gave him a thin smile. "I'm afraid I haven't had much of an appetite lately. I had some toast for breakfast. Elle made some chicken soup, but I couldn't eat anything."

"This lack of appetite could very well be part of your problem, Mariah," Dr. Stringer said sternly. "It would certainly account for your dizziness and lack of orientation prior to your injury."

I walked over to the other side of the bed and smiled down at Mariah. "So you only had toast? Nothing else?"

"No . . . wait!" Her eyes widened a bit. "Elle did give me a glass of warm milk before she left. She told me to drink it down. She said that if I didn't start eating like a normal person soon she was going to come over and start force-feeding me." A soft sigh escaped Mariah's lips. "I let it sit there for a while after she left, and finally I figured I'd better drink it. But it tasted, I don't know, not right. So I only drank half."

Hank and I exchanged a look and I knew we were both thinking the same thing. Had Elle Gardner drugged that milk? Could she have been the one who killed Jennifer and attacked Mariah?

Mariah was looking at us with wide eyes. "Something's wrong, isn't it? Did something happen that I should know about?"

Dr. Stringer cleared his throat. "I think that's enough visiting for now. Mariah needs her rest. Perhaps the two of you can come back tomorrow, when she's a bit stronger." The doctor leaned over and said to Mariah, "I'm going to keep you here at least two nights for observation, Mariah, just to be certain there are no ill aftereffects from that blow you got on your head."

She reached up and gingerly touched the bandage, then looked at me. "You said you found me in my garden? Maybe I did wander out there and trip somehow, hit my head on the concrete? Is that what happened?" When I didn't answer immediately, she said, "There's more to this, isn't there? What are you keeping from me?" Her eyes were wild. "Please, don't keep anything from me. Tell me the truth. If there's one thing I've learned, it's always better to know the truth."

Stringer moved forward. "Now, Mariah, there's no need to get upset. Your friends can come back tomorrow, and if you're stronger, they can fill you in on the details. For now, young lady, I want you to rest." He handed Mariah two pills and a small cup of water. "Take these."

"Rest," Mariah murmured. "That does sound good." She took the pills and almost immediately her eyes started to close. Stringer motioned to us, and we all left the room. Once we were in the hallway Stringer folded his arms across his chest and looked sternly at Hank and me. "Perhaps you two had better fill me in on the details I'm missing," he said.

"No need to bother them. I can do that."

We all turned as Dale Anderson strode over to us. She flashed her badge at Stringer. "Detective Dale Anderson, Cruz Homicide. I understand that Mrs. Blackthorne is awake. If so, I have a few questions for her."

Stringer frowned. "Questions? Regarding what?"

Dale's lips thinned. "Regarding the death of one Jennifer Hinkle. Mrs. Blackthorne was found lying near her body."

Stringer's frown deepened. He looked at Hank and me, and then back at Anderson. "I see," he said at last. "And why do you wish to question Mrs. Blackthorne? Do you think she had something to do with that woman's death?"

Dale held up her hand. "I don't think anything right now, Doctor. Right now I'm just gathering facts, and in order to do my job properly, I need to ask Mrs. Blackthorne a few questions."

"I'm afraid she wouldn't be of much help to you at the moment," Stringer said. "She's suffered a great shock, which of course has had an effect on her short-term memory. I'm afraid that her recall of recent events is sketchy at best."

"I see." I could practically read Dale's mind. The unspoken word *again* lingered in the air. "I'll still need to speak with her regardless. Any idea when that might be?"

Stringer took a moment to think. "I've given her a mild sedative so she will be asleep for several hours. You can leave your contact information at the desk and I'll notify you when she's strong enough to be questioned. Now, if you'll excuse me, I have other patients to see."

Stringer walked off in the opposite direction. Hank and I started to follow, but Anderson's voice rang out. "Just a minute, you two," she said. "Not so fast."

"Rats," I muttered, just loud enough for Hank to hear. I was hoping that Anderson hadn't seen us at the hotel. We both turned and I smiled sweetly at her. "Why, sure, Detective. How can we help?"

"You were allowed to see Mrs. Blackthorne, right? So, what did she have to say? Does she remember anything of what happened?"

I bit down hard on my lower lip, but Hank answered. "No, she does not. She recalls trying to take a nap in her living room after drinking a glass of milk prepared by her friend Elle Gardner. Her phone rang, and she went to answer it and then nothing."

"That's all? She doesn't remember going to the garden, or anything about Jennifer Hinkle being there?" Dale made a frustrated sound deep in her throat. "So what? This is just like six years ago? She's found near a dead body and can't remember a darn thing?"

"Amazing coincidence, isn't it?" remarked Hank. "Why, it's almost as if that's what someone wanted the police to think."

Dale arched a brow. "It almost sounds as if you think that scene was staged, Mr. Prince," she said.

"I realize that probably sounds a bit far-fetched to you, Detective, but I wouldn't discount it."

"Oh, don't worry, Mr. Prince. At this stage I don't discount anything. But I will say that there are entirely too many crime shows on television," Anderson grumbled. She pulled her notepad and pen out of her pocket. "You said a friend of hers fixed her a glass of milk? What was this friend's name again?"

"Elle—Elspeth—Gardner. She'd been staying with Mariah for a few days." I paused and then added, "You know, Detective, if you stop to think about it, Hank's theory makes perfect sense."

Dale looked up from her scribbling. "How do you figure that?"

"Mariah said on national television that she wouldn't rest until she resolved her husband's murder one way or the other. His real killer doesn't want that to happen. What better way than to kill someone who was irritating Mrs. Blackthorne and make it seem as if history repeated itself." When Dale remained silent, I added, "You know, it might not be a bad idea to put a police guard here. If Mariah's attacker finds out she's still alive, he or she will probably figure that Mariah might be able to identify them. They could try again." I shot her a pleading look. "I know you would feel terrible if anything were to happen to Mrs. Blackthorne."

Dale blinked, and I had the feeling she was fighting back an eye roll. "Okay, fine, Nora. As much as I hate to admit it, you do have a point. I'll assign a guard," she said.

"Thank you, Detective," Hank said. "That takes a load off my mind."

"Swell," Dale said dryly. "I'm so glad I could help ease your mind. Now, if you'll excuse me, I've got to get going."

"Oh, right. Back to the Cruz Inn," I blurted.

Anderson paused to pin me with her gaze. "How did you know that?"

I shrugged. "Just simple deduction. I know Jennifer was staying there, so it just seemed logical that you'd want to search her room."

"Logical. Right." Dale regarded me suspiciously for a moment and then said, "Well, I've got to get going. Try to stay out of trouble, please."

Dale turned and walked away. I sagged against the wall. "That was close."

Hank clapped me on the shoulder. "But a nice save. You'll make a good PI yet, Nora."

"Thanks." I glanced at my watch. "Let's go back to Hot Bread and we can call in the cavalry."

• • •

An hour later Hank, Louis Blondell and Ollie Sampson all sat grouped around my table in the back of Hot Bread's kitchen. Just as I thought, both men were more than happy to help. Louis brought his computer and Hank gave him the flash drive with Jennifer's phone info on it. While Louis and

Ollie pored over that, Hank inserted the flash drive with the files he'd downloaded from Jenn's laptop onto mine. Since none of us had eaten, I quickly cobbled together a platter of cheese, some cold cuts and crackers and set it in the middle of the table, then plopped in the chair next to Hank. I selected a cheese slice and a cracker and leaned forward. "What did I miss?" I asked Hank. "Did you open any of the files yet?"

"I was waiting for you to do that," said Hank, "but I did look up some details of that clipping Jennifer had stored away." He also reached for a cracker and a cheese slice and popped them into his mouth. He chewed, swallowed and then went on, "Anne Gillespi reported her husband, Tom Gillespi, missing and told officials that she last saw him before he went on a run. His body was discovered two days later about three miles from their home on a back road that ran through the park. He'd been shot in the head.

"Anne was arrested because various witnesses heard an argument between the couple in which Anne threatened to kill him; however, she had an alibi for the TOD. She was at some sort of graduation party at a neighbor's house. People testified they saw her there, but no one could commit to seeing her there the entire length of the party, which was four hours. Plus, the murder weapon, believed to be a Smith and Wesson Number Ten, .38-caliber special, was never recovered. Her attorney argued that there was no concrete evidence tying her to the crime, and that it would cause enough reasonable doubt for the jury to render a verdict of not guilty. In the end, the DA decided not to press charges. The case is still open.

"But here's the real interesting part. Anne Gillespi was under a psychiatrist's care at the time, a Dr. Fein. She was being treated for bouts of depression. And guess who Fein went to medical school with?"

I paused, cheese slice halfway to my lips. "Not Christian Blackthorne?"

"Close. Paul Lassiter."

"That is interesting," I said. "Maybe that's why Jennifer had the clipping, and not because she intended to research the case. Maybe her death isn't connected to Mariah's at all, but this Anne Gillespi's."

Hank leaned back in his chair. "Maybe, but I doubt it."

Louis let out a triumphant shout. "I got her phone listing," he cried. He tilted his laptop so we could see the screen. "Those are her last calls."

Hank peered over my shoulder at the list, which wasn't very long. Quite brief, in fact. There were four calls, two of which were to me. Hank tapped at one number. "That's Mariah's," he said. "So she did call her. That could have been the call Mariah was about to answer before she blacked out."

"Probably," I agreed. I pointed to the fourth number. "That's a local area code," I said. "It doesn't ring any bells, though."

"Well, there's only one way to find out," Ollie said. He took the phone from me and pressed the redial icon, then put the phone on speaker and set it in the middle of the table. A few minutes later a male voice answered. "T.C. Lock and Safe."

Hank and I exchanged a quick look, then he put a finger to his lips. He leaned over and said, "My name is Hank Prince. I'm a private investigator. With whom am I speaking?"

A pause and then, "I'm T. C. Crumm, the owner. You said you're a private investigator? What do you want with me?"

"Mr. Crumm, I'm working on a matter that concerns someone who made a call to your establishment recently. A Miss Jennifer Hinkle?"

"Hinkle, Hinkle. That name sounds familiar, let me think. Oh, yeah, I remember her. Tall, skinny blonde. She came to my shop with a key, wanted to know if I'd made it and if so, who for." He paused. "The key had my stamp on it, but I didn't recall the transaction offhand. I do a lot of key duplication. Anyway, I told her that I'd look up the work order and send her a copy. As a matter of fact, I did that just today."

Louis reached for the phone but Hank slapped his hand away. "I see. Can you tell me who the key was for?"

"Of course. It was a special order, for Dr. Christian Blackthorne. It was a strongbox key. He wanted another copy made quickly." Crumm paused to let out a soft chuckle. "That was one of his little eccentricities. He always liked to have spare keys on hand. I made spares for him for boxes, for locks in his house, even a few cars. I did this one the same day he asked for it. It's all in the email."

"I see. I don't suppose you could describe this key?"

"It's a standard strongbox key. Slim, gold, three circles on top."

I called up the photo I'd taken of the key on my phone. Crumm's description matched exactly. I showed it to Hank, who nodded and said, "Thank you, Mr. Crumm. You've been most helpful. If we need more information I'll be in touch."

Hank disconnected and handed Louis the phone. A few minutes later he had Jenn's email account up on the screen. The email from T.C. Locks was right on top, and Louis clicked on it. The email was brief:

Here is the receipt you requested. The order is for a spare key for Dr. Blackthorne's strongbox. Below was an attachment. Hank clicked on it, and it opened to reveal a scan of a receipt for a key, number 582, made for Dr. Christian Blackthorne. Scrawled below that, in spindly handwriting, were the words *Paid and picked up for today by J. Cutter.*

"J. Cutter," I breathed. "That has to be Jerry Cutter, Velma's son." I rubbed at my forehead as I struggled to recall the snatches of conversation I'd overheard between him and Jennifer in the Poker Face. Jerry had passed her an envelope. I looked at Hank. "I think that Jerry might have given this key to Jennifer, but how did he get it? Or did he have another copy made of the key before he gave this one to Blackthorne?"

"Excellent points," said Hank. "And ones I'd like answers to. And there's no time like the present."

Chapter Twenty

Hank put Jerome Cutter's name into the search engine, and ten minutes later we had his address in Cruz. I recognized it as being a not very nice neighborhood. We left Ollie and Louis combing through the files from Jenn's computer, and Hank, Nick and I set out for Cutter's apartment building.

Fifteen minutes later we arrived at our destination. The Astor Apartments was a run-down, three-story brick building located on the very end of South Street. The street was a dead end, and the apartments were right next to a large expanse of woods that at one time had been the proposed site of a shopping center that had never materialized. The apartments had no parking lot, so the tenants had to fight for parking on the street on a first-come, first-served basis. Tonight it seemed as if every tenant in the building must be home, because both sides of the street were packed. I finally found a space on Morton Street, two blocks over, and it was a tight squeeze at that. A light wind kicked up as Hank and I made our way to the apartment building, Nick at our heels. We climbed the few steps to the front door and the first thing we saw was a large sign: *Ring for entrance.*

"Really? In this neighborhood?" Hank said with a scowl.

"Apparently the management looks out for its tenants," I said dryly. I looked at the names above the bells and finally located one marked "Cutter" up at the top. I pressed the bell and we waited. A few minutes later the intercom gave a loud squawk, and a tinny voice asked, "Who's there?"

I leaned forward. "It's Nora Charles, Jerry. Do you remember me? We met at the bike shop. I was looking at that pink bicycle?"

There was a moment of silence and then, "Oh, yeah, I remember. So you've thought it over? Are you still interested?"

"Actually, I wonder if I might come up. I have a few questions."

I could picture his dark brows drawing together in a frown. "Now? It's getting kinda late, and I was getting ready for bed. I've got an early shift tomorrow. Can't we do this at the shop?"

"I know this is an imposition, but I have a rather busy day at Hot Bread myself tomorrow, and I wanted to get this matter squared away tonight, if possible," I said in a wheedling tone.

"I don't know," said Jerry. "I really need to get some sleep."

I glanced over at Hank, who mouthed, "Offer him money." I turned back to the intercom and said, "I'd be very grateful, and I'll certainly make this intrusion worth your while . . . say a fifty-dollar bonus?"

A brief silence, and then: "Third floor. Apartment 301. But let's make this quick, okay?"

The buzzer sounded, and Hank shot me a triumphant look as we pushed through the front door. "Works every time," he whispered.

We trudged up the narrow staircase to the third floor. The hall was dark and dingy. There were lights overhead, but I noticed that most of them had burned out and hadn't been replaced. We stood for a moment to get our bearings and suddenly the door at the end of the hall was jerked open. Jerry, attired in a ratty-looking bathrobe, stood framed in the doorway. "Over here," he called. The pleasant smile on his face turned into a scowl as he noticed Hank. "I thought you were alone," he said.

"This is my friend Hank Prince," I said. "He's a cycle enthusiast too."

"Yeah?" He looked at Hank a bit suspiciously, then held out his hand. "Pleased ta meetcha," he said.

"Merow."

Jerry started as he glanced down and saw Nick sitting right by my feet. "You brought a cat along?" he asked. "And a black one, too. They're usually bad luck."

Hank pushed past Jerry into the apartment, and Nick and I followed. As Jerry shut the door Hank remarked, "You're right about one thing, Jerry. Nick is bad luck, especially for criminals."

A flush stole up the side of Jerry's neck. "I'm no criminal," he said gruffly. "I haven't been in trouble for a long time." He shot me an accusatory stare. "I told you I turned over a new leaf, remember?"

"Yes, you did, and I believe you," I assured him. "But we need to ask you a few questions about Jennifer Hinkle."

He stared down at his feet, avoiding my gaze, and mumbled, "Jennifer Hinkle? I don't know anyone by that name."

"Are you sure?" I asked. "I'm certain I saw you with her in the Poker Face a few nights ago."

His eyes narrowed. "You were spying on me?"

I shook my head. "No, it was purely coincidental. I stopped in for a burger and a beer and noticed the two of you at a rear table. You see, I used to work with Jennifer, years ago. She'd come to Cruz and asked for my help with Mariah Blackthorne."

Jerry waved his hand in a careless gesture. "Yeah, she got hold of me too. Said that she was gonna write a book once she proved her innocence. Said that she was hot on the trail of who really killed the buzzard."

"Just how did Jennifer ask for your help, Jerry?" asked Hank.

Jerry frowned. "I don't know as I should say. She asked me to keep all this confidential, just between us. Why, I haven't even told my mother."

Hank reached into his pocket, whipped out a fifty-dollar bill. He dangled it in front of Jerry. "We know that you picked up a key for Blackthorne shortly before his death," he said.

A look of fear came into his eyes. "How . . . how do you know that? Did Jenn tell you?"

I stepped forward, put my face close to his. "We found the store receipt, which indicated that you picked up the key. You sold it to Jennifer, didn't you?"

Jerry's eyes flashed and he stood up a bit straighter. "I didn't sell nothing," he whined. "She gave me some money for my trouble."

I looked him right in the eye. "Don't lie, Jerry. I heard her tell you that she'd paid too much already."

He lowered his gaze and shifted his weight from one foot to the other. "So what if I made a few bucks? She was more than willing to pay."

"Well, for one thing, that key wasn't your property to sell. Technically it would belong to Mrs. Blackthorne."

"Mrs. Blackthorne wouldn't miss it. She never knew anything about it," Jerry maintained, a trifle belligerently. "It was to a private strongbox he kept in his office safe. The week before he died he came to me and said, 'Cutter—he always called me by my last name—Cutter, I need you to do an errand for me.' Then he gave me the name of the locksmith and told me to pick up the key and bring it to him, no questions asked. So that's what I did. When I brought him the key, he gave me ten bucks. Ten! Can you imagine! The old cheapskate." Jerry gave his head a derisive shake.

I sighed. Apparently that old saying about leopards not being able to change their spots was true. "How did you get that key, Jerry?" I asked. "Was it the same key you picked up? Or did you have another made?"

"I wouldn't waste my money getting another key," Jerry spat. "And I didn't steal that one either. I found it. It was that day when I was looking at those jade figurines. The bottom of one of 'em was hollow and the key fell out. I recognized it right off, and I took it. I figured he'd look for it sometime and when he couldn't find it, he'd want another made. He was anal that way about keys." Jerry shook his head. "I figured he'd probably ask me to go get it, and when I did, I'd just keep the money he'd give me and give him that one back."

"Surely the locksmith would have called when no one came for the key," I said.

Jerry shrugged. "Blackthorne never took those calls. My mother would have taken it, and she'd have told me. Then I was gonna call and tell them Blackthorne found his other key. That guy was used to this happening. He'd have just saved the key until the next time."

Hank and I exchanged a glance and then Hank asked, "Getting back to Jennifer. Do you know what she planned to do with that key?"

He frowned. "No idea. She didn't say and I didn't ask. To be honest, I didn't want to know. She was in kind of a bragging mode that night. Said she was real close to proving that Mrs. Blackthorne had nothing to do with her husband's murder. There was some detail, though, that had her pretty stumped. She said it came out of left field, and if she could just connect that up, she could blow the whole case wide open. I wished her luck. Heck, I was hoping she could do it. I always liked Mrs. Blackthorne." He sighed. "Anyway, she got a text and it looked like whatever was in it didn't make her too happy. I figured she wanted to be alone so I said goodbye and left. I haven't heard from her since, not that I expected to." He thrust his lower lip out. "Anything else you want to know?"

"Actually, there is. Do you happen to know where the doctor kept that strongbox?" asked Hank.

"Probably in his safe. It's behind a painting of some boats on the wall in back of his desk." He held up both hands. "Before you ask, no, I never tried to break into it. Not that I wasn't tempted, mind you, but I'd never do that to my mother. He'd have made her life even more miserable. Anyway, I was walking past his office one day and the door was open a bit. I peeked in and saw him putting something in the safe."

"Did you tell Jennifer where the safe was located?"

Once again, his gaze shifted down to study the tips of his shoes. "I told her he kept the box in the study, but I didn't tell her the exact location."

I had a feeling that location was what Jennifer had refused to pay more money for. No doubt she'd intended to find it herself. I was more convinced than ever that Mariah hadn't been dreaming that day, that Jennifer had been in her house hunting for the safe.

Hank looked at me and nodded. It was clear to both of us that was all the information we were going to get out of Jerry. "Well, Jerry, you've been very helpful," he said. "Sorry to have disturbed you."

"Yeah, sure." Jerry looked at me. "You're not interested in that bike, are you?"

I shook my head. "Not right now, anyway. But thanks. We appreciate your talking to us."

He ran a hand through his hair. "You know, if you don't believe me, you can ask Jennifer Hinkle. She'll corroborate everything I just told you."

Nick let out a mournful yowl. Jerry looked at the cat. "What's with him?"

I bent down and scooped Nick into my arms. He squirmed a bit, then settled himself against my chest. "I think he's trying to tell you that speaking to Jennifer would be rather difficult."

Jerry frowned. "Difficult? Why? Don't tell me she left town."

"I guess you could say she did, in a manner of speaking," Hank said. "She's dead."

• • •

Back out on the street, I set Nick down, then looked at Hank. "He's definitely a shifty individual, and I have serious doubts about his being able to stay on the straight and narrow. That being said, I believed his story," I said.

Hank nodded. "I did too. I'm also convinced that Jennifer was Mariah's mysterious intruder."

"I agree, but why was she in Mariah's bedroom? Jerry told her the box was in Blackthorne's study."

"Not sure. Maybe she couldn't find it and thought Mariah might have moved it."

"Or," I added thoughtfully, "maybe she was looking for something else."

"Like what?"

I sighed. "I have no idea."

My cell buzzed. I whipped it out of my pocket and saw Ollie's number. I hit the accept icon and the speaker button so Hank could hear. "Hey, Ollie. What's up? Find anything interesting on Jenn's computer?"

Ollie sounded smug. "Actually, we did. Something about one of your prime suspects. Elle Gardner. I think you'll find what's here most enlightening."

Hank and I raised our eyebrows in unison. "Can't you give us a hint?" I asked.

"I could, but I'd rather not over the phone. How soon can you get back here?"

"We'll be there in ten."

• • •

I did a brisk seventy all the way back to Hot Bread, cutting our arrival time to nine minutes. We burst into the shop through the rear door and I hurried right over to the table, where Ollie and Louis sat, hunched over Jennifer's phone, a half-eaten bag of potato chips open between them. "Okay, spill," I said. "What's this enlightening information?"

Ollie passed me the phone. "It seems that Mariah's friend Elle had been serving on the board of the Cruz Historical Society. Following the trial, she took a leave of absence for seven months."

I'd grabbed a chip and now I nearly choked on it. "Seven months. Don't tell me . . ."

Ollie shook his head. "No. She didn't disappear to have a baby. Jennifer obtained records that prove conclusively that Elle spent that time at Hope by the Sea."

I knew the name. It wasn't a fancy resort, but rather a rehab center located in San Juan Capistrano that specialized in drug and alcohol rehabilitation. "So Elle had a problem?"

"Apparently a large one. She was addicted to alcohol and painkillers. She registered under her mother's maiden name of Thorpe, which is probably why nothing shows up in a search. And it also means—"

"That she's not the pregnant mistress." I picked up another chip, popped it into my mouth. "That is kind of disappointing," I said. "I rather liked Elle in the role of murderess." I looked at Louis. "Cutter said that Jenn got a text that seemed to upset her that night I saw them in the Poker Face. Can you check her texts for the seventh? Around six?"

Louis's fingers flew over his keyboard, and a few minutes later he glanced up. "She got one from a Maverick107 at six oh-five. It says, 'Photo under separate cover.'"

I frowned. "Are there any photos in her mail account sent from a Maverick107?"

Louis fiddled some more with the keyboard. At last he looked up. "If she got an email from that person, she must have downloaded the attachment and then deleted the email. I can comb through her trash file, but I took a quick look and there are over two thousand deleted emails."

I let out a low whistle. "Swell."

"If it's there I can find it," Louis said confidently, "but it'll take some time." He tapped at the keyboard again and then said, "I've got some free time tomorrow morning. I can do it then."

"Please," I said. I looked at Ollie and Hank. "I just have this feeling we're getting close, but the only thing is, I'm not sure just what it is we're getting close to."

Nick had crawled underneath the table. Now I heard a scraping sound, and then some Scrabble tiles flew out. Ollie glanced down at the floor and smiled. "Looks as if little Nick has something to say."

When the tiles had stopped flying out, I bent down, picked them up, and laid them on the table. There was a J, an A, an E, an S, I, M and an N. I moved them around and then surveyed the word I'd made: jasmine. I looked at the cat. "What's with the names, Nick? First Violet and now Jasmine. Those names are pretty but they have nothing to do with Mariah's case."

Nick poked his head out from underneath the table. "Merow," he said.

"Little Nick isn't always that obvious," said Ollie. "Perhaps violet doesn't refer to a person's name, but to something else."

I gave Nick a stern look, and he ducked back underneath the table. "Such as?" I asked.

"Well . . ." Ollie drummed his fingers on the tabletop. "Violet's a color, right? A purple shade?"

"True," I agreed. "It's also a flower. But I can't see a connection between that and Mariah."

"Violet and jasmine are both used in perfumes," piped up Louis.

Ollie looked at him. "And how do you know that?"

"Because my sister works the cosmetics counter at Dillard's," Louis responded.

I looked at Louis. "I didn't know you had a sister."

He flushed. "I've got two of 'em, both older. Anyway, Daphne's worked in cosmetics for years. I remember she bought some perfume for our mother one Christmas, and she went on and on about the notes of jasmine, musk and violet in it. I did smell it and it was pretty nice. You'd have never have guessed by the name. Insolence."

My head jerked up. "What did you say?"

"You mean the name of the perfume? Insolence."

"Wait a second." I went over, grabbed my tote bag and came back. I pulled out the slip of paper that Nick had found in Jenn's apartment, pulled my laptop in front of me and started hitting the keyboard. A few minutes later I leaned back in my chair. I picked up the white slip of paper and held it aloft.

"The words on this paper Nick found," I said. "They're names of perfumes. Insolence, Ethereal, Amaranth. What's more, they're all perfumes that have notes of violet and jasmine in them. Plus, Amaranth is also a plant noted for its fragrant purple flowers and is often used in perfumes."

Nick let out a loud yowl. Ollie looked at him and grinned. "Looks as if little Nick has struck again."

"Maybe so," I said thoughtfully. I hadn't known Jenn well, but I'd known her well enough to know she'd written those names down for a reason. I just had to figure out what that reason was.

Chapter Twenty-one

"What is wrong, chérie? You look rather peaked."

Chantal shot me a concerned look. It was only a few minutes past eight a.m. and we'd been slammed from the moment I opened the door. Of course, the fact that it was Bargain Wednesday might have had something to do with it. All breakfast items served between eight and eleven a.m. were a dollar fifty, and all beverages were seventy-five cents. I'm proud to say that next to Fifty-Cent Friday, Bargain Wednesday was my most profitable day of the week.

"Do I?" I remarked. I poured coffee into a mug, set it on a tray with sugar packets and creamers and a fried egg sandwich, and handed it to Otis Bentley. As he shuffled off to grab the last remaining table, I said, "I didn't get much sleep last night. I keep running over everything that happened in my mind, trying to make some sense out of everything."

"You will, chérie," Chantal said. "Where is your partner this morning?"

Nick's head popped out from underneath the table. "Merow."

"Not you, Nicky," Chantal laughed. "I know where you are. I meant Nora's other partner, Mr. Prince."

Nick shot Chantal a baleful look, then vanished under the table.

"After Ollie and Louis left, he got a call from his boss. He needed Hank to work on something for him ASAP, so he's taking care of that today. He was a bit miffed, but . . . when duty calls."

Michaela, who was at the counter, turned toward us and said, "I need two cups of Joe and an egg salad sandwich on white toast."

Chantal pulled egg salad out of the refrigerator while I poured coffee into two mugs. Nick wandered out from under the table, his golden gaze fixed on Chantal as she put two slices of bread in the toaster and took the cover off the egg salad. "None for you, Nicky," she said. "Maybe some roasted chicken at lunchtime, though."

Nick let out a soft growl, went back underneath the table.

The toast popped up and Chantal started spreading egg salad on one slice. She glanced over at the counter, where Michaela was chatting with a tall man. "For a first day, Michaela seems to be working out well, doesn't she?"

I had to agree. Today was the girl's first day, and once the crowd started rolling in I had thought it might also have been her last. But the influx of people hadn't seemed to bother her; rather, she appeared to thrive on it. She took orders and refilled coffee cups way faster than Lacey ever had. "She's a godsend," I agreed. "She told me that when it gets a bit slower, she'd like to watch me make sandwiches so she could help with the cooking."

Chantal chuckled. "That's already a vast improvement over Lacey. Getting her to make a sandwich is an Olympic event. And speaking of your sister, I thought she was supposed to work this morning?"

"She said she had a migraine, but I think she's just sulking."

Chantal frowned. "Why? Did the interview not go well?"

"On the contrary, it went very well. Anderson offered her the job—on the condition it's approved by the Town Council."

Chantal clapped her hands. "She did! That's terrific!"

"Yeah, well, Lacey's antsy, of course. She thinks that Anderson should be down there trying to convince the mayor of the need for the position. I tried to explain to her that Anderson is tied up in Jennifer's investigation, but it was like talking to a wall. You'd think she'd understand how it gets with something like that, particularly since she was once in the center of an investigation."

"No offense, but Lacey will always be the center of Lacey's universe." Chantal arranged the sandwich on a plate, brought it over to the counter, then came back to stand in front of me. "I forgot to ask how you are coming with the investigation. Have you found anything to prove Mariah Blackthorne did not kill her husband?"

"Not yet, but . . ." I leaned my elbow on the counter. "I've got to admit this is a puzzling case. Perfume seems to play a part in this, but I can't figure out just what part."

Chantal frowned. "Perfume?"

I reached into my apron pocket, pulled out a white square of paper and handed it to Chantal. "Nick found that list in Jenn's room. Those are names of fancy perfumes. And she had an almost empty perfume bottle hidden in a shoebox in her closet."

Chantal looked at the list and let out a low whistle. "You're not kidding about these being fancy," she said. "Insolence sells for over one hundred a bottle, and Ethereal a little more. I'm not familiar with this third one, though."

"It's the name of a plant, but there is a perfume with that name too. I looked it up. It goes for two hundred a bottle. I checked out the bottles each scent comes in too, and none of them are a match for the bottle Jenn had hidden in the closet. I tried searching bottle shapes, but I couldn't find a match for this one."

"What did that bottle look like?" asked Chantal. "Maybe I'll recognize it. I've bought my fair share of perfume in my day."

That was true. Chantal changed her perfume almost as frequently as she changed underwear, choosing to spritz on whatever might strike her mood for the day. As for myself, for the most part I remained true to Estee Lauder's White Linen. I opened my middle drawer and pulled out my iPhone. I called up the picture I'd taken and showed it to Chantal. She studied the photo for a few minutes, then shook her head. "I have never seen a bottle like this before. Maybe perfume didn't come in it at all."

"Hmm, I never thought of that. I saw where a label had been removed, but maybe it wasn't a perfume label. The whole thing is odd." I set the phone down and added, "I think after we close today I'll take a trip down to Skin and Scents. Maybe Carm or Gillian might recognize the bottle."

Chantal clapped her hands. "That's a good idea! But be careful, chérie. Carm will never help you if she thinks your inquiry is connected to Mariah Blackthorne."

"That's for sure," I said. "Did you know Carm has a son?"

Chantal nodded. "Kenny. He's a sweet little boy. He was with her one day when she stopped to buy some flowers. He's got a birthday coming up soon, I think."

"So I heard. He's going to be six or seven, right?"

"Six, I believe. When he grows up he's going to be a real charmer." She wrinkled her nose. "Not like the father."

My head jerked up. "Did you know Carm's ex-husband?"

"I did not, but Remy did. Franco Carliotti liked to play the ponies, and his bad luck carried over into the marriage. From what I understand he pitched a fit when Carm told him she was pregnant. He wanted nothing to do with the child. I think he even hinted it might not be his."

I felt my pulse quicken. "So Kenny isn't his son?"

"Oh, no, he is. DNA proved it. It all came out in the divorce. Franco wanted nothing to do with the kid, and paid plenty for that privilege. Carm really got a bundle out of him. Between that and his gambling debts he barely got away with enough to live on. That's why he moved out West. Last I heard he was living with his mother." Chantal paused and peered at me. "You look disappointed, chérie?"

"I suppose I am." I told Chantal my suspicions about Carm being Blackthorne's mystery mistress. "This definitely shoots that theory all to pieces. I had to eliminate Elle Gardner too." I told Chantal what I'd learned about Elle's addiction. "They were my two best guesses for the role of the mystery mistress and now I've got zip."

"Well, do not worry." Chantal patted my arm. "You will figure it out, chérie. You always do. You and Nicky."

The cat in question poked his head out from underneath the table, meowed twice, then vanished again.

Chantal chuckled, then said, "And for what it is worth, even though you never asked my opinion, I think calling off looking into Nicky's past was the right thing to do." There was a catch in her voice as she added, "I could not bear it if someone else laid claim to Nicky either."

"Don't worry. No one's taking Nick, not if I can help it," I said. Suddenly I snapped my fingers. "Today's Wednesday," I said.

"All day," Chantal replied. "Why?"

"When we were in Carm's store the other day, Gillian mentioned that they have a perfumer coming in on Wednesdays and Saturdays. They're trying out selling specially blended scents. Maybe he'd recognize this bottle."

"It's worth a try," said Chantal. "Maybe I'll go with you, if Remy can spare me. I'd love to get a specially blended perfume for myself. Something mysterious and sexy." She eyed me. "It wouldn't hurt you to get a sexy perfume either, chérie. Men love that sort of thing."

I made a face, then fingered the paper with the perfume names on it. "I'll give you a call when I'm ready to leave. In the meantime, I'd better put this back." I opened my tote bag and replaced the paper in the zipper compartment. Chantal leaned forward, gave a sniff. "What is that delightful smell? It's coming from your bag."

I pulled out the white handkerchief. "It must be this," I said. "I soaked it with what was left in that perfume bottle I found. To be honest, I forgot it was here." I held it out to Chantal. "Does it smell familiar to you?"

Chantal took the handkerchief and sniffed. "It's not Insolence or Ethereal, that I know," she said. "It's a very sexy scent. Woodsy."

"Whew, new perfume?" We turned and saw Michaela grinning at us. "What is it?"

"That's what we're trying to figure out," I said. As Michaela raised an eyebrow I added, "Don't ask. It's too long a story to go into right now."

"No problem. But Chantal's right. That's a sexy scent." She frowned, and tapped her finger against her chin. "You know, I could swear I've smelled this scent on someone recently. If not that exact scent, one very close to it."

Now it was my turn to raise an eyebrow. "I don't suppose you remember where?"

Michaela's lips drooped down. "No, sorry. But I'll think about it. I'm sure it will come to me sooner or later." She leaned in close and whispered, "Is it for some mystery you and Nick are working on?" I gave a brief nod, and her grin stretched from ear to ear. "In that case, I'll try extra hard to remember. Oh, and by the way, I'm going to be whipping up a bunch of those cat cookies this weekend for the shelter. I'll save a dozen or so for Nick."

Nick's head popped out, and he licked at his lips. "Me-*row!*"

• • •

When three o'clock came I flipped the sign on the door from *Open* to *Closed* and set off for Skin and Scents. Chantal couldn't come. Remy had deliveries and needed her to mind the store. Hank was still preoccupied with the task his boss had assigned to him, so Nick and I jumped in my SUV and started off. When I got to Main Street, however, instead of making a right toward the business district I turned left. Nick, who'd been lounging in the passenger seat beside me, lifted his head and looked at me. "Yowr?"

"Yes, we are going to Carm's shop, but I just thought I'd check in on Mariah first. Maybe her memory has returned."

Ten minutes later I pulled into the parking lot at County Hospital. It was pretty full, but I found a space at the rear of the lot. Nick looked up drowsily as I parked, then he sat up, peered out the window. He turned back to me and let out a meow.

"Sorry, pal," I said as I shut off the engine. "You know the drill. No cats in hospitals. But I won't be long, I promise."

Nick made a grumbling sound deep in his throat, then stretched back out on the seat, flung his paws out and closed his eyes, resigned to his fate. "You're a real drama queen, Nick."

I went right to the reception desk and was informed that Mrs. Blackthorne had been moved to a private room on the fourth floor. "Name, please," said the nurse. "We need to clear visitors through Dr. Stringer. Police orders."

The requirement made me feel a bit better. Apparently Dale had taken my suggestion to heart. I gave my name and waited while the nurse made a phone call. A few minutes later she gestured to me. "You're cleared to go up, but only for fifteen minutes. Dr. Stringer doesn't want Mrs.Blackthorne to tire herself."

"No problem."

Mariah's room was at the end of the hall. A young officer sat in a chair in front of it, and I recognized him as Rogers, the same one who'd accompanied Dale yesterday. He looked up as I approached. "Oh, Ms. Charles," he said. "You're all cleared. Fifteen minutes."

"Thanks." I pushed open the door and went inside. It was a single room, and Mariah lay on the bed, her eyes closed, her face pale. I walked over and looked down at her. A few seconds later her eyes fluttered open. She managed a weak smile. "Nora. You came to visit. How nice." She paused and looked past me, then frowned. "You're alone?"

I heard the disappointment in her tone. "Hank's boss needed him to work on something. I'm sure he'll drop by later, though."

There was a chair beside the bed, and I lowered myself into it. "How are you feeling, Mariah?" I asked.

"Still weak, but I'm getting stronger." She touched the side of her head gingerly. "I still can't remember anything, though."

I hoped I didn't look as disappointed as I felt, and I patted her hand. "That's all right," I said. "I'm sure it will all come back to you in time."

"I hope so," she said with a sigh. "I'll tell you one thing, that lady detective who came here this morning didn't seem to like the fact I can't remember. I don't think she believed me."

"You mean Dale Anderson?"

"I think that was her name. She'd be pretty if she smiled once in a while. She seemed pretty hard-ass, but I guess in that job she has to be."

I chuckled inwardly at Mariah's spot-on description of Anderson. "Did Dr. Stringer say when you could go home?"

She made a face. "He wanted to keep me here a few more days for observation, but I told him that wasn't necessary. I want to go home today. I can rest just as well in my own bed."

"If you're feeling up to it, there's something I'd like to show you." I pulled my phone out, called up the photo of the perfume bottle. I handed

Mariah the phone. "Do you recognize that?"

Mariah frowned. "It looks like a perfume bottle."

"Does it seem familiar? I mean, would it be one of yours?"

Mariah shook her head. "Oh, no. The only perfume I've used for years was Midnight Lace, and the bottle didn't look anything like that. This bottle is pyramid-shaped. Midnight Lace's bottle was long and slender. It had a deep blue hue too. This one looks like it might be genuine crystal." She handed me back the phone. "Was it important?"

"More puzzling than anything else. Hank and I found this bottle in Jennifer Hinkle's hotel room."

Mariah's nose wrinkled upon hearing Jennifer's name. "It would appear she had expensive taste in perfume." She closed her eyes for a moment, then opened them and sighed. "I just know that detective thinks I had something to do with her death. I mean, the woman was a complete nuisance, but would I kill her because of that?" Mariah's hands clutched at the thin blanket that covered her. "Honest, Nora, I wish I could remember what happened, why I was in my garden and how I got there but I . . . I can't."

I saw she was getting agitated, so I reached out, grabbed her hand and gave it a squeeze. "It's all right, Mariah. You're the victim here. No one is upset that you can't remember. According to Dr. Stringer it's perfectly normal."

Her lips twisted into a crooked smile. "That's what they said the last time. The memory would come back, I had to be patient. There was something buried deep in my subconscious—some sound or smell or something I saw fleetingly. They all told me that eventually something, somewhere would trigger it and the memory would just come flooding back." Her sigh was audible. "I don't mind telling you I'm tired of waiting. I need to know the truth, no matter what it is."

"I can't say I blame you," I replied. "If you're feeling up to it, Mariah, there's something else I'd like to show you."

I started to open my tote to remove the perfumed handkerchief, but just then the door to the room opened and a nurse stuck her head in. "Your fifteen minutes are up, Ms. Charles. I'm sorry, but you'll have to leave now. Doctor's orders."

"Of course." I shut my tote, pushed back my chair and rose. I leaned over and gave Mariah a light kiss on the forehead. "You just rest and get better."

"Oh, I will. I'm getting out of here today and going home no matter what," Mariah said, her lips thinning.

I exited the hospital and went back to my SUV. Nick was still dozing in the passenger seat, and didn't even look up when I slid behind the driver's seat. I was just about to press the ignition button when my phone rang. I fished it out of my pocket, saw Louis's number on the screen, and hit the accept icon. "Hey, Louis."

"Well, I found Maverick107's email," he said without any preamble. "It took me all morning, but I got it. I'm sending it to your email now. I think this Maverick guy's probably a PI, like your friend Hank Prince. At least, it sounds that way from the email. You'll see. And you can thank me later. Right now I'm late for a meeting."

Louis disconnected and I called up my email. The one from Louis was right on top. He'd forwarded me Maverick's email to Jenn, which was brief, only two lines:

As per instructions. I think you might find these interesting.

There were two attachments. I opened the first one. It was a very blurry photograph of a woman. Only the side of her face was visible. I frowned as I looked at it. Something about her seemed vaguely familiar, but I couldn't pinpoint what.

I opened the second photo and let out a sharp gasp. This photo was of a man and a woman, and it was much clearer. I recognized Christian Blackthorne immediately. He was with a woman who was most definitely not Mariah. And even though she had to be at least twenty pounds heavier and her hair was cut in a most unflattering short bob, I recognized her immediately.

The woman with Blackthorne was none other than Carmela Reis.

Chapter Twenty-two

For a moment I just sat there in stunned silence, studying the photograph. The dark background suggested a somewhat intimate location, like a bar perhaps. Carmela's lips were parted in a smile and she had her hand on Christian's chest. Blackthorne was looking down at her adoringly. I bit down hard on my lower lip, remembering my earlier conversation with Hank. Well, if she and Blackthorne had been involved, as this photo suggested, it might account for her animosity toward Mariah.

I did a split screen and looked at the two photos side by side. I didn't think Carm was the woman in the blurry photo, but it was hard to be certain. The PI's note to Jenn had said that she would find these interesting. Why?

At any rate, I'd discovered why she had wanted to speak to me about Carmela.

Nick had awakened and was now leaning across the console, staring at my phone. He looked at me, blinked twice and let out a loud meow. His paw reached out, and he swatted at the screen. I recalled the Post-it he'd found, the one that said *Photo AG?* I stared at the photo, and then I pulled up the article and looked at the photo there. Once again, it was hard to make a definite identification. Both photos could be of Anne Gillespi. But why would Jenn's PI say she'd find these interesting. The two cases weren't related.

Or were they? Could it be that the blurred photo was actually a photo of . . .

"The pregnant mistress?" I mused aloud. "Anne Gillespi?"

"Yowzer!"

I looked at Nick, who swatted at the screen again. "You think so too, don't you? I sure wish this photo was clearer." I went over everything I knew in my mind. The main reason Anne Gillespi had gotten off being tried for her husband's murder was the fact the murder weapon had never been found. She'd vanished shortly afterward, presumably to make a fresh start. Cruz, California, was certainly a good distance away from Bledsberg, Ohio. No one would have heard of her here, and even if they had, if she changed her name and her appearance . . . I stared at the photo. Was it possible that Carm could be Anne Gillespi?

Nick pawed at my sleeve. "Yes, I know. Carm's son isn't Blackthorne's.

But she could have lied to Blackthorne about being pregnant. They do it all the time on soap operas. Or it might not be Carm, but someone else. If so, who? *Aah!"* I gave one auburn curl a vicious tug. "I need better photographs," I said.

I dialed Hank's number, which went straight to voicemail. I left a message that I might have come across a break in Mariah's case, and I'd explain when I got home. Nick let out a loud meow. "Yes, it is a puzzle," I said as I pressed the ignition button. "And even more out of left field than that perfume. Maybe Hank knows someone who can help with those photos, but in the meantime, let's head over to Carm's shop. Maybe we can get some more answers there."

• • •

But when I arrived at Skin and Scents, neither Carm nor Gillian were there. A young girl around sixteen years of age was behind the counter. I recognized her as Rosetta Bieber, who was a junior at Cruz High and a regular at Hot Bread. As I approached, she looked up and gave me a wide smile. "Ms. Charles! Nice to see you."

I returned her smile. "You too, Rosetta. You're working here now? Do you like it?"

Her head bobbed so hard her ponytail shook back and forth. "Oh, yes, it's pretty cool. I get free samples, plus I get a fifteen percent discount on anything I buy. I'm learning so much about makeup and cosmetics, I'm thinking about going to beauty school to become a cosmetologist. Ms. Reis said that if I did, she'd hire me to give makeup demos."

I smiled at the excitement in the girl's voice. "It certainly sounds like a dream job," I said.

"Yeah. Makes me wish I was graduating this year, like Mollie." Mollie Travis was my former part-timer and I recalled that she and Rosetta were on the cheer squad together. She let out a sigh and then said, "So what can I help you with today? Are you looking for something in particular?"

"Actually, yes. Gillian—Ms. Spence—mentioned custom scents the last time I was here, and I'd like to learn a bit more about them. I understand the perfumer is here today?"

Her head bobbed up and down. "Oh, yes. Jacques is here. He's at the back counter." She waved her hand in the general direction. "Those scents have become quite popular. We've had quite a few people inquire about them. They're a bit on the pricey side, but from what I hear, well worth it. Do you have an idea of the type of scent you want?"

I removed the handkerchief from my bag and handed it to Rosetta. "I was thinking something like this."

Rosetta took a sniff. "Wow, that's really . . . strong. And kind of sexy. I don't think we have any perfume in stock that's similar, but Ms. Reis or Ms. Spence would know for sure. If not, I'm sure Jacques can whip up something very similar for you."

I thanked her and made my way to the rear of the store. A tall, olive-skinned man stood behind the counter, which was littered with perfume bottles of all shapes and sizes. He flashed me a smile as I approached. "Good afternoon. I am Jacques, the perfumer. Are you interested in a personal scent?"

I picked up one of the bottles, sniffed at it. "I'm considering it. This one smells nice."

"I've created hundreds of personal scents," Jacques said proudly. He picked up a small glass bottle, removed the stopper and tipped it toward me. "Offhand, I can see you with a clean, fresh scent, something along the lines of this."

I took a sniff. Scents of cherry, pine and sandalwood wafted up. "That is nice."

"Only nice? Hmm." Jacques frowned, then put his finger to his lips and took a step back, studying me. "Perhaps a scent with a touch more sophistication . . . and a dash of mystery?" He picked up another bottle and held it out to me. "This one has lovely top notes."

I dutifully sniffed again, inhaling the clean lemon and vetiver scent. "That one is very nice," I said. "But to be truthful, I'm looking for something that smells more like . . . this."

I pulled the handkerchief out of my purse and handed it to him. Jacques took a sniff, frowned, sniffed again. He looked at me and shook his head. "This perfume wouldn't suit you at all," he said.

"No? Why not?"

He put his finger to his lips and studied me for a moment before he answered. "You give off a fresh, girl-next-door aura," he said at last. "This scent's emphasis notes are jasmine, musk and violet. The combination is, well . . . sexy." He gave his head an emphatic shake. "No offense, but it's not you at all. Trust me. I've been blending scents for people for as long as I care to remember."

"I trust your opinion," I assured him. "Actually, this scent is a favorite of a friend of mine. She's been searching for it but can't find it anywhere." I pulled out my phone and showed him the photo of the bottle. "I thought perhaps you might be familiar with it."

Jacques squinted at the photo. "Beautiful bottle," he murmured. "Looks like Waterford crystal . . . definitely pricey . . . hmm." He was silent for a few moments then said, "I might be able to find something in my files. It will take me a few minutes, if you don't mind waiting?"

Jacques vanished into the back room. I strolled back out front and saw Rosetta alone at the counter, a magazine spread out in front of her. She looked up rather guiltily as I came closer, closed the magazine and stuffed it underneath the counter. "How'd you make out?" she asked. "Isn't Jacques divine?"

"Yes, he is," I said. "He's checking something out for me." I paused and then asked, "Will Ms. Reis be in at all today?"

"Actually, she's got the day off," said Rosetta. "Her son was sick this morning. She'll probably be in tomorrow, though. Today it's just me. Ms. Spence called in too. Something about a doctor appointment she'd forgotten about." She gave a quick glance at the clock on the wall. "It's a good thing we close at five today. I'm beat." She made a motion of wiping sweat from her brow.

She pulled the magazine back from underneath the counter and I made my way back to the specialty scent counter. Jacques was just emerging from the back room. He had a paper in one hand, a tablet in the other. "I found it," he said triumphantly. "It's called Requiem, and has been discontinued for a few years. I printed the information out for you."

He passed me the paper, and I saw the image of the pyramid-shaped bottle printed there. I read the printed description: *A sexy, ultra-feminine scent with notes of musk, vetiver, jasmine and violet.* My eyes widened as I saw the price and I raised my startled gaze to Jacques. "Wow! This sold for five hundred an ounce?"

"Yes. And as I thought, that bottle is genuine Waterford crystal, which also adds to the price tag."

"I see. Do you know where I might be able to find a bottle?"

"That will be difficult." He lifted his hand, scratched behind his ear. "You might be able to locate a bottle on eBay, or there are a few shops in Beverly Hills that cater to an exclusive clientele. They might still have a bottle around."

"That's it?" I cried as Jacques fell silent. "No store around here that might carry it?"

Jacques tapped on his tablet for a few moments, then looked at me. "You're in luck," he said. "There are a few specialty shops in this area who might have a bottle lying around. But just be prepared—it's not gonna come cheap." He vanished into the back room again, returning seconds later with a sheet of paper, which he handed to me. "There's a list, but tell your friend that creating a signature fragrance would be far less costly."

I stuffed the paper into my tote. "I'll keep that in mind," I told him. "And thanks."

• • •

I returned to my SUV, and as soon as I opened my door, Nick rose, stretched, and hopped over to settle himself in the passenger seat.

"Good news, bad news," I told the cat. "The bad news is Carm wasn't there, so I couldn't quiz her about knowing Blackthorne. But the good news is I think we've identified the mystery perfume." I paused. "And you were right. It had violet and jasmine in it."

Nick blinked twice, then stretched out on the seat and closed his eyes, apparently unimpressed by my confirmation of his kitty psychic abilities. I pulled out the paper and looked at the list. There were six shops in total, and five were in towns ten or more miles away. The last store on the list, the Giftery, was located on Gilbert Place right here in Cruz. I hit the ignition button and ten minutes later turned onto Gilbert Place. I found a parking spot at the end of the block and eased my SUV into it. When I went to get out of the car, Nick rose from the passenger seat and jumped clear across my lap and out onto the street. "Okay, okay," I said. "You can come with me, but you might have to wait outside."

Nick's black tail swished to and fro. I took that as a sign that waiting outside probably wasn't an option.

The Giftery was located in the middle of the block, sandwiched in between a dry cleaner and a dry goods store. Nick and I both peered in the large front window. One side had a display of kitchen items, and there was a cookie jar in the shape of a black and white cat who could have been Nick's twin. The other side of the window was mostly fragrances, and one display in particular caught my eye. It was a spectacular array of perfume bottles and crystal atomizers that glinted in the afternoon sun. I glanced at the listing of hours on the front door. They were open till nine tonight. I pushed the door open and Nick and I went inside. Almost immediately a woman wearing a long midnight blue silk skirt and white ruffled blouse came toward me. "Good afternoon," she said in a soft, sultry voice that held just a trace of Texas twang. "Welcome to the Giftery. I'm Dolores, the manager. How can I help you?"

"I'm looking for a particular scent that's been discontinued. The perfumer over at Skin and Scents thought perhaps you might have a bottle of it in stock."

Dolores pursed her ruby red lips. "We do carry some discontinued scents," she said. "Most of them are quite pricey, though." Her gaze traveled downward, settled on Nick, and her posture stiffened. "I'm sorry, but we don't allow animals in the store." She made a sweeping gesture with her hand. "I know some places in Cruz are rather lenient, but we've got too many breakables here. I've been meaning to put a sign in the window."

"I can understand your concern," I assured her, "but Nick is a very good kitty. Very well behaved. I run a sandwich shop myself, and he's in there all the time."

"Sandwich shop? Wait . . . are you Nora Charles?" At my nod her expression softened. "I've heard a lot about your store, Hot Bread, and you and your cat too. You like to solve mysteries."

Nick sat up straight at that remark and let out a soft meow of assent. Then he held out his paw.

Dolores laughed and bent down to shake Nick's paw. "You're a little charmer, aren't you?" she crooned. She looked at me over her shoulder. "I suppose I can make an exception to my no pets rule for him. Just don't tell anyone, okay?" Dolores smiled at Nick, then turned to me. "Now that's settled, back to business. What scent were you interested in?"

I pulled the paper with the perfume description out of my tote and handed it to her. "This one. I was hoping to be able to find a bottle for a friend of mine. It was her favorite, and she's almost out of it. She's going through a rough patch right now and would really appreciate it."

Dolores's eyes widened as she looked at the paper. "Requiem," she said. "That's a definite blast from the past. Like I told the other girl who was in here asking about it, we haven't carried this scent for years."

My ears perked up. "Other girl?"

"Yeah, Judy something. Or maybe it was Jan. No, Jennifer. It was Jennifer. She had a friend who wanted a bottle of it too. Asked me if I had a record of the last sale. She thought she could contact the purchaser, see if he might know where she could get a bottle."

"That's not a bad idea," I said. "Could you give me that information?"

"I can print out another copy," Dolores said. "But I'll tell you the same thing I told her. This perfume isn't cheap." She made a face and rubbed her fingers together. "Prepare to open up your bank account."

Dolores vanished into the back room, returning less than five minutes later waving a piece of paper. "Here it is," she said. I took the paper, glanced at it, and did a quick double take. Dolores noticed my expression and said, "I told you. Pricey."

"You weren't kidding." I shoved the paper into my tote and pulled a twenty out of my wallet. "Oh, and by the way. Could you put that cat cookie jar in the window on hold for me? I'll pick it up later in the week."

"Sure." Dolores took the bill and smiled. "I can see why you'd want it. He's a twin for your cat."

"Actually, it's a birthday gift for another friend of mine." Chantal's birthday was next week, and I knew she'd love that cookie jar. She might even decorate it with one of her famous collars.

Once Nick and I were back on the street, I pulled out the sales slip copy and looked at it again. I wasn't sure which had startled me more, the perfume's fifteen-hundred-dollar price tag or the name of the purchaser. It wasn't Christian Blackthorne after all. It was Dr. Paul Lassiter.

"Another curveball," I said. "Well, I know where our next stop is."

I started toward the spot where I'd parked the SUV. As I paused before the driver's door, I heard a screeching of tires. I looked up and saw a black car coming down the street way too fast—and headed straight for me!

Nick yowled, and the two of us dashed in front of my vehicle. The black car didn't slow down at all, just roared past us. I leaned against the hood of the SUV to catch my breath.

The driver would surely have hit me if I hadn't moved. But had I been the target of a driver out for a joyride, or a vicious killer?

Chapter Twenty-three

In the end I opted not to call the police. After all, I had no definite way of knowing if the driver had been aiming for me or not, and I didn't have any information to offer other than it had been a black sedan. I hadn't gotten a license plate number or seen the driver.

Hank was in my kitchen drinking a cup of coffee when I walked in. "Well, it's about time. Don't keep me in suspense," he barked out. "What's this about a break in Mariah's case?"

"The perfumer at Skin and Scents was able to identify the perfume. It's called Requiem, and it's pretty pricey. I was also able to track down someone who bought it around the same time Blackthorne was killed. Dr. Paul Lassiter." I handed Hank the receipt. "Jennifer was in that store too, and the owner gave her the same information."

"So that probably means that Jennifer had a bottle of Requiem. But that's not Mariah's perfume."

"No, it's not, but I've got a feeling that Lassiter might have purchased it as a favor for Blackthorne."

Hank looked puzzled for a moment, and then he nodded. "Oh, I get it. A gift for the mystery woman?"

"That's what I'm thinking and I bet Jennifer did too. And there's more."

I showed Hank the two photographs. He was silent for a long moment, twisting his lips as he thought. Finally he said, "As a professional courtesy, I'll refrain from saying I told you so when it comes to this photo of Blackthorne and Carmela. But who's this other photo of?"

"Remember the note Nick found? *Photo AG?* I was wondering if the woman in that photo could be Anne Gillespi."

"Anne Gillespi, eh?" Hank's brows drew together to form a slight ridge in his forehead. "I suppose, considering the article we found, it's a possibility."

"Here's another one. Do you think it's possible Anne Gillespi could be the mystery woman?"

Hank's eyes popped. "That's quite a stretch," he said at last. "But as we well know, anything's possible."

"Now I'd like to take it a step further. Jenn's message to me said she wanted to ask me about the woman in Skin and Scents." I took a deep breath, exhaled it. "I wonder if perhaps Jenn suspected that Carm might be Anne Gillespi?"

Hank was silent for a few moments and I could tell from the ridge between his eyebrows he was digesting what I'd just told him. Finally he asked, "What do you know about this Carmela Reis? Has she always lived in Cruz, or could she have moved here from somewhere else?"

"Like Ohio, you mean?" I said. "I don't know much about her personally, but according to the Cruz gossip chain, she moved here about six years ago with her husband, Franco Carliotti. They had a rather rocky marriage and she finally divorced him a year ago, and from what I understand, took him to the cleaners. I have no idea where she lived before that."

"The dates might fit." Hank picked up his phone. "And she could have changed her name and then remarried. Let's see what I can find out."

While Hank made his phone call, I refilled Nick's water bowl and spooned some of his favorite Fancy Feast Tuna into his food bowl. He let out a grateful merow and hunkered down for his snack. Just as I finished, Hank set his phone down. "Okay, I've forwarded those photos to a buddy of mine. He's got access to a photo recognition program, but he's not sure how much success he'll have with them. He's also going to contact his guy in the Ohio PD to find out more about this Anne Gillespi. He warned me it could take a few days though."

"That long?" I gritted my teeth. "We don't have the luxury of time. Whether the killer is Carm or not, once they realize Mariah is still alive, I'm sure they'll try to finish the job. Anderson had a guard on Mariah's hospital room, and I hope she continues it when Mariah returns home. When I was there she mentioned that she wanted to go home today."

Hank's phone buzzed with an incoming text. He looked at the screen and then at me. "Speaking of Mariah, she just texted me that she has been released, under protest from Dr. Stringer. Elle is taking her home, but she can't stay long. She wants to know if we can stop by."

"Good," I said. "Tell her we'll be there in an hour. There's a stop we need to make first."

• • •

Twenty minutes later I slid my SUV into a parking space across the street from Lassiter's office. Hank and I exited the car, and Nick jumped out as well. Hank raised an eyebrow and jerked his thumb at Nick. "Are you sure him tagging along is a good idea?" he asked.

Nick cocked his head at Hank, then sat up on his haunches and swiped his paw in the air. *"Merow!"*

I chuckled. "Nick disagrees. He likes to be where the action is."

Hank let out a chuckle. " I guess worst-case scenario he could wait out in the hallway."

We all trooped into the building and over to the reception desk. A different girl sat there, this one a pretty blonde. Her gaze was fixed on her computer monitor, but she glanced up as we approached. She gave Nick a wary glance before asking, "Can I help you?"

"We'd like to see Dr. Lassiter," Hank said.

She eyed Nick again, then looked at Hank. "Do you have an appointment?"

I stepped forward. "No, but if you tell him it's Nora Charles and I have some important information regarding Mariah Blackthorne to discuss with him, I'm sure he'll see us."

She frowned, then picked up the phone and dialed a number. She spoke softly into the receiver for several seconds, then replaced it and looked at us. "He's just finishing up with a patient. He said you should go right up." She paused. "I guess the cat can go too," she added.

I thanked her and we made our way over to the bank of elevators. Once again *Beethoven's Fifth* played in the background as we rode up. We reached the second floor in a matter of seconds, and I led the way down the now familiar pink and beige shag carpeting to Lassiter's office. I pushed open the dark paneled door and we all went inside. Unlike my last visit, there was no receptionist sitting at the desk, so Hank and I settled into the comfortable chairs along the wall, Nick sprawled at my feet. After a few moments the door to Lassiter' s inner office opened and a short, elderly woman in an expensive-looking blue suit came out, followed by Lassiter. The woman smiled at him and said, "Thank you so much for seeing me on such short notice, Doctor. I always feel better after my sessions with you."

"Just keep on doing what you've been doing, Mrs. Gracie," Lassiter returned. He patted her arm. "You're doing fine. I'll see you in two weeks."

The woman turned, saw us sitting there and smiled. She did cast a curious glance at Nick, however, before exiting the office. Lassiter's smile vanished the moment the woman was out the door. He walked over to where we sat, his posture erect. "Ms. Charles," he said. His gaze flicked over Hank, and one eyebrow jutted skyward when he saw Nick. "I see you've brought an entourage with you."

"Nick is my cat," I said. "And this is Hank Prince. He's a good friend of mine, and of Mariah's." I paused and then added, "Mr. Prince is also a private investigator."

Hank extended his hand. "Pleased to meet you," he said.

Lassiter made no move to return the gesture. He ignored Hank and turned to me. "My assistant said you had important information to tell me about Mariah?"

"It's more like a puzzle. I was hoping you could help put the pieces together." I pulled out my phone and called up the photo of Blackthorne and Carmela, then handed it to Lassiter. "Do you recognize that woman?"

Lassiter's eyes narrowed. "Of course I do. That's Carmela Carliotti."

"Could I ask where you know her from?"

He hesitated, then said, "She was my patient."

"*Your* patient?" I could barely keep the surprise out of my voice. "That's not what I was expecting."

Lassiter's lips twisted. "That other woman who came here wasn't expecting that answer either. I'm sorry to have disappointed both of you."

"So Jennifer Hinkle did come here? Would you mind sharing what she asked you about?"

"She wanted to know if I knew how Blackthorne met Carmela. I told her they met here, at my office. Carmela had just finished her session and Christian dropped by to pick me up. My car was at the shop, and he'd offered to buy me a drink and then take me home. He took a fancy to her almost at once and spent the entire evening talking about her."

"So it was what, love at first sight?"

Lassiter frowned. "In Christian's case, more like lust. Carmela was smitten, I know that. A few weeks later he mentioned to me that they'd started seeing each other. Since they were both married, their liaisons had to be very secretive."

"I imagine it must have been awkward for you, considering she was seeing you professionally," I murmured.

Lassiter shook his head. "It ended up being a moot point. A few weeks into their relationship Carmela stopped seeing me."

"She did? Did she then start seeing Dr. Blackthorne professionally?"

"I don't think so, but I can't be certain. Anyway, the relationship didn't last long. One day Christian just remarked out of the blue he'd broken things off with her, and that she hadn't taken it very well."

"Did he mention why he broke things off? Was Carmela getting too serious?"

Lassiter paused and then said, "Christian confided in me that he'd told Carmela he wanted to concentrate on his marriage to Mariah, but that wasn't the case. The real reason he broke up with her was because he'd become infatuated with someone else."

I pulled out the receipt for Requiem and handed it to Lassiter. "Do you remember buying that?"

He looked at the receipt and nodded slowly. "I picked this up as a favor for Christian. It was a present for that woman. Her favorite perfume, he'd said. That store was the only one around here that carried it, and since he often bought perfume for Mariah there, he didn't want a record of this purchase." He handed me back the receipt and said, "You know, I told all this to that other reporter. You could just ask her."

I shoved the receipt back into my bag. "That's not possible, but even if I could, I doubt she'd have told me anything. Just one more question, Dr. Lassiter. You went to medical school with a Dr. Howard Fein, correct?"

Lassiter frowned. "Yes, but I haven't spoken to Howie in ages. What's he got to do with Mariah's case?"

"This is on an entirely different matter. I was wondering if you had a number where I could reach him."

Lassiter hesitated, then went over to his desk. He scribbled something on a notepad, tore the page off and handed it to me. "That's his cell number. And now I'll say good night again. It's been a long day, and there's a glass of port and a good book at home calling my name."

• • •

Once we were back in my SUV, Hank turned to me. "What was all that about Fein?"

"You mentioned that Anne Gillespi was being treated by Fein," I reminded him. "I thought perhaps I could find out more from him."

"I doubt he'll be able to tell you much. Doctor-patient confidentiality, remember."

"I know," I sighed. "But it's worth a try."

Hank took the paper from me. "I have a pretty good contact in Ohio," he said. "Let me give him this and see what he can do. He'd be more likely to weasel the information out of Fein than you."

"Chantal told me that Carm's ex had a DNA test run on their son, and the kid is his. If Carm is indeed the mystery woman, aka Anne Gillespi, I'm betting she either had an abortion or else wasn't pregnant in the first place."

"She lied to try to get Blackthorne to leave Mariah?" Hank pursed his lips. "She wouldn't be the first woman to try a stunt like that. I've been thinking though. From what you've told me about the woman, it seems her animosity is directed at Mariah more than Blackthorne. If she had been going to kill anyone, it seems more likely it would have been Mariah."

"Unless she thought framing the woman she saw as an obstacle would bring her more satisfaction." I shook my head. "I think Jennifer was on the same track that we are, and reached the same conclusion. The key to the whole puzzle is finding out just who this mystery woman is, whether she's Carm, or Anne Gillespi, or someone else entirely. She said that something out of left field was puzzling her and I'm willing to bet the Anne Gillespi connection is it."

Hank leaned his head back against the leather headrest and rubbed at the spot between his eyes. "This whole case is starting to give me a huge headache. I'll tell you, if it weren't to help Mariah, I'd dump the whole thing. There are too many twists and turns in it for my taste."

"Hank Prince," I cried, "I've never known you to be a quitter on anything."

He twisted his lips into a rueful grin. "Yeah, well, there's always a first time."

Nick's head popped up. "Yowzer," he said. He waved his paw emphatically.

"See, even Nick can't believe you'd give up on this," I said.

"Maybe we should let Nick solve it," grumbled Hank. "He's done pretty good in the past. After all, he did spell out violet and jasmine, which ended up being the main scents in that mystery perfume. I say we give him his Scrabble tiles and let him have at it."

I looked at Nick. "Okay, buddy. Feel free to give us your insights. What do you make out of all this?"

Nick cocked his head at me. Then he blinked twice, turned around, stretched out and laid his head on his paws. He closed his eyes. A few seconds later he let out a loud snore.

Hank chuckled. "Apparently Nick is baffled, or else he's mulling over possibilities." He glanced at his watch. "Elle will be leaving soon. We should get over to Mariah's."

I pressed the ignition button. "We will. There's just another stop I want to make."

* * *

Twenty minutes later we were walking into Bikers Cycle and Fitness. Fortunately, Jerry Cutter was behind the counter, just finishing up with a customer. "You can pick up the bike Saturday," he told the bearded man. "You've made a great choice."

The customer left and I walked swiftly up to the counter. Jerry smiled as I approached. "Can I help—oh, it's you!" The smile faded from his face as recognition kicked in. "What do you want?" he asked sullenly. "Come to tell me about more dead people?"

"I just want to show you something." I pulled out my phone and opened the photo of Blackthorne and Carmela. I passed it over to Jerry. "Take a good look at the woman in that photo. Does she seem familiar to you at all?"

Jerry took the phone and looked at the picture, then shook his head. "Nope. Never saw her around the mansion." He grinned. "And I'd remember her. She's a babe."

I took the phone back, called up the other photo . "How about this one?"

Jerry took the phone and stared at the screen for what seemed an eternity. "That's a terrible photo," he said at last. He squinted at it again and then handed the phone back to me.

"Well?" I asked. "I realize it's not a very clear picture, but did anything about her seem familiar to you?"

Jerry looked from me to Hank then back to me, then he nodded. "I can't be one hundred percent certain, but there's something about her posture, the way she stands, that makes me think . . . yes. Like I said, I can't swear to it, but she could be the woman I saw arguing with Blackthorne."

Chapter Twenty-four

When we arrived at Mariah's house, I looked around but didn't see any sign of a police guard. I parked and then the three of us went up to the front door. As I lifted my hand to ring the bell, the door was flung open and Elle stood there, her eyes blazing.

"Well, it's about time you got here," she said. She held up her wrist and pointed to her watch. "I've got to leave soon, and Mariah is terribly anxious. She expected you'd be here already. She's terribly upset about that police guard too. She doesn't think he's necessary."

I blew out a sigh of relief at hearing that Anderson hadn't canceled the guard. "I'm sure she is," I said. "But it's for her own good."

Elle held up both hands. "You don't have to convince me, even though the policeman looks like he's about twelve. I think it's a good thing. Mariah just refuses to believe she could be in danger."

"Where is she, by the way?" Hank asked.

"In the kitchen. She wanted to make some fresh iced tea for you."

Hank gave my arm a squeeze. "I think I'll go see her. Excuse me." He turned and started off toward the kitchen. I started to follow, but Elle laid her hand on my arm. "A moment, please, Nora," she said. "I have something to say to you."

I had a pretty good idea what that was, and I held up my hand. "Look, I'm sorry about putting Anderson on your case," I said. "But Mariah mentioned that the milk you gave her tasted funny, and she had that episode right after drinking it. It just seemed . . . I thought it was something Anderson should know, that's all."

"I was a bit miffed at first," Elle admitted. "But then I realized why you did it. You were trying to protect Mariah." Her lips twisted into a crooked smile. "There have been many people over the years who also thought Mariah needed protection from me. They were convinced that I was an opportunist, a femme fatale out to snatch Christian away from her."

I eyed Elle, surprised by the admission. "And were you?"

"At first, yes. They were all correct. I did cultivate a friendship with Mariah to get closer to Christian. I confess I was taken in by his charming manner, as many other women were." She paused and then added, "You were right about the milk too. I did put a sedative in it, but it wasn't for any nefarious purpose. I just wanted her to get some rest and I knew she'd balk at taking it otherwise. Had I known . . ." She spread her hands. "I'd cut off my arm before I'd intentionally let anything happen to Mariah. We honestly, truly, did become fast friends. And I know, deep down, she had nothing to do with her husband's death. Mariah wouldn't hurt a fly. She's the type who would trap it and let it back outdoors. That's why I stuck by her all these years."

I found myself believing Elle. One thing bothered me though. "You said your original intention for being friendly with Mariah was to get closer to her husband."

Elle flushed. "Yes. It's not something I'm exactly proud of. Suffice it to say that my husband was consumed with his business at the time, and I felt neglected. I know it's no excuse, but . . ." She spread her hands. "Mariah was always gushing about Christian back then, and she made him seem like a god. I fell, and fell hard." Her breath came out in a gentle whoosh. "I confess that it took awhile, but in the end I did see Christian for what he truly was . . . a selfish, arrogant, vain man who didn't deserve the passionate love Mariah gave him." She shook her head. "Mariah refused to accept the truth about Christian for a long time. And even then, when she knew what a cheating louse he was, she'd never have killed him. It's just not in her." She glanced at her watch. "I really have to get going. Morrie and I have an important dinner at the country club tonight."

"One last thing." I pulled my phone out of my bag and called up the photo of the mystery woman. I held the phone out to Elle. "Do you recall ever seeing this woman around here?"

Elle looked at the picture, then slowly shook her head. "It's not a very good photo, but offhand I'd have to say no."

Elle left and I went into the kitchen. Hank and Mariah were seated around the small oak table, drinking iced tea. Mariah jumped up from her chair as I entered. "Nora. Would you like some iced tea?"

I waved my hand as I slid into the chair beside Hank. "No, thanks. I was just speaking with Elle. She admitted that she put a sedative in your milk."

Mariah sat back down, took a sip of her iced tea before she answered. "I know she meant well." She ran a hand through her lustrous black curls. "If I hadn't been drugged, things might have been much different. For one thing, I doubt I'd have wandered out to the garden or have had anything to do with that Jennifer Hinkle."

Hank took Mariah's hand. "Her phone shows a call placed to you that night. That could have been the call that you got up to answer."

Mariah sighed. "I wish I could remember it. For the life of me, I can't imagine why she might have been calling. I'd made it quite clear I wanted nothing to do with her."

I shot Hank a significant look, and then I leaned across the table and said, "She might have been calling you about this." I called up the photo of the key and showed it to Mariah. She looked at the photo and let out a gasp of surprise.

"Why, that looks like the key to Christian's strongbox."

"You knew about that," I said.

"Of course." A sly smile played across her lips. "He thought I didn't know about it, but I did. I assumed it had something to do with his practice. He kept it in his wall safe in his study." She frowned. "How did that woman get this key anyway?"

"He had another copy made and Jerry Cutter picked it up for him. Later on he found where your husband had hidden it and took it. He gave it—or rather sold it—to Jennifer."

Mariah's lips thinned. "What nerve. To think of all the times I defended him, in deference to his mother. Turns out he's a common thief after all. He had no business taking that key, let alone selling it."

"I'm not defending him by any means, but he didn't think you knew about the box, so to his mind you wouldn't have missed it," I said.

"So that reporter had the key," Mariah mused. Her eyes suddenly snapped wide. "Nora! Do you think that it was her that day in my bedroom! That she broke in here looking for the safe?"

"I do," I admitted. "I also think that whatever your husband kept in that box might very well be the reason he was murdered."

Mariah's eyes widened. "Are you certain? You'd think that if that were the case, the killer would have tried to break in here while I was in prison to search for the box."

Hank shrugged. "There could have been many reasons. The killer might have gone away, or maybe even have been convicted of another crime and been in prison as well. Or maybe he or she decided that as long as you were in prison, their secret was safe. But when you returned and announced that you were determined to find out the truth, they decided that they might not be safe very much longer. Especially when Jennifer started poking around."

Mariah tilted her head to one side, pondering my words, and then nodded. "I suppose that makes sense," she said slowly.

"Well, we won't know anything for sure until we find out what your husband had hidden in that box," I remarked.

Abruptly she pushed her chair back and rose to her feet. "Then what are we waiting for? Let's get that box and open it at once," she cried.

"Whoa, whoa, slow down," said Hank. He laid a restraining hand on her arm. "It might not be that easy. We don't have the combination to the safe, and I admit, I'm not too skilled in safecracking. We might have to call in an expert."

"Oh, there's no need for that," Mariah said airily. "I found the combination to that safe years ago and I memorized it, just as he did." She tapped at her temple. "It's our birthdays."

"Clever girl," Hank said approvingly. "But even if we get into the safe, we can't open the box without a key."

Mariah smiled mysteriously. "Not a problem. So come on, what are we waiting for? It's time we solved this mystery once and for all."

• • •

Blackthorne's study was large and imposing, just the sort of home office I imagined a successful doctor would have. It screamed of masculinity and ego, from the deep chocolate oak-paneled walls right down to the matching oak flooring. A thick rug in an Oriental pattern lay in front of the fireplace that occupied the far wall. The fireplace wall was constructed with a ledger stone façade, and the hearth with granite tiles. The oaken mantel was filled with photographs, all of Christian with people I assumed were clients. I did note, though, that there wasn't one photograph of Mariah, either with Christian or alone, among them. A massive executive desk in an L shape, also in dark oak, took up most of the floor space. There was a large leather chair behind the desk, and two club chairs that looked to be made of the same buttery soft leather in front. To the left of the desk was a massive, five-tier bookcase. The top of the bookcase was trimmed with cutouts of what I imagined were either pixies or angels, in various poses.

Mariah went directly to the desk and ran her hand along its edge. "Isn't it beautiful," she murmured. "Christian had this whole room and everything in it specially built. He had the specs lying out one day, and I looked at them." She chuckled. "I'm sure he thought I wouldn't be able to read them, but he was wrong. I had a cousin I used to be very chummy with who was an architect." Her fingers went to a piece of molding just above the center drawer. "He had a secret compartment built in, and you have to press the wood just right—there!"

The molding shot open, revealing a small drawer. Mariah pulled it all the way out. There were a few papers inside . . . and a small black velvet pouch. Mariah picked up the pouch, and a second later a key identical to the one we'd found in Jenn's room dropped onto the desk. She shot us a triumphant smile. "He always kept his key in that drawer, he never carried it on his person. I doubt any thief would ever have found this hiding place." She picked the key up and handed it to Hank. Then she walked over to the picture of a beautiful seascape with ships docking and tipped it to one side, revealing a wall safe. She spun the dial quickly, gave the handle a tug . . . and the door creaked open, revealing the outline of a box inside. She looked over her shoulder at Hank. "Do you want to do the honors?" she asked.

Hank lifted the box out of the safe, set it on the desk. He frowned. "Feels pretty light," he said. He shook it and looked at Mariah. "The box feels empty to me, but maybe what's inside doesn't weigh very much. Let's have a look." He went to insert the key into the lock, and then frowned. "This key doesn't fit this lock," he said.

Mariah looked puzzled. "Really? That's strange."

"Did your husband have more than one strongbox?" I asked.

Mariah shrugged. "I suppose he could have. I honestly don't know."

"Well, we don't need a key here," Hank announced. "The box isn't locked." He flipped back the lid, and we all gathered around to stare at its contents. A lone sheet of paper was inside. Hank picked it up, unfolded it, and held it out so that we could all see what was written there: *Fooled you.*

Mariah looked at us, perplexed. "Who on earth did he think he was fooling?" she asked. "Me? He wasn't aware I knew about his secret hiding place."

"Maybe he was setting someone up," suggested Hank. "Someone he thought might have a key to this particular box."

"There has to be another box somewhere," I said. "It might explain why he wanted a duplicate key made right away. He switched boxes." I looked around the room. "But where did he hide it? Here, or somewhere else in the house?"

"I'd say it would be either here or his bedroom," said Mariah. She glanced around the study, and her gaze fell on a tall oak cabinet beside the fireplace. "He always put his papers and notebooks in that cabinet. Maybe there's some clue there. It's worth a look, right?"

I pushed up my jacket sleeves. "What have we got to lose?"

Mariah and I both started toward the cabinet, but Hank paused, reaching inside his jacket pocket for his phone. He looked at the screen and then motioned for me to come closer. When I was next to him he whispered, "My contact just texted me," he said. "Good news and bad news."

"Okay, let's get it over with and have the bad news first."

"He's had no luck so far with the photo. He's sending it to one of his contacts to see if they can improve the quality." Hank's frown morphed into a smile. "Now here's the good news. You don't have to worry about contacting Dr. Fein. My guy was able to get in touch with Fein's old nurse and found out the real reason Anne was seeing him."

It was my turn to frown. "It wasn't for depression?"

"It started out that way, but she was also seeing him because she found it hard to deal with her injuries. Apparently shortly after the DA dropped the charges, she was in an auto accident and got pretty badly burned. She had three surgeries, but still had a scar along the left side of her face. According to the nurse it really wasn't all that bad but she was horribly self-conscious about it, thought it made her look like a monster." He paused. "Apparently Anne was pretty vain about her looks."

"A scar, huh?" Something was niggling at the edges of my memory. There was something I was missing. Nick came over, raised himself on his hind paws, and tapped at the sleeve of my jacket. I looked down and saw a slight smudge there. That made me think of the tan stain I'd noticed on Jenn's jacket when I found her body. Could it be . . .

"Makeup," I burst out, startling both Nick and Hank. I looked at both of them sheepishly. "Sorry," I said. "But I've just remembered something that may be important."

I went over, got my tote bag, and found the card Adam Porter had given me. I punched the number into my cell and a few minutes later I had him on the line. "Hello, Mr. Porter. I don't know if you remember me. This is Nora Charles. I was in a few days ago."

"For a trim. Nora C! Of course I remember you," he said warmly. "I hope you're calling to tell me you've changed your mind about a makeover?"

"I'm still considering it," I lied. "But right now I have a question for you."

"Not the news I was hoping for, but sure, anything I can do to help you. What's your question?"

"You mentioned that you were able to locate hard-to-find beauty products. Did anyone ask you to find one for them recently?"

"Funny you should ask. Yes, someone did. She asked if I could locate a bottle of PermCover. It's used specifically to cover up deep acne scars and the like." He chuckled. "I'd hate to tell you how many movie stars cover up their acne-pitted skin with it."

"Tell me, could that cream also cover up a burn scar?"

Adam chuckled. "My dear, it could cover up any scar. That's why movie studios use it exclusively."

"Thanks, Adam. One last thing. I don't suppose you remember this woman's name?"

He sounded insulted. "Why of course I do. She only gave me her first name, but I remember it. It's Anne, the same as my mother's name."

I fought to keep the excitement out of my voice. "Could you describe her?"

He was silent for a few moments and I could picture him, eyes squeezed shut as he tried to remember details. "She was average height," he said at last. "Five-five, five-six tops. She had on big sunglasses that covered most of her face and a horrible purple print scarf tied around her hair. Some sort of striped sweater on underneath a jacket that seemed way too big for her."

It sounded to me like Anne was in disguise. "There's nothing else?" I asked Adam. "No distinguishing characteristics that you recall?"

"Other than she had no sense of style, nothing," Adam said. "She just came in, paid cash and left immediately. I'm sorry I can't be of more help."

"That's okay, Adam. I appreciate it. If she should come back . . ."

"I'll call you at once."

I thanked him again and hung up before he could reiterate his offer of a makeover and looked at Hank. "I think I've figured something out," I said. I told Hank about the smudge on the jacket and my conversation with Adam Porter. "I'm positive that the woman who ordered that makeup from Adam Porter is Anne Gillespi, and she's the one who killed Blackthorne and Jennifer. We need to find out her new identity, fast."

Mariah looked over from her post at the file cabinet. "Yoo-hoo," she called. "Are either of you going to help me look?"

"You start," Hank whispered. "I'll go make some more calls. I'll check on that police guard too, while I'm at it. It's odd he hasn't checked back in.

Mariah said he went patrolling well over an hour ago." He went over to Mariah. "I've got some business I need to tend to, but Nora and Nick here will start. I'll catch up later."

He gave her arm a quick squeeze and hurried out. Mariah turned to me. "Just like a man, leaving the grunt work to the women," she said. "Oh, well, let's get started."

She pulled out some notebooks and papers from the file cabinet's top drawer. She handed half of them to me and then settled herself in the leather chair behind the desk. I eased myself into one of the leather club chairs and opened one of the notebooks Mariah had given me. I felt a tug on my pants leg and looked down to see Nick looking up at me. He pawed again at my pants, digging the tips of his claws in. "Yowzer," he said.

"You're bored, I know. Wait a sec." I rummaged in my tote and pulled out the pouch that contained his Scrabble tiles. I opened the pouch and let the tiles spill across the thick carpet. "There you go. Your favorite toy should keep you amused while we humans toil away."

Nick pounced on the tiles immediately, swatting them to and fro with his paw. Mariah glanced over, and her lips curved upward as she watched Nick. "My, he is cute, isn't he. And he's so intense with those tiles. It almost looks as if he's picking out certain letters."

I looked at my cat and saw that Mariah was right. Nick hunched over the group of tiles, picking at each one with his paw. He'd edge one out, then swat it back into the pile. "What's up with that, buddy?" I asked.

Nick glanced up, blinked. "Yowzer," he said. Then he went back to swatting at the tiles.

My phone buzzed just then and I picked it up, looked at the screen. Seeing Michaela's name, I hit the accept icon. "Hey, Michaela. What's up?"

"Ms. Charles. I'm sorry to call so late, but—I just remembered where I smelled that perfume. It was in Skin and Scents. The woman behind the counter had it on."

I felt my stomach lurch. "Ms. Reis was wearing it?"

"No, not her. It was the other woman, Ms. Spence. I even remarked on it and she smiled and thanked me. Said it was her signature scent, and every girl should have one. To be honest, I think she was making a pitch for those specially blended scents . . ."

I glanced down at the pile of tiles Nick was accumulating. So far I could see an S, two E's, a P, an N and a C. Spence?

Michaela chattered on, but I didn't hear a word she was saying. I was visualizing Gillian, with her mousy stringy hair and that pink and gray striped cardigan she always wore. The same color pink as the thread I'd found in Mariah's bedroom. I was remembering something else too. Carm talking about the heavy makeup Gillian wore, and Gillian self-consciously touching her face.

The left side of her face.

"Ms. Charles?"

I shook my head and tried to focus. "Sorry, Michaela," I said. "It's been a long day. I appreciate you calling me with the information."

"Oh, no problem. I'll see you tomorrow, bright and early."

I hung up and leaned back, my thoughts whirling. Gillian was so self-deprecating, so unassuming. She could definitely be described as nondescript. She'd moved to Cruz about seven years ago following a nasty divorce—or so she said. And that day in Hot Bread she'd mentioned that she'd seen a shrink for a time.

I ran my hand through my hair. This was crazy, wasn't it? And yet . . .

Nick had wiggled under the desk, and now some Scrabble tiles came flying out. I leaned down and picked them up. A G, two I's, two L's, an A and an N. I didn't have to put them in order to know they spelled out Gillian.

I knelt down and peered under the desk. Nick was hunched next to the velvet case, a pile of tiles in front of him. "I need to borrow these a minute, Nick," I said. He let out a sharp meow as I swept all the remaining Scrabble tiles into a pile, then placed them on the desk. I moved them into position so that they spelled Gillian Spence. Then I slowly moved them around again. When I finished, I leaned back, hardly daring to believe my eyes.

Gillian Spence's name had just become Anne Gillespi.

I thought back to the message Jenn had left. She'd said she wanted to talk to me about the woman *in* the perfume shop, not the woman *who owned* the perfume shop. Now I was positive she'd suspected Gillian, not Carmela, of being Anne Gillespi, but she hadn't been sure how to prove it. That had to be what she'd needed my help with.

I swallowed, unsure of what to do next. I could call Anderson, but I really had no proof other than my gut and the name anagram. I needed to get Hank, and thinking of him made me frown. He should have returned by now. I was getting concerned about that police guard too. From what Elle had said, I was pretty sure that it was Rogers. I was just about to tell

Mariah I was going to look for him when she let out a sharp cry. She turned to me, her face flushed. "I think I've found something," she said excitedly. She held up a notebook and pointed to a notation in the margin on one of the pages. "He talks about having additional work done on the bookcase, and here in the margin he's written, 'Angels guard where man fears to tread, on the wings of justice.'" She looked up at me. "Christian was a very methodical man. He also didn't mince words. If he wrote this here, in this particular section, then it held some special meaning for him."

I walked over to the bookcase. "Some of those carved figures resemble angels," I said. I peered more closely at them. The figure on the far left side definitely had wings on its back. I reached up and pressed my fingers against the figure. Nothing. I moved my fingers up, pressed on the wings. A drawer shot out from the bottom of the bookcase, almost hitting me in the ankle. I bent down and found myself staring into a dark cavity. I called up the flashlight app on my phone and shone the light inside. "There's a box in here," I said.

I reached inside and pulled out a strongbox that looked almost identical to the one we'd found in Christian's safe. I took it over to the desk, pulled at the lid. "It's locked."

"Try the key." Mariah handed it to me, and I stuck it into the lock. It turned easily, and I swung back the lid. I stared at what was inside, hardly daring to believe my eyes.

"What's inside?" Mariah came and peered over my shoulder. She let out a gasp. "A gun? What on earth?"

I swung around to look at her. "I take it this isn't Christian's?"

Mariah shook her head. "No. I mean, I don't think so. I know he always wanted to learn to shoot, but I told him I would never permit a gun in the house. But if it's not his, then who does it belong to?"

"I have an idea, but we need to find Hank and that police guard pronto."

Nick suddenly let out a loud hiss. His black tail bristled out in back of him and he leapt onto the top of the desk. At that same moment, I became aware of a faint odor in the air. I sniffed. I wasn't mistaken. It was definitely Requiem.

Mariah smelled it as well. She put a hand to her head. "That aroma," she murmured, and started to sway. "Oh, my," she murmured as she leaned into me. She pressed a hand to her head.

I pulled out the leather chair, eased Mariah into it. "Are you all right?" I asked. "Should I call a doctor?"

Mariah shook her head. "No, no, it's just . . . that odor. That fragrance." She blinked a few times, trying to regain her equilibrium, and then her eyes snapped wide open and she stared at me. "That fragrance . . . violet and jasmine. It's the missing piece of the puzzle," she cried triumphantly. "It's my elusive memory. I got a whiff of it in here that afternoon, right before I saw Christian stretched out on the floor, and I blacked out."

I set my lips. I reached over, slammed down the lid of the box. "Mariah," I said, "we've got to get out of here. Right now."

"I'm afraid it's too late for that," said a raspy voice behind us.

We both whirled around. Gillian Spence, née Anne Gillespi, stood in the study doorway, and the gun she held was pointed directly at us.

Chapter Twenty-five

Gillian moved farther into the study, her lips curved downward in a sneer. She waved her gun in the direction of the box. "I see you found the gun," she said. "Saves me a lot of time and trouble. I wasn't too successful the first few times I tried looking for it."

Mariah let out a sharp gasp. "So it wasn't a dream! You broke into my house?"

"The first two times after you went to prison, yeah." Gillian's lips twisted in a wry smile. "This time I didn't have to. You really should be more careful, Mariah. That side door was unlocked." She reached into the pocket of her pink and gray sweater and held up a key. "I lifted this from Christian's pocket one evening. He'd bragged about that strongbox and how it was the perfect place to keep the gun. How he would keep it safe for me there, and no one, especially the police, would ever find it." Her gaze traveled to the bookcase. "I would never have figured that for a hiding place in a million years."

"So Dr. Blackthorne knew your real identity?" I asked. "That you're Anne Gillespi?"

Her eyes widened a bit, and then she barked out a laugh. "So you did figure it out? I guess I shouldn't be surprised, considering your reputation."

"Your makeup—you wear that heavy foundation to cover up a scar from an auto accident," I said. "And Requiem . . . the part-timer smelled it on you."

"Ah, the perfume." Gillian waved the gun in the air. "I brought the bottle in one day. I wanted to see if Jacques could duplicate it. We were busy that day, though, and I never got the chance to ask. I'd deliberately avoided wearing it since Mariah came back because, well, you know, I was afraid if I ever ran into her and she smelled it she might remember. That particular day I'd used up almost all the perfume I had left, so I decided to get rid of the evidence, so to speak. I went out back to throw it in the dumpster. I had no idea that reporter was lurking around back there. She saw me and I guess she got suspicious. She dug the bottle out of the trash."

"Jennifer suspected your true identity?"

"I'm not sure. I know she talked to that Adam Porter." Gillian's hand flew to her left side, and she touched her cheek lightly. "Three plastic surgeries that took all my money, and still they couldn't fix this scar. That darned foundation is the only one that covers it completely so I don't look like a freak, but I was running out of that too. I knew I was taking a chance asking Porter to get me some, but I had no choice. He's the only one around here who could lay his hands on it."

"Why did you kill Jennifer?" I asked. "Was she getting too close to discovering your real identity?"

"I kept an eye on her. Like Carm, I figured she was trouble, but for a different reason. I overheard her on her phone, talking to the PI she hired. She was trying to piece things together, trying to find out more about Anne Gillespi's past. My past. I knew she had to be stopped before she put everything together." She waved the gun in the air. "I followed her, and I heard her leave you a message. When she mentioned the woman in the perfume store, I figured she wanted to pick your brain about me. Then she called Mariah, but Mariah didn't answer the phone. I figured she was going to ask Mariah about the key and the perfume, and I knew I had to silence her before she did."

She turned to Mariah. "I knocked you out that day but I had no idea if you'd seen me or not. Later on when I learned you'd been seeing Dr. McDowd, I pretended to be from the temp agency and I looked through your file. You told her that you sensed something before you fainted, either a sound or a smell, and that if you could only pinpoint that, then you might remember what happened. When you went to prison I broke in twice to hunt, but both times neighbors called the cops and I had to make a run for it. I came back again and saw the alarm company here, but I figured as long as you were in prison I was safe. Then they released you. You made a big deal about trying to remember, to learn the truth. I knew I had to keep an eye on you and make certain you never remembered, or worse yet, found that box."

"But I never saw you," said Mariah. "I could never have identified you as Christian's killer."

"No, but you could identify my perfume. Then it would only be a matter of time before a smart cop put it all together—or a PI." She waved the gun in my direction. "After all, Nora here figured it out."

I licked at my lips. Gillian's eyes glittered and I had the distinct feeling she was only a short hop away from total insanity. I figured our only hope right now was to keep her talking, until either Hank would return, or possibly the police guard. Where were they, anyway? I looked at Gillian. "It was clever of you, to change your real name into an anagram."

Gillian preened. "I thought so. And Christian thought so too. That's why I went to him originally, you know. I needed to confess to someone, and I knew he'd be bound by doctor-patient confidentiality. Dr. Fein mentioned him several times, said he was a friend of Lassiter's."

"That's not entirely true," interrupted Mariah. "That rule can be superseded if the doctor believes a crime has been committed."

Gillian's lips curved in a sneer. "Your husband didn't seem to care much about that," she said. "Christian liked to make his own rules." Her eyes took on a faraway look. "I met him one evening at a bar. He bought me a drink, said he was a shrink, and he could see something was eating at me. He said that he could help me if I wanted. I told him I'd rather date him. We started going out a few nights a week. Finally I broke down and told him the whole story, how Randy used to beat and verbally abuse me, until I was finally pushed to the point where I couldn't take it any longer." Her expression cleared and her jaw tightened. "I told Christian I wasn't one bit sorry. To my mind, I'd rid the world of something evil. But I knew the only reason I'd gotten off was because the murder weapon hadn't been found. I was terrified that someday I'd get caught with it. So he told me to give it to him. He'd keep it safe. He'd keep me safe. Fool that I was, I believed him."

She turned toward Mariah. "I told him I wanted him to leave you, divorce you and marry me. He was hesitant. He said that he'd built up a good practice here, and that he was very well-regarded. He said that his marriage to you was important to his standing in the community. That was when I realized that Christian only loved me as long as it was convenient for him. The minute it disrupted his perfect little life, he was ready to run."

"I heard him on the phone with you that day," Mariah interrupted. "You were carrying his child. What happened to the baby?"

"Oh, grow up, Mariah," Gillian spat. "I only wanted him to think that. I thought that maybe if he thought a child was on the way, he'd be amenable to leaving you. Instead he told me that he'd pay for an abortion. When I told him no, he said that he wasn't about to give up everything for me and some ill-conceived brat. He told me to have the abortion, or else he'd get that gun out of its hiding place and expose me for the murderess I was. He gave me a choice: I could have the child but if I did, I'd lose my freedom. The child would end up in an orphanage. That was when I decided he was no better than Randy, and he had to die too."

Mariah's eyes blazed. "So you came here when I was out, killed my husband and decided to frame me for his murder?" she cried.

"I didn't intend to frame you, not at first," Gillian said. "But when you walked in the study right after I'd killed him, I had no choice but to knock you out. And then the opportunity was just too good. I figured you'd get a good lawyer and get off. Imagine my surprise when they sent you to prison, but . . ." She shrugged. "At that point I figured better you than me."

"You really are a monster," hissed Mariah. "So what do you plan to do now? Kill both of us? You'll never get away with it." She lifted her chin. "Hank Prince will be back any minute. He'll make sure you rot in prison for a long, long, time."

"Oh, your PI friend? I don't think he'll be of much help." She twirled the gun in her hand. "I snuck up behind him and clocked him good. He'll be out for hours. As for you two, you're going to be the victims of a robbery gone horribly wrong. And I, and my gun, will be long gone before anyone finds your bodies."

"You're forgetting the police guard," I blurted.

She threw back her head and let out a harsh laugh. "Hardly. I took care of him too. Anderson shouldn't have sent that green kid to guard you. Gets distracted too easily. It was a piece of cake to knock him out cold, tie and gag him and shove him behind that rosebush in the garden." She pulled a black mask out of her pocket, dangled it before us. "I made sure he saw me wearing this before I got him with the butt of my gun. He'll be able to testify that it was indeed a robber who broke in here and killed the two of you."

She raised the gun, pointed it at Mariah. "You don't know how truly sorry I am to have to do this," she said. "I never had anything against you, Mariah. I didn't even blame you for Christian not wanting to leave you to marry me, unlike Carm. I'm afraid she's nursed a grudge against you over the years. She never saw the big picture with Christian, I'm afraid. Never realized just what a cad he was. No, I blamed Christian. He deserved what he got." She lowered the gun for a moment and glanced at me. "And I'm especially sorry about you, Nora. I had a lot of respect for you and your detecting abilities. I'm just sorry you got involved. I tried to warn you off, but you didn't take the hint."

"So you made that phone call to me? And tried to run me down with your car?"

"Guilty," she admitted. "Although I wasn't trying to kill you, then. Just scare you. And now, I'm afraid, it's time to say goodbye."

Mariah paled, and I was afraid she might faint. "You're forgetting one thing," I said.

Gillian frowned. "What's that?"

"Me-oooooooow!"

The high-pitched shriek, like the battle cry of an ancient warrior, rent the air. Gillian took an involuntary step backward and lowered her gun again as Nick, who'd been squatting on the desk, launched himself directly at the woman, his claws extended. He flew right at her and landed *plop!* right on her shoulder. He hissed as he dug his claws in.

Gillian let out a cry like that of a wounded animal. She shouted a string of obscenities as she tried in vain to dislodge Nick from her upper body. She reached her free hand up and Nick lifted one claw and swatted at it, drawing blood. Gillian screamed and dropped the gun, trying to grasp Nick with both hands now.

Mariah moaned and pitched forward. I caught her before she fell and eased her back into the chair. Then I looked around, saw the gun had skidded over right in front of the file cabinet. I started toward it, but at that moment Gillian managed to dislodge Nick's claws from her shoulder. She grasped him around the middle and flung him to the other side of the room. Nick struck the fireplace mantel and slid to the ground. I hesitated, torn between seeing to my cat and grabbing the gun. Unfortunately, I hesitated a second too long. Gillian lurched forward and grabbed my wrist, pulling me back.

"Where do you think you're going," she rasped. I could see blood freely welling in the series of claw marks that ran down one side of her neck. Nick had definitely done some damage, I thought in satisfaction. But at what cost?

I stole a quick glance over at the fireplace. No Nick anywhere. Apparently he hadn't been badly hurt, but where was he?

Gillian had pushed me away from the cabinet and now leaned over, reaching for the gun. Before I could move, I saw a black and white blur streak past, and then Gillian let out another shriek and grabbed at her arm. Nick had gone into stealth mode, silently leaping up and sinking his teeth this time into her upper arm. His sharp fangs had penetrated right through the threadbare fabric of Gillian's pink and gray sweater. Gillian, however, wasn't done. She slipped her arm out of the sweater and flung it to one side, taking Nick with it. Nick yowled as he attempted to free his claws from the worn fabric.

Gillian huffed a stray lock of hair out of her eyes and looked over at Nick with disgust. "God, what an annoying creature that cat is," she mumbled. She retrieved the gun and took a step backward, aiming the revolver directly at Nick. "Time to put him out of my misery."

That was all the incentive I needed. "Oh no you don't," I cried. I charged forward, hitting her in the solar plexus with my head. We both went down, and the gun went flying out of Gillian's hand again.

"Don't you dare to hurt Nick," I cried. As Gillian staggered, I smashed my foot into her instep. Gillian stumbled back in pain, and I lunged for the gun. I snatched it up an instant before Gillian's hand snaked out, grabbed my ankle. She gave a hard pull, and I stumbled. I fell down hard, my temple smacking against the hardwood floor.

"Stupid woman. Did you really think you or your cat could stop me," Gillian mumbled. She rose to her feet, a trifle unsteadily, and looked around. She spied the gun, which had tumbled form my hand when I fell and now lay against the edge of the desk. Gillian stepped over me, snatched it up. She whirled, pointed it at me. "I'll take care of your cat after I finish you off," she said.

"Mer-oooooo."

Nick was still struggling to free his claws from the sweater. I swallowed and looked at Gillian as she leveled the gun at me. "Please, Gillian. You don't want to do this."

"On the contrary, I've never wanted anything more—oooh."

Gillian swayed, then dropped to the floor. I blinked as I saw Mariah standing behind her, holding the gun from the box in one hand. Nick freed himself from his fabric prison and raced over to where I lay. He leaned close to me and his pink tongue darted out, licked my cheek.

"Hands up!"

And then the study door flew open and Hank stood framed in the doorway, gun in hand. Behind him, albeit a bit shaky, was Rogers. He also had a gun drawn. Both men looked at the scene before them, then at each other. Rogers rubbed at his neck. "What the heck?" he said.

Mariah was the first to speak. "I see our backup has arrived," she said.

I struggled to a sitting position, drew Nick into my arms and gave him a hug. "Yeah," I said with a wink. "Too bad we didn't need 'em. As you can see, we've got everything under control."

Epilogue

"Who wants another Leonardo DiCaprio? Or a Meryl Streep?"

It was two days later. I'd decided to close the shop for the day and Hank, Louis, Ollie, Mariah, and I were all gathered in Hot Bread's kitchen for a celebratory lunch. Samms was there too. Upon returning from his debrief, he'd been informed of what had happened by Dale Anderson and had wasted no time in rushing right over to make sure that I was, as he put it, "still alive and kicking and in one piece."

Now he popped the last of his John Travolta, a rib eye steak and avocado on a long roll, into his mouth. "I could go for another one of those," he said with a grin. "After all, I skipped breakfast."

I eyed him. "Since when do you need to skip a meal to have seconds?"

He patted his stomach. "Since I put on about five extra pounds the past few months eating your fabulous sandwiches. But worry not, I plan to work it off at the gym later."

Ollie looked up from his Leonardo DiCaprio, otherwise known as a chipotle chicken club sandwich. "Yeah, that's what I tell myself too. But somehow I never make it there."

I went over to the refrigerator, pulled out another steak, and slapped it on my grill. Nick looked up from the chicken he was noshing on, sniffed the air, and then went back to eating.

I returned to the table, eased myself into the chair next to Samms. He reached out and grabbed my hand. "That was definitely one of your closer calls," he said.

"That's for sure," I agreed. "Gillian—I guess I should say Anne, since that's her real name—was crazy, and there's no doubt in my mind that if it hadn't been for Mariah, she would have shot me."

Mariah flushed. "I didn't do anything spectacular," she demurred. "I just took advantage of an opportunity. She was so fixated on you and Nick, she wasn't paying any attention to me. I didn't even think about it, it was just a reflex action. I grabbed the gun out of the box and clocked her one." She looked over at Nick. "If you ask me, the real hero is Nick. If he hadn't attacked her like that, she would have shot both of us point-blank."

Nick looked over at us, yawned, then went back to his chicken.

I chuckled. "All in a day's work for my kitty. At least Anne is finally behind bars where she belongs."

"Thank goodness," said Mariah. "Although I was a bit worried at first that Detective Anderson might bring charges against me for tampering with evidence. After all, when I grabbed the gun Anne used to murder her husband, I most likely smudged her fingerprints on the murder weapon."

"Well, according to Dale, Anne sang like a little birdie once they got her in the interrogation box. She seemed proud of the fact that she'd killed three people, and nearly two more. She signed a confession, so even if you smudged the fingerprints on that gun, it doesn't matter," Samms said.

"I honestly would never have suspected her," I said. "Jerry Cutter was right when he described her as nondescript. I was more inclined to think Carm might have had something to do with Blackthorne's death, especially after I saw that photograph."

"Jennifer suspected Carm at first too," said Ollie. "I managed to get in touch with her informant, who was able to fill in some of the blanks. Apparently Jennifer thought the mystery woman was Carm, and she asked her CI to find out if she'd ever had any plastic surgery done. But then she happened to go into Skin and Scents and saw Gillian. Jennifer noticed the heavy makeup Gillian wore, and also noticed that she was rubbing at the left side of her face. Apparently she was having an allergic reaction to her new makeup, which was why she sought out Porter's help getting PermCover. Anyway, when Jenn attempted to ask Gillian about her makeup, Gillian went off in a huff. That made Jennifer suspicious, so she asked her CI to do some digging on Gillian as well. When he told her that he couldn't find a record of Gillian Spence prior to her moving to Cruz, Jennifer decided to keep an eye on her. The following day she caught a break when she saw Gillian toss that perfume bottle into the dumpster. Unfortunately for Jennifer, Gillian saw her take the bottle, and she decided to also keep an eye on her."

"I'm convinced that was what she wanted my help with," I said. "Figuring out which one, Carm or Gillian, might be Anne. I think she had an idea that perhaps Blackthorne might be hiding Anne's murder weapon in the strongbox in his safe. She tried to get the info out of Jerry Cutter, but balked when he wanted more money for that information. She figured she could find it by herself."

"But it wasn't her who came into my bedroom that day," put in Mariah. "It was Anne."

"Right," Hank said. "Anne was also conducting her own search. She found the original strongbox right after she killed your husband. Imagine her surprise when she found that note instead of her gun. She figured that Christian must have discovered that she'd taken his spare key and he'd no doubt hidden the gun somewhere else. She made a few attempts to find it after you went to prison, but after the alarm system was installed she figured as long as you were in prison anyway, she was safe. But when you were released early and made a public showing of wanting to regain your memories of that night, coupled with Jennifer's showing up, well, that pushed her over the edge. She had to redouble her efforts to find that gun. She probably intended to dispose of the gun, then move away and change her identity yet again."

"Gillian, I mean Anne, admitted that she overheard Jenn call Mariah and leave a message," Samms said. "She wanted to meet Mariah in the garden. She said that it would be in her best interests to help her find the safe because she was convinced that whatever her husband had in there was the real reason he was killed. Anne figured she couldn't take a chance that Mariah would help Jenn and they'd find the gun, so she snuck up behind Jenn and bashed her head in with that owl statuette. And then lo and behold, Mariah comes wandering into the garden in her drugged state. It was déjà vu for Anne all over again." Samms looked at Mariah. "She knocked you out, made the scene look similar to Blackthorne's, then went into your house and erased the message Jennifer had left you. When she saw Nora and Hank pull up she hightailed it out of there before they'd see her."

"She admitted making that phone call and almost running me down with her car," I said. "She was willing to go to any lengths to keep her real identity a secret." I shook my head. "And to think I thought she was dull."

Samms raised his glass. "So now it would seem we've tied up all the loose ends. Anne will be in prison for a long time to come. Thanks to you, she can also be tried for the murder of her husband as well as Blackthorne."

"One thing I am still curious about," admitted Ollie. "Who was skimming the company funds? Was it Lassiter or Blackthorne?"

"Without an examination of their books no one will ever know for sure," said Hank. "But I'm thinking it was both of them. Lassiter for his gambling and Blackthorne for his women."

Mariah wrinkled her nose. "As hard as some of it is to hear, I've always thought it's best to know the truth," Mariah said. "Secrets always come out, and they have a way of biting you in the you-know-where. I must admit, though, I'm especially glad it all turned out in my favor. I confess I had my doubts."

Ollie looked at Mariah. "And now that you're finally free in every sense of the word, what are your plans? Are you going to stay here in Cruz?"

Mariah slid a glance Hank's way. "I may relocate here permanently eventually, but right now I thought I'd take a little trip to Chicago. I was there once, with Christian at a seminar, and it seemed like such a lovely city. I think I'd like to spend some time there." She tossed Hank a fond glance. "And after that, well, who knows? Perhaps I'll decide to stay awhile."

Hank cleared his throat, and I noticed the tips of his ears were red. "I—ah—told Mariah I'd be glad to give her the grand tour of Chicago."

He reached out and covered Mariah's hand with his own, and they looked deeply into each other's eyes. I couldn't stifle a grin. "Well, whatever you decide to do, Mariah," I said, "I'm sure that you'll be very happy." I looked at Hank. "You too."

Louis raised his glass of iced tea. "And I shall be extremely happy once you write up this article for next month's *Noir*. I see a large circulation jump in *Noir*'s future."

I clinked my glass with Louis's and then, as he took a sip, I asked, "Does that also mean a raise is in mine?"

Louis nearly choked on his iced tea. "We'll discuss that later," he managed to say.

Suddenly the door to the upstairs apartment burst open and Lacey hurried over to our table. "Nora," she cried, "Anderson just called me. The mayor approved my job! I start on Monday!"

I jumped up and enveloped my sister in a hug. "That's great news, Lacey. I'm so happy for you."

"Thanks."

Samms reached out to grab Lacey's hand. "That is wonderful news," he said. "I'm sure you'll be a great addition to the Cruz PD."

Lacey smiled at him. "Thanks, Lee. I'm sure your recommendation helped a lot, too. Oh, and I nearly forgot the best news of all. Dale got the job approved for full-time, not part-time." My sister turned to give me a sheepish glance. "Which means, Nors, that if I'm to start on Monday, I'm not giving you two weeks' notice. I am so sorry."

"No, you're not, but it's okay." I waved my hand. "Michaela is working out fine, and Mollie informed me that if her schedule allows, she'll be happy to work one or two days a week if I need her and help with the catering jobs. So it's all good."

Nick went over, twined his portly body around Lacey's legs. "Meow," he said softly.

Lacey bent down to give Nick a scratch behind the white spot on his ear. "I know you'll miss me," she said. "But you're happy for me, right?"

Nick stood up on his haunches and pawed at Lacey's pants.

I chuckled. "The final seal of approval. Oh, and I almost forgot." I went over to the counter and picked up a plate. "Michaela dropped these off for you, Nick. Her special recipe."

I took one of the cat cookies from the plate, crumbled it into his bowl. Nick let out a satisfied yowl, then scurried over to the bowl, hunkered down. A few minutes later we all heard the sound of contented chewing.

"Guess Michaela's cookies are a hit," I remarked. "Maybe I'll add them to the menu."

"Not a bad idea," agreed Samms. "That way you can increase your customer base to include those with four feet."

Nick glanced up from his bowl, let out a loud meow, and went back to eating.

• • •

It was a little after two o'clock when Hank, Mariah, Ollie and Louis finally left. Samms lingered behind, eating the last piece of key lime pie and drinking his third cup of coffee. When he'd consumed the last bite of pie he drained his cup, then pushed his chair back and patted his stomach. "I'll need to put in at least three hours at the gym to work all of this off."

I arched a brow. "Three hours? From all you've eaten, I'd say it would be more like five or six."

"That's because you're such a good cook," he said with a grin. "But I may as well postpone the gym until after Saturday."

I started loading dishes into the dishwasher. "Saturday? What's Saturday?"

Samms's face fell slightly. "How fast we forget. Don't you remember? We have a date for Saturday night."

"Oh, right. Felipe's." I hesitated and then said, "Are you sure you want to go out? Felipe's is so expensive. Lacey's going out with Peter Saturday, so we'd have the apartment to ourselves. I could make us a nice dinner here."

"I can afford Felipe's," said Samms. "And you're missing the point. I

197

wanted to take you out for a nice dinner. You cook every darn day. You deserve a break."

I arched a brow. "Are you sure that's all there is to it?"

He pursed his lips, let out a small sigh. "I see I can't fool you, can I, Nora? Okay, I admit it. I wanted to soften you up a bit. I—I have something I want to ask you."

I felt my heart skip a beat. "A-ask me?" I stammered.

He nodded. "Yeah. I know we've only been dating a short while, but, well, to be honest, Red, it seems longer."

I swallowed. Was I ready for this? I wasn't even certain I was entirely over Daniel. "Samms, I . . . I hate surprises. You know that."

He leaned in closer. "You're right. I do know that. Okay, then, I'll ask you now. But we're still going to Felipe's."

I squeezed my eyes shut. Oh my gosh, what was about to happen?

"I know how you guard those recipes of yours, but my sister would love that one for eggplant carbonara. She's a vegetarian, you see, and she's always looking for a good recipe."

My eyes flew open. "You want my recipe," I said slowly. "That's what you wanted to ask me?"

"Why, sure." His eyes were twinkling, though, as he added, "What did you think I was going to ask?"

I swallowed. "Oh, nothing. Nothing at all."

"Good. Then I've got to be going. See you Saturday."

Samms gave me a quick kiss on the lips and then was gone. Nick leapt onto the back counter. I went over and gave him a chuck underneath his chin. His lips tipped up, and I'd bet every last nickel in my cash register that he was laughing at me.

I plopped my chin in my hands and said, "You know, Nick, maybe Mariah is right. Maybe it's better to know the truth. After all, everyone else seems to be coming to grips with their past, maybe it's time we did too." I leaned over, dropped a kiss on the top of his head. "Because no matter what, we are now, and always will be, a team. And nothing, and no one, can change that. So . . . it's time to call out the big guns."

Nick cocked his head and watched me thoughtfully as I took out my cell phone and punched in a number. A few minutes later Hank's voice boomed over the wire. "Hey there," he drawled. "I didn't expect to hear from you this soon. Did you forget something?"

"No—yes. Actually, I need a favor."

"After what you did for Mariah, I'm at your command. So what do you need?"

I looked over at Nick. He blinked his eyes twice. I let out a breath. It was now or never. "I need whatever you can find out on a Philip Castorelli. He used to own a magic shop in Cruz . . ."

From Nora's Kitchen

John Travolta's Steak Sandwich

hoagie rolls
extra-virgin olive oil
½ pound rib eye, thinly sliced
salt and pepper
coleslaw
olives or pickles (if desired)

Split hoagie roll, drizzle with olive oil and put on griddle or grill.

Season steak with salt and pepper and cook in pan in olive oil until juicy and tender.

Remove from pan, drain and place on roll.

Add coleslaw on top, add olives or pickles if desired.

Leonardo DiCaprio's Chicken Club

1 stalk finely chopped celery
½ cup mayo
1 tablespoon dill, chives or parsley
3 cups chopped chicken
salt and pepper
6 slices bacon
12 slices sandwich bread, crust removed.
Sliced tomato

Mix celery and mayo in bowl. If preferred, add in dill, chives or parsley (recommend only adding one).

Season chicken with salt and pepper, then mix into bowl with celery, mayo, and dill, chives, or parsley.

Cook bacon in pan, set aside (if you're pressed for time, you can use precooked bacon).

Toast sandwich bread, spread mixture on one side of bread when done.

Top with bacon and tomato slice, then top with slice of bread. Repeat spreading on mixture, with bacon and tomato on top again.

Top with remaining slice and serve. Makes 4 sandwiches.

Jimmy Kimmel Sandwich

hoagie roll or 2 slices of thick rye bread, whichever you prefer
1 tablespoon mayonnaise
¼ pound each of roast beef and provolone (if you want to switch out these
for your favorite meat and cheese, that's okay too!)
¼ cup hot or sweet peppers
½ cup shredded lettuce
¼ cup thinly sliced onion (optional)
salt and pepper to taste

If using roll, slice lengthwise.

Spread mayo on roll or bread.

Layer the cheese and meats.

Top with peppers, lettuce, and onion if desired

Sprinkle salt, pepper over all and serve!

About the Author

While Toni LoTempio does not commit—or solve—murders in real life, she has no trouble doing it on paper. Her lifelong love of mysteries began early on when she was introduced to her first Nancy Drew mystery at age ten—*The Secret in the Old Attic*. She and her cat pen the Nick and Nora Mysteries, the Urban Tails Pet Shop Mysteries, and the Cat Rescue Mysteries. Catch up with them at Rocco's blog, catsbooksmorecats.blogspot.com, or her website, tclotempio.net.